Daguerreotypes

and Other Essays

Translations from the Danish in this volume
are by
P. M. Mitchell and W. D. Paden

Daguerreotypes

and Other Essays

Isak Dinesen

Foreword by
HANNAH ARENDT

The University of Chicago Press

Isak Dinesen was the pen name of Baroness
Karen Blixen of Rungstedlund (1885–1962).
Her many works include *The Angelic
Avengers* and *Carnival: Entertainments and
Posthumous Tales,* both of which are pub-
lished by the University of Chicago Press.

The University of Chicago Press, Chicago 60637
William Heinemann, Ltd., London

©1979 by the Rungstedlund Foundation
All rights reserved. Published 1979
Printed in the United States of America
93 92 91 90 89 88 87 86 85   76543

Library of Congress Cataloging in Publication Data

Blixen, Karen, 1885–1962.
  Daguerreotypes, and other essays.

  Translation of Essays.
  Bibliography: p.
  CONTENTS: Arendt, H.   Isak Dinesen, 1885–1962.
—On mottoes of my life.—Daguerreotypes. [etc.]
  I. Title.
PT8175.B545A26   1979   839.8'1'472   78–27543
ISBN 0–226–15305–3

Contents

Foreword

Isak Dinesen, 1885-1962

Hannah Arendt

*Les grandes passions sont rares
comme les chefs-d'oeuvre.* —BALZAC

The Baroness Karen Blixen née Karen Christentze
Dinesen—called Tanne by her family and Tania first
by her lover and then by her friends—was the Danish
woman author of rare distinction who wrote in English out of loyalty to her dead lover's language and,
in the spirit of good old-fashioned coquetry, half hid,
half showed her authorship by prefixing to her
maiden name the male pseudonym "Isak," the one
who laughs. Laughter was supposed to take care of
several rather troublesome problems, the least serious of which, perhaps, was her firm conviction that it
was not very becoming for a woman to be an author,
hence a public figure; the light that illuminates the
public domain is much too harsh to be flattering. She
had had her experiences in this matter since her
mother had been a suffragette, active in the fight for
women's franchise in Denmark, and probably one of
those excellent women who will never tempt a man to
seduce them. When she was twenty she had written

© 1968 by Hannah Arendt. Reprinted from her volume *Men in
Dark Times* by permission of Harcourt Brace Jovanovich, Inc.
(New York) and Jonathan Cape Ltd. (London). First published
in *The New Yorker* as a review of Parmenia Migel's *Titania:
A Biography of Isak Dinesen*.

and published some short stories and been encouraged to go on but immediately decided not to. She "never once wanted to be a writer," she "had an intuitive fear of being trapped," and every profession, because it invariably assigns a definite role in life, would have been a trap, shielding her against the infinite possibilities of life itself. She was in her late forties when she began to write professionally and close to fifty when her first book, *Seven Gothic Tales*, appeared. At that time, she had discovered (as we know from "The Dreamers") that the chief trap in life is one's own identity—"I will not be one person again. . . . Never again will I have my heart and my whole life bound up with one woman"—and that the best advice to give one's friends (for instance, Marcus Cocoza in the story) was not to worry "too much about Marcus Cocoza," for this means to be "really his slave and his prisoner." Hence, the trap was not so much writing or professional writing as taking oneself seriously and identifying the woman with the author who has his identity confirmed, inescapably, in public. That grief over having lost her life and her lover in Africa should have made her a writer and given her a sort of second life was best understood as a joke, and "God loves a joke" became her maxim in the latter part of her life. (She loved such mottoes to live by and had started with *navigare necesse est, vivere non necesse est*, to adopt later Denys Finch-Hatton's *Je responderay*, I shall answer and give account.)

But there was more than the fear of being trapped that caused her, in interview upon interview, to defend herself emphatically against the common notion of her being a born writer and a "creative artist." The truth was that she never had felt any ambition or particular urge to write, let alone *be* a writer; the little writing she had done in Africa could be dismissed, as it had only served "in times of drought" in every sense to disperse her worries about the farm and relieve her boredom when no other work could be done. Only once had she "created some fiction to make money," and though *The Angelic Avengers* did make some money, it turned out "terrible." No, she had started writing simply "because she had to make a living" and "could do only two things, cook and . . . perhaps, write." How to cook she had learned in Paris and later in Africa in order to please her friends, and in order to entertain friends and natives alike, she had taught herself how to tell stories. "Had she been able to stay in Africa, she would never have become a writer." For, "*Moi, je suis une conteuse, et rien qu'une conteuse. C'est l'histoire elle-même qui m'intéresse, et la façon de la raconter.*" ("I, I am a storyteller and nothing else. What interests me is the story and the way to tell it.") All she needed to begin with was life and the world, almost any kind of world or milieu; for the world is full of stories, of events and occurrences and strange happenings, which wait only to be told, and the reason why they usually remain untold is, according to Isak Dinesen, lack of imagination—for only if you can imagine what has happened anyhow, repeat it in imagination, will you see the stories, and only if you have the patience to tell and retell them (*"Je me les raconte et reraconte"*) will you be able to tell them well. This, of course, she had done all her life, but not in order to become an artist, not even to become one of the wise and old professional storytellers we find in her books. Without repeating life in imagination you can never be fully alive, "lack of imagination" prevents people from "existing." "Be loyal to the story," as one of her storytellers admonishes the young, "be eternally and unswervingly loyal to the story," means no less than, Be loyal to life, don't create fiction but accept what life is giving you, show yourself worthy of whatever it may be by recollecting and pondering over it, thus repeating it in imagination; this is the way to remain alive. And to live in the sense of being fully alive had early been and remained to the end her only aim and desire. "My life, I will not let you go except you bless me, but then I will let you go." The reward of storytelling is to be able to let go: "When the storyteller is loyal ... to the story, there, in the end, silence will speak. Where the story has been betrayed, silence is but emptiness. But we, the faithful, when we have spoken our last word, will hear the voice of silence."

This, to be sure, needs skill, and in this sense storytelling is not only part of living but can become an art in its own right. To become an artist also needs time and a certain detachment from the heady, intoxicating business of sheer living that, perhaps, only the born artist can manage in the midst of living. In her case, anyhow, there is a sharp line dividing her life from her afterlife as an author. Only when she had lost what had constituted her life, her home in Africa and her lover, when she had returned home to Rungstedlund a complete "failure" with nothing in her hands except grief and sorrow and memories, did she become the artist and the "success" she never would have become otherwise—"God loves a joke," and divine jokes, as the Greeks knew so well, are often cruel ones. What she then did was unique in contemporary literature though it could be matched by certain nineteenth-century writers—Heinrich Kleist's anecdotes and short stories and some tales of Johann Peter Hebel, especially *Unverhofftes Wiedersehen* come to mind. Eudora Welty has defined it definitively in one short sentence of utter precision: "Of a story she made an essence; of the essence she made an elixir; and of the elixir she began once more to compound the story."

The connection of an artist's life with his work has always raised embarrassing problems, and our eagerness to see recorded, displayed, and discussed in public what once were strictly private affairs and nobody's business is probably less legitimate than our curiosity is ready to admit. Unfortunately, the questions one is bound to raise about Parmenia Migel's biography (*Titania. A Biography of Isak Dinesen.* Random House, 1967) are not of this order. To say that the writing is nondescript is putting it kindly, and although five years spent in research supposedly yielded "enough material . . . for a monumental work," we hardly ever get more than quotations from previously published material drawn either from books and interviews of the subject or from *Isak Dinesen: A Memorial,* which Random House published in 1965. The few facts revealed here for the first time are treated with a sloppy non-workmanship which any copy editor should have been able to spot. (A man who is about to commit suicide [her father] cannot very well be said to have "some premonition . . . of his approaching death"; on p. 36 we are instructed that her first love should "remain nameless," but he doesn't, on p. 210 we learn who he was; we are informed in passing that her father "had sympathized with the Communards and had leftist leanings" and are told, through the voice of an aunt, that "he was profoundly saddened by the horrors he had witnessed during the Paris Commune." A disabused man, we would conclude, if we did not know from the above-mentioned memorial volume, that he had later written a book of memoirs "in which ... he rendered justice to the patriotism and idealism of the 'communards.'" His son confirms the sympathies with the Commune and adds that "in parliament his party was the Left.") Worse than the sloppiness is the wrong-headed *délicatesse* applied to the by far most relevant new fact the book contains, the venereal infection—the husband from whom she was divorced but whose name and title she kept (for "the satisfaction of being addressed as Baroness," as her biographer suggests?) had "left her a legacy of illness"—from whose consequences she had suffered all her life. Her medical history would indeed have been of considerable interest; her secretary relates to what an extent her life was consumed by a "heroic fight against the overwhelming odds of illness ... like one human being trying to stem an avalanche." And worst of all is the occasional, rather innocent impertinence, so typical of the professional adorers to be found in the surroundings of most celebrities; Hemingway, who quite generously had said in his acceptance speech for the Nobel Prize that it should have been given to "that beautiful writer Isak Dinesen," "could not help envying [Tania's] poise and sophistication" and "needed to kill in order to prove his manhood, to extirpate the insecurity which he never did really conquer." All this would not need saying and the whole enterprise would best be passed over in silence, if it were not for the unhappy fact that it was Isak Dinesen herself (or was it the Baroness Karen Blixen?) who had commissioned, as it were, this biography, had spent hours and days with Mrs. Migel to instruct her, and, shortly before her death, reminded her once more of *"my* book," exacting a promise that it would be finished "as soon as I die." Well, neither vanity nor the need for adoration—the sad substitute for the supreme confirmation of one's existence which only love, mutual love, can give—belongs among the mortal sins; but they are unsurpassed prompters when we need suggestions for making fools of ourselves.

No one, obviously, could have told the story of her life as she herself might have told it, and the question why she did not write an autobiography is as fascinating as it is unanswered. (What a pity that her biographer apparently never asked her this obvious question.) For *Out of Africa,* which is often called autobiographical, is singularly reticent, silent on almost all the issues her biographer would be bound to raise. It tells us nothing of the unhappy marriage and the divorce, and only the careful reader will learn from it that Denys Finch-Hatton was more than a regular visitor and friend. The book is indeed, as Robert Langbaum, by far her best critic, has pointed out, "an authentic pastoral, perhaps the best prose pastoral of our time," and because it is a pastoral and not dramatic in the least, not even in the narration of Denys Finch-Hatton's death in an airplane crash and of the last desolate weeks in empty rooms on packed cases, it can incorporate many stories but only hint, by the most tenuous, rarefied allusions, at the underlying story of a *grande passion* which was then, and apparently remained to the end, the source of her storytelling. Neither in Africa nor at any other time of her life did she ever hide anything; she must have been proud, one gathers, to be the mistress of this man who in her descriptions remains curiously lifeless. But in *Out of Africa,* she admits her relation only by implication—he "had no other home in Africa than the farm, he lived in my house between his Safaris," and when he came back the house "gave out what was in it; it spoke—as the coffee-plantations speak, when with the first showers of the rainy season they flower"; then "the things of the farm were all telling what they really were." And she, having "made up many [stories] while he had been away," would be "sitting on the floor, crosslegged like Scheherazade herself."

When she called herself Scheherazade in this setting she meant more than the literary critics who later followed her lead, more than mere storytelling, the "*Moi, je suis une conteuse et rien qu'une conteuse.*" The Thousand and One Nights—whose "stories she placed above everything else"—were not merely whiled away with telling tales; they produced three male children. And her lover, who "when he came to the farm would ask: 'Have you got a story?',"" was not unlike the Arabian King who "being restless was pleased with the idea of listening to the story." Denys Finch-Hatton and his friend, Berkeley Cole, belonged to the generation of young men whom the First World War had made forever unfit to bear the conventions and fulfill the duties of everyday life, to pursue their careers and play their roles in a society that bored them to distraction. Some of them became revolutionists and lived in the dreamland of the future; others, on the contrary, chose the dreamland of the past and lived as though "theirs was . . . a world which no longer existed." They belonged together in the fundamental conviction that "they did not belong to the century." (In political parlance, one would say that they were antiliberal insofar as liberalism meant the acceptance of the world as it was together with the hope for its "progress"; historians know to what an extent conservative criticism and revolutionary criticism of the world of the bourgeoisie coincide.) In either case, they wished to be "outcasts" and "deserters," quite ready "to pay for their wilfulness" rather than settle down and found a family. At any rate, Denys Finch-Hatton came and went as he wished, and nothing was obviously further from his mind than to be bound by marriage. Nothing could bind him and lure him back but the flame of passion, and the surest way of preventing the flame from being extinguished by time and inevitable repetition, by knowing each other too well and having already heard all the stories, was to become inexhaustible in making up new ones. Surely, she was no less anxious to entertain than Scheherazade, no less conscious that failing to please would be her death.

Hence *la grande passion*, with Africa, still wild, not yet domesticated, the perfect setting. There one could draw the line "between respectability and decency, and [divide] up our acquaintances, human and animal, in accordance with the doctrine. We put down domestic animals as respectable and wild animals as decent, and held that, while the existence and prestige of the first were decided by their relation to the community, the others stood in direct contact with God. Pigs and poultry, we agreed, were worthy of our respect, inasmuch as they loyally returned what was invested in them, and . . . behaved as was expected of them . . . . We registered ourselves with the wild animals, sadly admitting the inadequacy of our return to the community—and to our mortgages—but realizing that we could not possibly, not even in order to obtain the highest approval of our surroundings, give up that direct contact with God which we shared with the hippo and the flamingo." Among the emotions, *la grande passion* is just as destructive of what is socially acceptable, just as contemptuous of what is deemed "worthy of our respect," as the outcasts and deserters were of the civilized society they had come from. But life is lived in society, and love, therefore—not romantic love, to be sure, that sets the stage for marital bliss—is destructive of life too, as we know from the famous pairs of lovers in history and literature who all came to grief. To escape society—couldn't that mean to be granted not just passion but a passionate life? Hadn't that been the reason why she left Denmark, to expose herself to a life unprotected by society? "What business had I had to set my heart on Africa?" she asked, and the answer came in the song of the "Master" whose "word has been a lamp unto my feet and a light unto my path"—

> Who doth ambition shun
> And loves to live i' the sun,
> Seeking the food he eats,
> And pleas'd with what he
>   gets,
> Come hither, come hither,
>   come hither:
> Here shall he see
> No enemy
> But winter and rough weather.

> If it do come to pass
> That any man turn ass
> Leaving his wealth and ease,
> A stubborn will to please,
> Ducdame, ducdame, ducdame:
> Here shall he see
> Gross fools as he,
> And if he will come to me.

Scheherazade, with everything the name implies, living among Shakespeare's "gross fools" who shun ambition and love to live in the sun, having found a place "nine thousand feet up" from where to laugh down "at the ambition of the new arrivals, of the Missions, the business people and the Government itself, to make the continent of Africa respectable," intent upon nothing except preserving the natives, the wild animals, and the wilder outcasts and deserters from Europe, the adventurers turned guides and safari hunters, in "their innocence of the period before the Fall"—that is what she wanted to be, how she wanted to live, and how she appeared to herself. It was not necessarily how she appeared to others, and particularly to her lover. Tania he had called her, and then he had added Titania. ("There is such magic in the people and the land here," she had said to him; and Denys had "smiled at her with affectionate condescension. 'The magic is not in the people and the land, but in the eye of the beholder. . . . You bring your own magic to it, Tania . . . Titania.'") Parmenia Migel has chosen the name as title for her biography, and it wouldn't have been a bad title if she had remembered that the name implies more than the Queen of fairies and her "magic." The two lovers between whom the name first fell, forever quoting Shakespeare to each other, knew of course better; they knew that the Queen of fairies was quite capable of falling in love with Bottom and that she had a rather unrealistic estimate of her own magical powers:

> "And I will purge thy mortal grossness so
> That thou shalt like an airy spirit go."

Well, Bottom did not transform into an airy spirit, and Puck tells us what is the truth of the matter for all practical purposes;

> "My mistress with a monster is in love . . . .
> Titania wak'd and straightway lov'd an ass."

The trouble was that magic once more proved utterly ineffective. The catastrophe that finally befell her she had brought about herself, when she decided to stay on the farm even when she must have known that coffee growing "at an altitude so high ... was decidedly unprofitable," and, to make matters worse, she "did not know or learn much about coffee but persisted in the unshakable conviction that her intuitive power would tell her what to do"—as her brother, in sensible and tender reminiscences, remarked after her death. Only when she had been expelled from the land that for seventeen long years, supported by the money of her family, had permitted her to be Queen, Queen of fairies, did the truth dawn upon her. Remembering from afar her African cook, Kamante, she wrote, "Where the great Chef walked in deep thought, full of knowledge, nobody sees anything but a little bandy-legged Kikuyu, a dwarf with a flat, still face." Yes, nobody except herself, forever repeating everything in the magic of imagination out of which the stories grew. However, the point of the matter is that even this disproportion, once it has been discovered, can become the stuff for a story. Thus, we meet Titania again in "The Dreamers," only now she is called "Donna Quixota de la Mancha" and reminds the wise old Jew, who in the story plays the role of Puck, of "dancing snakes" he once saw in India, snakes that have "no poison whatever" and kill, if they kill, by sheer force of embrace. "In fact, the sight of you, unfolding your great coils to revolve around, impress yourself upon, and finally crush a meadow mouse is enough to split one's side with laughter." In a way, that is how one feels when one reads on page after page about her "successes" in later life and how she enjoyed them, magnifying them out of all proportion—that so much intensity, such bold passionateness should be wasted on Book-of-the-Month-Club selections and honorary memberships in prestigious societies, that the early clear-headed insight that sorrow is better than nothing, that "between grief and nothing I will take grief" (Faulkner), should finally be rewarded by the small change of prizes, awards, and honors might be sad in retrospect; the spectacle itself must have been very close to comedy.

Stories have saved her love, and stories saved her life after disaster had struck. "All sorrows can be borne if you put them into a story or tell a story about them." The story reveals the meaning of what otherwise would remain an unbearable sequence of sheer happenings. "The silent, all-embracing genius of consent" that also is the genius of true faith—when her Arab servant hears of Denys Finch-Hatton's death, he replies "God is great," just as the Hebrew Kaddish, the death prayer said by the closest relative, says nothing but "Holy be His name"—rises out of the story because in the repetition of imagination the happenings have become what she would call a "destiny." To be so at one with one's own destiny that no one will be able to tell the dancer from the dance, that the answer to the question, Who are you? will be the Cardinal's answer, "Allow me . . . to answer you in the classic manner, and to tell you a story," is the only aspiration worthy of the fact that life has been given us. This is also called pride, and the true dividing line between people is whether they are capable of being "in love with [their] destiny" or whether they "accept as success what others warrant to be so . . . at the quotation of the day. They tremble, with reason, before their fate." All her stories are actually "Anecdotes of Destiny," they tell again and again how at the end we shall be privileged to judge; or, to put it differently, how to pursue one of the "two courses of thought at all seemly to a person of any intelligence . . .: What did God mean by creating the world, the sea, and the desert, the horse, the winds, woman, amber, fishes, wine?"

It is true that storytelling reveals meaning without committing the error of defining it, that it brings about consent and reconciliation with things as they really are, and that we may even trust it to contain eventually by implication that last word which we expect from the "day of judgment." And yet, if we listen to Isak Dinesen's "philosophy" of storytelling and think of her life in the light of it, we cannot help becoming aware of how the slightest misunderstanding, the slightest shift of emphasis in the wrong direction, will inevitably ruin everything. If it is true, as her "philosophy" suggests, that no one has a life worth thinking about whose life story cannot be told, does it not then follow that life could be, even ought to be, lived as a story, that what one has to do in life is to make the story come true? "Pride," she once wrote in her notebook, "is faith in the idea that God had, when he made us. A proud man is conscious of the idea, and aspires to realize it." From what we now know of her early life it seems quite clear that this is what she herself had tried to do when she was a young girl, to "realize" an "idea" and to anticipate her life's destiny by making an old story come true. The idea came to her as a legacy of her father, whom she had greatly loved—his death, when she was ten years old, was the first great grief, the fact that he had committed suicide, as she later learned, the first great shock from which she refused to be parted—and the story she had planned to act out in her life was actually meant to be the sequence of her father's story. The latter had concerned *"une*

princesse de conte de fées whom everybody adored,"
whom he had known and loved before his marriage,
and who had died suddenly at the age of twenty. Her
father had mentioned it to her and an aunt had later
suggested that he had never been able to recover
from losing the girl, that his suicide was the result of
his incurable grief. The girl, it turned out, had been a
cousin of her father, and the daughter's greatest ambition became to belong to this side of her father's
family, Danish high nobility to boot, "a race totally different" from her own milieu, as her brother relates it.
It was only natural that one of its members, who
would have been the dead girl's niece, became her best
friend, and when "she fell in love 'for the first time
and really forever,' [as] she used to say," it was with
another second cousin of hers, Hans Bror Blixen, who
would have been the dead girl's nephew. And since
this one took no notice of her, she decided, even at
the age of twenty-seven, old enough to know
better—to the distress and the amazement of everybody around her—to marry the twin brother and
leave with him for Africa, shortly before the outbreak
of the First World War. What then came was petty
and sordid, not at all the stuff you could safely put
into a story or tell a story about. (She was separated
immediately after the war and received her divorce in
1923.)

Or was it? As far as I know, she never wrote a story
about this absurd marriage affair, but she did write
some tales about what must have been for her the
obvious lesson of her youthful follies, namely, about
the "sin" of making a story come true, of interfering
with life according to a preconceived pattern, instead
of waiting patiently for the story to emerge, of repeating in imagination as distinguished from creating

a fiction and then trying to live up to it. The earliest of
these tales is "The Poet" (in *Seven Gothic Tales*); two
others were written nearly twenty-five years later
(Parmenia Migel's biography unfortunately contains
no chronological table), "The Immortal Story" (in
Anecdotes of Destiny) and "Echoes" (in *Last Tales*). The
first tells of the encounter between a young poet of
peasant stock and his high-placed benefactor, an elderly gentleman who in his youth had fallen under
the spell of Weimar and "the great Geheimerat
Goethe," with the result that "outside of poetry there
was to him no real ideal in life." Alas, no such high
ambition has ever made a man a poet, and when he
realized "that the poetry of his life would have to
come from somewhere else" he decided on the part
"of a Maecenas," began to look for "a great poet"
worthy of his consideration, and found him con-
veniently at hand in the town he lived in. But a real
Maecenas, one who knew so much about poetry,
could not very well be content with shelling out the
money; he had also to provide the great tragedies
and sorrows out of which he knew great poetry
draws its best inspirations. Thus, he acquired a
young wife and arranged it so that the two young
people under his protection should fall in love with
each other without any prospect of marriage. Well,
the end is pretty bloody; the young poet shoots at his
benefactor, and while the old man in his death agony
dreams of Goethe and Weimar, the young woman,
seeing as in a vision her lover "with the halter around
his neck," finishes him off. "Just because it suited
him that the world should be lovely, he meant to
conjure it into being so," she said to herself. " 'You!,'
she cried at him, 'You poet!' "

The perfect irony of "The Poet" is perhaps best

realized by those who know German *Bildung* and its
unfortunate connection with Goethe as well as its
author did herself. (The story contains several allusions to German poems by Goethe and Heine as well
as to Voss's translation of Homer. It could also be
read as a story about the vices of *Bildung*.) "The Immortal Story," on the contrary, is conceived and written in the manner of a folk story. Its hero is an
"immensely rich tea-trader" in Canton with very
down-to-earth reasons for having "faith in his own
omnipotence," who only at the end of his life came
into contact with books. He then was bothered that
they told of things that had never happened, and he
got positively outraged when told that the only story
he knew—about the sailor who had come ashore, met
an old gentleman, "the richest man" in town, was
asked by him to "do your best" in the bed of his
young wife that he might still have a son, and was
given a five-guinea piece for his service—"never has
happened, and . . . never will happen, and that is
why it is told." So the old man goes in pursuit of a
sailor to make the old story, told in all harbor towns
the world over, come true. And all seems to go
well—except that the young sailor in the morning
refuses to recognize the slightest similarity between
the story and what had happened to him during the
night, refuses the five guineas, and leaves for the lady
in question the only treasure he possesses, "one big
shining pink shell" of which he thinks "that perhaps
there is not another one like it in all the world."

"Echoes," the last one in this category, is a belated
sequel to "The Dreamers" in *Gothic Tales*, the story
about Pellegrina Leoni. "The diva who had lost
her voice" in her wanderings hears it again from
the boy Emanuele, whom she now proceeds to make

into her own image so that her dream, her best and least selfish dream, should come true—that the voice which gave so much pleasure should be resurrected. Robert Langbaum, whom I mentioned before, noticed that here "Isak Dinesen pointed the finger of accusation against herself" and that the story, as the first pages suggest anyhow, is "about cannibalism," but nothing in it bears out that the singer had "been feeding on [the boy] in order to restore her own youth and to resurrect the Pellegrina Leoni whom she buried in Milan twelve years ago." (The very choice of a male successor precludes this interpretation.) The singer's own conclusion is, "And the voice of Pellegrina Leoni will not be heard again." The boy, before starting to throw stones at her, had accused her, "You are a witch. You are a vampire . . . . Now I know that I should die if I went back to you"—for the next singing lesson. The same accusations, the young poet could have hurled at his Maecenas, the young sailor at his benefactor, and generally all people who, under the pretext of being helped, are used for making another person's dream come true. (Thus, she herself had thought she could marry without love because her cousin "needed her and was perhaps the only human being who did," while she actually used him to start a new life in East Africa and to live among natives as her father had done when he had lived like a hermit among the Chippeway Indians. "The Indians are better than our civilized people of Europe," he had told his small daughter, whose greatest gift was never to forget. "Their eyes see more than ours, and they are wiser.")

Thus, the earlier part of her life had taught her that, while you can tell stories or write poems about life, you cannot make life poetic, live it as though it were a work of art (as Goethe had done) or use it for the realization of an "idea." Life may contain the "essence" (what else could?); recollection, the repetition in imagination, may decipher the essence and deliver to you the "elixir"; and eventually you may even be privileged to "make" something out of it, "to compound the story." But life itself is neither essence nor elixir, and if you treat it as such it will only play its tricks on you. It was perhaps the bitter experience of life's tricks that prepared her (rather late, she was in her middle thirties when she met Finch-Hatton) for being seized by the *grande passion* which indeed is no less rare than a chef-d'oeuvre. Storytelling, at any rate, is what in the end made her wise—and, incidentally, not a "witch," "siren," or "sibyl," as her entourage admiringly thought. Wisdom is a virtue of old age, and it seems to come only to those who, when young, were neither wise nor prudent.

On Mottoes of My Life

A short while ago an interviewer asked me whether—after having lived for many years, having felt at home in more than one country and amongst different races, and known both good and bad luck—I could sum up the events and experience of my life in what is called a motto.

He was wise, I think, to address his question to a person of my generation. The idea of what is called "a motto" is probably far from the minds of young people of today. As I look from the one age to the other, I find this particular idea—the word, *le mot*, and the motto—to be one of the phenomena of life which in the course of time have most decidedly come down in value. To my contemporaries the name *was* the thing or the man; it was even the finest part of a man, and you praised him when you said that he was as good as his word.

Very likely it will be difficult for the younger generation to realize to what extent we lived in a world of symbols. We might, at this moment, lay before us a plain matter-of-fact object, a piece of cloth, and en-

This essay was first published in the *Proceedings of the American Academy of Arts and Letters and the National Institute of Arts and Letters*, 2d set., no. 10 (1960):345–58.

deavor to agree in defining and placing it. A young man or woman would say to me: "You may give this thing a name of your own choice, but actually, in reality and for all working purposes, it is a length of bunting, of such and such measurements and such and such colors, and worth so and so much a yard." The person brought up with symbols, genuinely surprised and shocked, would protest: "What do you mean? You are all wrong. The thing before us, in reality and for all working purposes, is a thing of tremendous power. Put it to a test in real, actual life—it can at any moment call up a hundred million people and set them marching. It is the Stars and Stripes, it is Old Glory, it is the United States of America."

Children of my day, even in great houses, had very little in the way of toys. Toy shops were almost unknown; modern mechanical playthings, which furnish their own activity, had hardly come into existence. One might, of course, buy oneself a hobby-horse, but generally speaking an individually selected knotty stick from the woods, upon which imagination might work freely, was dearer to the heart. We were not observers, as children today seem to be from birth, of their own accord; and not utilizers, as they are brought up to be; we were creators. Our knotty stick, for all working purposes, in appearance and as far as actual horsepower went, came nearer to Bucephalus and eight-hoofed Sleipner, or to Pegasus himself, than any magnificently decorated horse from a smart store.

In a similar way we liked to christen an enterprise, an epoch or a task, by hoisting our colors above it in the form of a motto, proclaiming to the whole world what this undertaking was meant to be. *In hoc signo vinces.* The word, the motto, here was both the starting-shot or program, and the summing-up. It existed before the activity or deed itself, and remained when these had been brought to their conclusion; it was the opening verse, "in the beginning was the Word," and the final statement, the sacred Amen—"so be it."

And the word, taken in such earnest, is a mighty thing. You choose your motto and have it set in your seal, but before you are aware of it the motto has sealed and stamped you. There are in my own country families who for centuries have lived under the influence of a motto; I have known members of several generations of them and have found them to vary in many ways, but the stamp has been recognizable in each of them, and the people who have lived under the sign of *Nobilis est ira leonis* will differ in countenance and even in instincts from those under *Amore non vi.* I am related to and have been friends with old and young members of a family born and brought up with the motto "And yet." They were all staunch people, difficult to argue with.

Now in going through those mottoes of my own life, which at different times I have selected for myself, which I have looked upon as belonging to me, and which have most likely finished up by making me belong to them, I feel myself walking in the steps of Jacques:

> All the world's a stage,
> and all the men and women merely players.
> They have their exits and their entrances;
> and one man in his time plays many parts,
> his acts being seven ages.

Or, as in my own case, only five such ages.

Denys Finch-Hatton, my English friend in Africa, used to laugh at me. He called me "the Great Emperor Otto." For

> The great Emperor Otto
> could never decide on a motto.
> He hovered between
> "l'Etat c'est moi" and "Ich dien."

In my particular case Denys took it that the first statement expressed my attitude towards people of my own race, and the second my state of mind in my dealings with natives, and he was probably right.

To the little girl in my mother's house the great Emperor Otto's dilemma was felt as wealth, a multitude of possibilities. On the covers of old exercise-books, now found in attics, mottoes in red and blue pencil come and go. The one that recurs most often is a highly laudable maxim: *Essayez!* Others, in a Latin which unfortunately I have now forgotten: "Still I am unconquered," or "Often in difficulties, never afraid," I take to have been written down in some kind of bitterness or rebellion against higher powers sitting on the child—our governesses, most likely, for I have never gone to school, but was taught by governesses at home, to which circumstance I owe, I think, the fact that I am totally ignorant of many things that are common knowledge to other people. Still these young or elderly women were ambitious persons; at the age of twelve we were called upon to write an essay on Racine, a task that I should fear to undertake today, and to translate Walter Scott's "The Lady of the Lake" into Danish verse, passages of which were frequently on the lips of my sisters and myself years later. Other mottoes, in themselves more appropriate to my present age than to that of eleven or twelve at which they were written down, I take to have been picked for the sake of the beauty of the words themselves: *Sicut aquila juvenescam.*

I think it must have been at the age of seventeen, when I had got my own way and was studying painting at the Royal Academy of Copenhagen, that the rich possibilities consolidated into one, and that I chose the first real motto of my youth.

Navigare necesse est, vivere non necesse! This audacious order was flung from the lips of Pompey to his timid Sicilian crew when they refused to set out against the gale and the high seas to bring provisions of grain to Rome.

It is not an original motto to choose; many young people will have made it their own. In their hearts the longing and the will to dare are waiting for the magic of *the word* to send them off. It came naturally to me to view my enterprise in life in terms of seafaring, for my home stands but a hundred yards from the sea, and through all the summers of our youth my brothers had boats in the fairways between Copenhagen and Elsinore.

To young people, who think in paradoxes, the paradox of Pompey—for a paradox it is, since that all-important voyage to Rome had for its purpose the maintenance of life, and since, in any case, if you are no longer alive you can no longer sail—appears as the true, clear logic of life. No compass-needle in the world was as infallible to me as the outstretched arm of Pompey; I steered my course by it with unswerving confidence, and had any wiser person insisted that there was no earthly sense in my motto, I might have answered: "Nay, but a heavenly sense!" and have added perhaps: "And a maritime!"

Before this gale I was swept, on the eve of the First World War, under all plain canvas to Africa. I was at that time engaged to my cousin, Bror Blixen; a mutual uncle had come back from a big-game safari to what was then the Protectorate of British East Africa, and had displayed to us a Fata Morgana of tremendous farming possibilities there. In the true spirit of Pompey: "It is necessary to farm, it is not necessary to live," we set out.

Genuine simplicity of heart at times will call forth unexpected indulgence in the governing powers of the universe. The goddess Nemesis herself is swayed by it into a gentler course. The goddess might have answered me: "All right, have it your own way. Sail on, and give up the idea of living!" This, I take it, was her answer to the Flying Dutchman. To me her answer came differently: "Bless you, you fool! *I* shall set your sails, and *I* shall turn your wheel, and I shall have you sailing straight into life!" Under the flag of my first motto I sailed into the heart of Africa and into a Vita Nuova, into what became to me my real life. Africa received me and made me her own, so thoroughly that, unconsciously faithless to the motto which had united us, I exchanged it for another.

The family of Finch-Hatton, of England, have on their crest the device *Je responderay*, "I will answer." They have had it there for a long time, I believe, since it is spelled in such antiquated French; it is a long time too since Hatton Garden in London was a garden, and a long time since it was known about one of the members of the family, a favorite of Queen Elizabeth I, that

Sir Christopher Hatton he danced with much
  grace,
He had a fine form and a very sweet face,

but that all the same he came to a sad end, for the
Devil took him.

I liked this old motto so much that I asked Denys,
an earlier pioneer in Africa than myself—although all
we settlers who had come out before the war looked
upon ourselves as one family, a kind of Mayflower
people—if I might have it for my own. He generously
made me a present of it and even had a seal cut for
me, with the words carved in it. The device was
meaningful and dear to me for many reasons, two in
particular.

The first of these was its high valuation of the idea
of the answer in itself. For an answer is a rarer thing
than is generally imagined. There are many highly
intelligent people who have no answer at all in them.
A conversation or a correspondence with such persons is nothing but a double monologue—you may
stroke them or you may strike them, you will get no
more echo from them than from a block of wood. And
how, then, can you yourself go on speaking?

In the long valleys of the African plains I have been
surrounded and followed by sweet echoes, as from a
sounding board. My daily life out there was filled
with answering voices; I never spoke without getting
a response; I spoke, freely and without restraint, even
when I was silent. One explanation of this was, I
believe, that I lived so high up, more than 6,000 feet
above sea-level, so to say on the roof of the globe,
where the air is felt to be the dominant element and is
apt to turn all hearts into aeolian harps. Another was
that I was here in contact with the African natives and
with African big game. I have always loved animals

7

very much, and to meet them now on their own ground, not imported into human existence—to ride straight into a herd of zebra or eland and to hear from my bed the distant, mighty roar of the hunting lion, I felt as a return to those happy days when Adam gave names to the beasts of Eden. The natives of Africa I had not met before; all the same they came into my life as a kind of answer to some call in my own nature, to dreams of childhood perhaps, or to poetry read and cherished long ago, or to emotions and instincts deep down in the mind, for I have always felt that I resembled the natives more than did other white people in the Protectorate. From the very first day an understanding sprang up between them and me, so that I may say that my love of them, of both sexes and all ages, as of all tribes—above all with the Masai, the warrior-tribe, who were my neighbors when I rode across the river—was as strong a passion as I have ever known. The dark figures around me answered me, even without speaking, in their noiseless, gentle movements and quiet, keen glances. When we were alone together the echo grew stronger. I have been out on safari, a hundred miles from another white person, with native companions only, and have become one with my surroundings, with the landscape, animals, and human beings and with the hours of day and night. This feeling was enhanced by the natives giving us white people native names, characterizing us in words of their own language. Most of these were animals' names, although there were exceptions to this rule, and one very unsociable nieghbor of mine was known as *sahani modya*, one plate or cover, and my Swedish friend Eric von Otter was given the fine name of *resarsi modya,* one cartridge, since he never needed more than one for any head of game. My husband and I were *wauhauga,* the wild geese. Later, when I was alone on the farm, my old Somali gunbearer, after returning to his own country, wrote me a letter addressed to "Lioness Blixen" and beginning "Honourable Lioness," which resulted in all my friends in the colony calling me the Lioness. I feel very sure that, to a woman at least, the presence of echoes in her life is a condition for happiness, or is in itself a consciousness of rich resources. I advise every husband: answer your wife, make her answer you.

Secondly I liked the Finch-Hatton device for its ethical content. I will answer *for* what I say or do; I will answer *to* the impression I make. I will be responsible.

I cannot quite account for the overlapping of the words and the ideas of answer and responsibility. My audience, so many of whom certainly will be better versed in etymology than I, may be able to furnish the reason. The connection exists in the languages that I know—the Danish word for responsibility is plain "Ansvar." In a colony it is a sad thing to see to what extent people who in their own country have stuck to an orthodox code of behavior, in surroundings where they cannot possibly be called to account will feel themselves free of any code. It is a very good thing there, it is probably a very good thing anywhere, to have *Je responderay* harmoniously in your blood.

Were I now, after my return from those happy hunting grounds, to advise a person looking for a motto, I should tell him that *Je responderay* is a happy sign under which to live. In looking back on my nearly twenty years in Africa, I feel that the fact that all things worked together for the good of a human being goes to prove that this human being did indeed love God.

Readers of my book *Out of Africa* will know, however, that this state of things did not last for me. When in the early thirties coffee prices fell, I had to give up my farm. I went back to my own country, at sea-level, out of earshot of the echoes of the plain— the big, wild, debonnaire inhabitants of those plains and the dark, friendly figures of the manyattas sinking below the horizon all around me. During this time my existence was without an answer from anywhere. It had often happened to me during my life to imagine things, and to find it somehow difficult to bring them into reality. Here it was the other way round: things were realizing themselves on all sides, and very insistently at that, without its being in the least possible for me to imagine them.

Under the circumstances I myself grew silent. I had, in every sense of the word, nothing to say.

And yet I had to speak. For I had my books to write.

During my last months in Africa, as it became clear to me that I could not keep the farm, I had started writing at night, to get my mind off the things which in the daytime it had gone over a hundred times, and on to a new track. My squatters on the farm, by then, had got into the habit of coming up to my house and sitting around it for hours in silence, as if just waiting to see how things would develop. I felt their presence there more like a friendly gesture than a reproach, but all the same of sufficient weight to make it difficult for me to start any undertaking of my own. But they would go away, back to their own huts, at nightfall.

And as I sat there, in the house, alone, or perhaps with Farah, the infallibly loyal, standing motionless in his long white Arab robe with his back to the wall, figures, voices and colors from far away or from nowhere began to swarm around my paraffin lamp. I wrote two of my *Seven Gothic Tales* there.

Now I was back again in my old home, with my mother, who received the prodigal daughter with all the warmth of her heart, but who never quite realized that I was more than fifteen years old and accustomed, for the past eighteen years, to a life of exceptional freedom. My home is a lovely place; I might have lived on there from day to day in a kind of sweet idyl; but I could not see any kind of future before me. And I had no money; my dowry, so to say, had gone with the farm. I owed it to the people on whom I was dependent to try to make some kind of existence for myself. Those Gothic Tales begin to demand to be written, and first of all they demanded a motto for the book they were to make. "Give us," they cried out, "a sign in which"—not to conquer, for I could not then conceive the idea of conquest, but—"to run, to move!"

Unexpectedly, as if on its own, the third motto of my life swooped down upon me. Even at the time I did not understand the meaning of it, it just took possession of me.

In the gypsy-moth plane in which I flew with Denys over Africa there was room for two only, the passenger sitting in front of the pilot with nothing but air in front of him. You could not, there, help feeling that you were, like one of the characters of the Arabian Nights, carried through the heavens upon the palms of a djinn. In the morning or afternoon, when I had no need to fear the sun, I used to take off my flying-helmet, and the current of African air would seize me by the hair and drag back my head, so that I felt it difficult to keep it in place. In the same way I was now, in Denmark, grasped by a current of life that seemed to know what it was about, although I myself did not know.

For it so happened that I had read in the papers about the boat of a French scientific expedition which had gone down below Iceland with her flag flying. And the boat had been named *Pourquoi pas?*—"Why not?"

Now again this motto had all the nature of a paradox, and I cannot, in so many words, account for the meaning of it. But it worked. It was encouraging and inspiring. "Why?" by itself is a wail or lament, a cry from the heart; it seems to ring in the desert and to be in itself negative, the voice of a lost cause. But when another negative, the *pas*, the "not," is added, the pathetic question is turned into an answer, a directive, a call of wild hope.

Under this sign—at times very doubtful about the whole thing, but still, as it were, in the hands of an exacting and joyful spirit—I finished my first book. And this third motto of mine may be said to stand over all my books. It will stand, I think, over whatever books I may still come to write.

My friend in Africa, Hugh Martin, when I sent him my first Tale for his personal comment, answered me in a verse by Kipling:

Old Horn to all Atlantic said:
Now where did Frankie learn his trade?
For he ran me down with a three-reef mainsail,
All round the Horn.

Atlantic answered: Not from me.
You'd better ask the cold North Sea.
For he ran me down under all plain canvas,
All round the Horn.

I might make this answer my own. I had, at the
time, no teacher or adviser; I could not, at the time,
have been taught or advised. I was taken and forced
on by the French boat gone down in the cold sea
below Iceland: *Pourquoi pas?*

"They have their exits and their entrances. . . ." So
have programs and mottoes. But in a good play an
exit is not a disappearance—even after his final exit a
character still forms part of the play. The next motto
of my life came into it very quietly, without chasing
out the *Pourquoi pas?*, as if by a law of nature, like the
change of the seasons, which no one really wants to
alter.

An old English town had three walls around it. In
each wall was a gate, and above each gate an inscription. Above the first gate was written: "Be bold,"
above the second: "Be bold," above the third: "Be not
too bold."

Will this sound like a come-down to the ears of my
audience? To me it is not so. A person who all through
his life, like Mussolini, has declared: *"Non amo i
sedentari"*—"I do not like sedentary people"—will
recognize the moment for choosing a chair and settling down in it, trusting that "trees where you sit will
crowd into a shade." The craving to impress your will
and your being upon the world and to make the
world your own is turned into a longing to be able to
accept, to give yourself over to the universe—Thy will
be done. Which of the two is the most truly bold? I

13

have been very strong, unusually so for a woman, able to walk or ride longer than most men; I have bent a Masai bow and have felt in a moment of rapture a kinship with Odysseus. The pleasure of having been strong is still with me; the weakness of today is the natural continuation of the vigor of former days. Nietzsche has written: "I am a yea-sayer, and I have been a fighter, so that one fine day I shall have my arms free to bless"—the latter attitude being not in opposition to the former but a consequence of it.

Can a human being, fully aware of the eternity behind and before him or her, fully value and appreciate the passing hour? An hour of watching the woods or the sea or of listening to music, an hour given to friendly talk with friends? One might say in the manner of the bird in the poem which perches on a frail branch, knowing that the branch will not support it, but knowing at the same time that it has wings which, when the moment comes, will do so. Indeed, *Pourquoi pas?* The older motto after its exit upholds the new.

I have come over here to America under the sign of "Be bold. Be bold. Be not too bold." I may wish that I had been able to come earlier, in the years when the necessity of sailing was plainer to me than the necessity of living. And yet I feel that the arrangement is no come-down—it may even be, in its own way, a joke. It is probably a good thing for me, at this moment and while speaking to you, to be warned against being too long-winded, if not too bold.

I shall finish up my talk on the mottoes of my life with a short tale, which a friend of mine told me.

An old Chinese mandarin, during the minority of the young Emperor, had been governing the country for him. When the Emperor came of age the old man gave him back the ring which had served as emblem of his vicariate, and said to his young sovereign:

"In this ring I have had set an inscription which your dear Majesty may find useful. It is to be read in times of danger, doubt and defeat. It is to be read, as well, in times of conquest, triumph and glory."

The inscription in the ring read: "This, too, will pass."

The sentence is not to be taken to mean that, in their passing, tears and laughter, hopes and disappointments disappear into a void. But it tells you that all will be absorbed into a unity. Soon we shall see them as integral parts of the full picture of the man or woman.

Upon the lips of the great poet the passing takes the form of mighty, harmonious beauty:

> Nothing of him that doth fade,
> but doth suffer a sea-change
> into something rich and strange.

We may make use of the words—even when we are speaking about ourselves—without vainglory. Each one amongst us will feel in his heart the inherent richness and strangeness of this one thing: his life.

Daguerreotypes

*W*hen I tried to describe over the radio some customs and thoughts of an earlier time, I did not plan that my *causeries* should appear in print. The *Daguerreotypes* were conceived as an oral transmission of things which had reached me orally. I am now allowing them to appear in a book as the result of requests which have reached me from many sides—though I do not mean to shift the responsibility upon those who have suggested the publication.

It is not without some diffidence that I send forth the *Daguerreotypes*. Not everything said in conversation can endure the severe test of being made immortal and subjected to criticism. I will ask my readers to imagine they are my auditors. This little book is no work of literature, but a memento of the two evenings last winter when you honored me by being my guests.

I

I have given the simple sketches which I shall have the honor of showing you—on a couple of evenings,

This essay was originally published as *Daguerrotyper* (Copenhagen, 1951).

here in front of the fireplace at Rungstedlund—the title of *Daguerreotypes*. The daguerreotype was the earliest form of photography and made its appearance and evoked great excitement a century ago; it was named for the Frenchman, Daguerre, who was born in the very year of the revolution, 1789, and made his invention public in a lecture in 1839. I have chosen the name for two reasons.

The first reason is that the old pictures were in no way art, nor did they pretend to be. They were content to be faithful representations of reality. Here and there, in some older houses, old faded daguerreotypes still hang on the walls of the guest-rooms, and they seem to us to be very simple and sober compared with the artistic and skillful portraits made in later days. It was presumably something of a trial to be "taken" by a photographer in the days of the daguerreotype. The client had to sit in a fixed position with a rod running down his back for a full half-minute, without blinking. And it was probably seldom a really pleasant surprise for people who had grown up knowing the portrait painter's interpretation of them, to see themselves in photographic reproduction. Princess Caroline, Prince Ferdinand's spouse, had had her portrait painted many times in her life—but when she was given the first daguerreotype of herself she looked at it silently for a long time and then said, "Well, I am ver-ry thankful that my friends have stood by me." But the daguerreotype could reply to complaints with a righteous insistence on its veracity: it said, "That's the way you look!"

It is not a picture of people from an earlier day that I shall hold up for your inspection; it is rather a reproduction of their ideas and concepts and of their view of life. But I think I share the old Frenchmen's ambition: to reproduce things as they were.

The other reason I have named my sketches after Daguerre is that, in the consciousness of my listeners, he presumably belongs well back in the past. They are not my own memories I shall relate to you, nor my own ideas and concepts I shall present to you: I want to talk about things that were old and antiquated when I first made their acquaintance. I was myself photographed by Elfeldt in the proper fashion, carrying a large bouquet of roses, and I have laughed at the old picture on a metal plate which time left behind in its flight.

I am older than many of my listeners, but I am not Daguerre's contemporary—he would be one hundred and sixty-two years old today. Yet, in another way of thinking, I am much older than Daguerre: a group of my young friends have determined that I am three thousand years old. Therefore, I cannot be personally responsible for the pictures I shall show you any more than someone three thousand years ago could have been responsible for the daguerreotypes. In this matter, as in others, I subscribe to Goethe's remark, "He who cannot account for three thousand years lives only from hand to mouth."

I have wondered from time to time during my life about the fact that mute objects which are put aside in drawers and on shelves, and which are not attacked by moths or rust, undergo drastic changes in their forgotten existences during the course of years.

I have seen it happen in Africa with my party dresses which I bought in Europe and hung up in a closet—and when I took them out to wear after two or three years they had in some way or other stretched or shrunk so that they turned out to be much too long or much too short. They had not changed, but were nevertheless changed. The styles and my own eyes were responsible for the change. After my mother's death I went through some drawers in an old chest. One of them contained albums and loose photographs. They set me to thinking. Here was a photograph that at one time had been "the last word," a very modern portrait of a young woman of fashion. At another time, a generation later, it had been taken out, inspected, and laughed at, for it had turned out to be a quite ridiculous picture of my Aunt Amalie in her youth, in a dress and coiffure which one cannot suppose anybody in the world would invent. Today it is a part of cultural history. The small yellowed surface has acquired depth, an admonishing perspective. We hold in our hand a symbol of the structure and ideology of an epoch, and we sense from all this, as from a long-preserved *potpourri,* the fine, true essence of a departed culture.

We understand while we look at it that there is nothing accidental here: there is a mystical inner connection between the principles, ideals, ambitions, prejudices, and dreams of an age—and its sofas, bouquets, and women's hats. Because Estrup as minister of state was prepared to carry out the defense of Copenhagen, cost what it might; because the czar of Russia as a happy and attentive son-in-law was paying a summer-holiday's visit at Fredensborg Palace; because *A Doll's House* had just been performed at the Royal Theater and had occasioned violent discussion in the newspapers and within families; because on other evenings, on the same stage, Emil Poulsen as Ambrosius had caused young ladies to dissolve in tears; and because Edison had just astonished the world by inventing the phonograph—because of all this, my mother's old friend, the wife of Admiral Bardenfleth, had—at an early stage of her life, as a young seaman's bride—to be photographed with a shy little smile, beneath a complex of braids and curls, and in a dress with tucks, flounces, pleats, and a train, before a background of agitated waves in which could be seen pieces of a wrecked ship and—as a symbol of hope—an anchor.

This strange, passive development is also undergone by comments, assertions, and judgments which we heard uttered many years ago and which have since lain unheeded in our minds until one day some accident causes us to bring them to light again. How they have changed in the interim! Once they had been accepted, orthodox points of view. A generation later, perhaps at the very time we rediscovered them, they were quite unreasonable, indeed offensive or alarming. Today they are history.

At what point does this decisive change take place from a thing rejected and useless to a thing significant to us because we can learn from it? From the used to the everlasting, from the antiquated to the "antique"? A five-year-old hat is dreadfully démodé—"from seventeen hundred and something," as we Danes say. A hat which really dates from the year 1700 is a bit of historical evidence. No doubt a hat ages more quickly and acquires its patina more quickly than a convention, but, for both, the process is certainly completed in a century. When one is sufficiently beyond fifty years of age to have been old enough, fifty years ago, to understand what people were saying; and if one then lived with and listened to old people, one then received intimately and orally views of life which were developed and matured a hundred years ago.

So one can—as I now can—intimately and orally transmit century-old ideas to the youth of a new era. We ourselves made their acquaintance in a day when they were antiquated and useless, and we revolted against them. Can the youth of today learn anything by listening to them, can they put them to any use? A hundred years, that is a twentieth of the time since the birth of Christ—time enough to have aged every wine.

Many young people will answer me as I once answered the people who wanted to teach me about the ways and customs of past times: "What good is your history to us?"

I had a young Norwegian friend in Africa who systematically refused to read any book that was written before 1900. "The modern authors," he said, "have read the classics and learned from them. It is unreasonable to suppose that we need take the same trouble. We want to learn what sort of time we are living in. That is what is of importance to us; that is all we need."

Nevertheless, we say, when a man has lost his memory, that he doesn't know who he is. Of course, he doesn't even know by what name he was christened—though there are people who change their names without losing or changing their personalities in so doing. And in many ways such a man knows very well who he is at the moment. He knows or can find out how much he weighs and what his height is, and in a mirror he can clearly see what he looks like. He knows whether he is well or ill, which colors and which kind of wine he likes, whether he enjoys music, whether he can drive a car, and what he wants to do in the morning. Nevertheless we maintain that, being devoid of experience or an overview of his life, he really doesn't know who he is. And it has always been the case that a self-conscious nation looks to its own history in order fully to understand what it really is.

In a similar way it seems to me that my old daguerreotypes may, for the young person who tonight looks at them, contain certain, perhaps obscure insights—the hints of hitherto unsuspected concatenations.

My first daguerreotype is a remark which, around the turn of the century, I heard made by my old uncle, my father's brother, Court Chamberlain Dinesen of Katholm.

It was probably pronounced for the first time on a summer evening with the doors of the sun porch opened out towards the avenue of linden trees, with cut roses in the room, and long-tailed falling stars in the heavens—for we regularly spent our summer vacation at Katholm.

The hospitality of the old estate was then almost unlimited. When we—my mother and the five of us children, together with our old nursemaid, Malla—arrived intent on settling down in my uncle's home for a month, we always found, in addition to a couple of spinster aunts, several other summer guests: distant relatives, former schoolteachers of some generation of the family, and some of my uncle's former fellow officers. Yet the house was ready and willing to receive any additional guests who would do it the honor of presenting themselves.

My old uncle presided at the table and led the conversation in the sun porch after dinner; he did not otherwise let his daily life be affected by the number of people he had under his roof.

Daguerreotypes

People like him aren't to be found nowadays. I could tell many anecdotes about him. His life bore the mark of his having been sent to Russia as a twenty-two-year-old officer of the Royal Guard as a gentleman-in-waiting when Princess Dagmar went there to marry the Grand Duke and Crown Prince, who later became Czar Alexander III. As my uncle had neither a title nor much money I can only assume he was selected for the elevated mission because of his exceptional good looks. My father, his younger brother, said he was the only perfectly handsome man he had seen in his lifetime. Now, being sent to Russia as a kind of representative of the Danish nation, and being received with waving flags and martial music, could go to one's head. It had gone somewhat to my uncle's head—he liked to recount his memories of the Russian capital and the Winter Palace, and it was interesting to hear him. He had been a brave officer in 1864; he was also a widely traveled old gentleman who felt quite as much at home in Paris as in Copenhagen. But Katholm was for him clearly the center of the universe. He was a blusterer and a domestic tyrant whom a pretty woman or a clever old retainer could wrap around their little finger. I could tell just as many stories about his generosity as about his prejudices.

The conversation this summer evening must have turned to bicycles, which were scarcely a recent invention but which at the time were making rapid headway in all social circles, and among ladies. It was the last fact which incensed and upset my uncle. He began by saying it was damnable to see ladies on bicycles; he met with disagreement—something he really couldn't stand—and he grew so excited he finally struck his knee with his clenched fist and proclaimed in a resounding voice from his military days, "When I see a lady riding a bicycle it seems to me I damn well have the right to warm her bottom!"

I was myself so young I didn't dare raise my voice to refute him. Though I had just been given my first bicycle, I swallowed my indignation in silence. I had two pretty young cousins ten or twelve years older than I who rode elegantly on bicycles and did not let the matter rest; in their high, clear voices they boldly stood up to defend them. They couldn't hold their own, of course, but in the end one of them fired a parting shot: "Well, there's no way you could do that, uncle, for in the first place she would be riding away from you, and in the second place she would be sitting on it!" My uncle was somewhat taken aback, and was unable to come up at once with an answer. "No," he said finally, with great emphasis and with the profound conviction of the just, "No, but the right! The *right* to do it—I would have that, by God."

Late that evening we youngsters continued the debate among ourselves in the tower room and the adjacent large guest room. My two cousins were still hot under the collar. "Right!" they shouted. "What sort of right does uncle think he has? I should really like somebody to explain that to me!"

That is what I now, fifty years later, am trying to do.

One hundred years ago a gentleman's education was an elaborate and costly matter. He was produced through specially predetermined, dignified, and complicated processes. And it is difficult at the present day fully to understand how many of these were intended to give him the proper feeling for women's nobility and the correct attitude towards it. A true gentleman was known primarily by his position on this matter. "Yes, he drinks too much," women could say about him. "He never pays his tailor. We know well he can be brutal." Yet if he was irreproachable in the first article of faith, they would conclude, "But he's a real gentleman." In the English officers' messes it was forbidden under any circumstances whatsoever to mention a lady's name. To break this law was a greater breach of the gentleman ideal than any other.

It will be still more difficult to explain today how the skirt—the long garment—had become such a significant, indeed decisive, symbol of women's nobility and her legs the one sacrosanct taboo. Women of those days were not reticent about displaying their physical charms above the belt. But from the waist to the ground there were mysteries, holy secrets.

Personally, I imagine the explanation to be that trousers are in reality a dubious item of clothing, an item without dignity—even for men they were called "unmentionables" in the days of the daguerreotypes—or that in reality it is a debatable matter whether a dressed person should have two legs. It is often said that trousers are not suitable for women, and I agree, but I must add that they are not suitable for men either. When I think of the robes my friends among the Arabs and Somalis wore, and of the dignity and expressiveness which robes communicated to the movements of their slim figures, I deplore our European men in their sheathings. In Berlin I saw a King Lear appear on the stage in tight-fitting trousers and I understood at once that the garment made it impossible for the actor to play the great, mad king's role, in which the folds of clothing must respond to the mighty outbursts of human passion, and to the gestures. The great dramatic scenes of antiquity—Socrates' death, the murder of Caesar at the Capitol—are incompatible with any image of trousers. Moses in trousers could never have brought forth water from a rock.

In any case, that was the way it was. Long skirts were the most sacred attribute of womanly nobility.

The English author Samuel Butler tells a story about a little boy whose world collapsed when he, on a vacation, was quartered in a room with two young aunts and saw them come out from behind their crinoline, long-legged and bifurcated, whereas he until that moment had believed that ladies were made all in one piece from the waist to the ground.

The nineteenth century laid particular emphasis on this taboo. Queen Caroline Mathilda had ridden in male costume in the more frivolous eighteenth century, but when Carl Ploug attempted to describe the incident, he hesitated to go any farther than

> . . . the riding habit's sable flow
> undulating, allowed to show—
> defying custom, womanly mode—
> to each bold glance, as on she rode,
> the splendor of soft, rounded forms
> half hid when dressed by manly norms.

He could tolerate the queen's erotic excesses, but to go so far as to say she had galloped through the woods in trousers—that was too much.

When, shortly after the turn of the century, women began to ride astride horses, a curious garment, the "divided skirt," was created for them. In most cases it was a skirt on each leg. Nevertheless this had a piquant touch, and a race horse at the Klampenborg track that bore the name "Divided Skirt" was viewed in a frivolous light. But one must assume that honor was preserved.

In my father's book, Boganis's *Letters from the Hunt,* he writes, "It is all very well when ladies are on guard duty but it will be no good when they decide to hunt on foot with guns over their shoulders. However charming a girl's well-formed calf can be when revealed by a carelessly lifted dress, there is nothing at all attractive about chopped-off skirts that show the entire leg up to the knee."

"For," he adds, "the secret of woman's strength lies in suggestion."

I shall tell you two brief anecdotes which illustrate this secret, symbolic importance of the female leg.

The first you can find in Karl Gjellerup's novel *Romulus.* The hero of the book enters a riding school and by chance hears two riders talking about the young lady whom he loves. One asks the other if he has ever glanced up her ankles a bit when helping her into the saddle—then still a side-saddle—and the other answers yes, that has happened. At this the young hero who is in love naturally feels obliged to knock the bold horseman to the ground—and from this develops the plot of the entire novel.

The second was told me by an elderly French gentleman. One evening he had been sitting by the fireplace facing a very pretty young woman, in fact, a princess of the blood. In order to warm her tiny feet in her fine shoes, she had drawn her skirts up a bit above the ankle. *"Ah, Madame,"* said my old friend, *"ça donne envie de voir plus*—that makes one want to see more!" *"Eh bien!"* said the princess, "to please an old friend!" and with this she threw back a whorl of skirts, probably half-way up to her knees, and stretched out a pair of slender silk-clad legs towards him. From the tone of the narrative I deduced that this moment of unusual and lovely favor was for him the apex of his long life.

It should therefore be comprehensible to us that those men who subjected themselves to such hard and lengthy discipline, and who faithfully held to the primary requirement of a gentleman, saw with disapproval, indeed with a touch of real personal bitterness—as if they were being made fools of by the very persons who owed them so much—ladies sit on a bicycle and ride off with both legs boldly displayed. It is comprehensible that, under the circumstances, they felt it a gentleman's duty—even to the extent of employing extreme means—to hinder the misled creatures from tossing away their greatest treasure, in accord with the principle that he

> Who checks the king's evil counsel
> Is the king's best friend.

"But what," the young men and women of the twentieth century will ask, "what was, for the generation born and raised in the first quarter of the nineteenth century, what was the 'woman's nobility' that should not be sacrificed and that could be ruined by transgressions which in no way would compromise a man?"

In his novel *Homeless*, Meïr Goldschmidt gives a kind of poetic explanation of the relationship when he writes, "The theory is, that men are made of stuff that doesn't show spots, whereas women are made of white silk." But modern young people will perhaps not be satisfied with a poetic explanation; they demand a straightforward answer. The exhibitor of daguerreotypes is forced to reply: "I am not able to give a straightforward explanation. The relationship was *per se* poetic. Woman's nobility was contained in woman's mystery. That is the secret strength of the eternal feminine: suggestion."

In trying to explain this matter, it has seemed to me as if the men of that older generation viewed women from three points of view or as three groups—that is to say, viewed or judged them officially in such a manner (but that is a point to which I shall return). Women were for them either guardian angels or housewives or, in a third group, what the Swedish poet Viktor Rydberg calls the priestesses of pleasure, the dancers, and what I here, to use a nice word—for there are a good many that are not so nice—shall call the bayadères.

The ideal woman of real life was a mixture of guardian angel and housewife. In art the most admired and most popular ideal was a mixture of angel and bayadère. We know that from *La Dame aux camélias* and a long series of later novels and plays, right down to *Trilby*.

The guardian angel—unadulterated—shed a heavenly light at a man's side and protected him against the power of darkness. Bjørnson depicts her in a poem in which he describes how a youth "is wounded deep by Eden's serpent and doubts"; he continues:

And on the sunny height
with bridal wreath his childhood dream:
in love's eyes bright,
faith's heav'nly dream.
As from his mother's arms he came
and stammering Jehovah's name,
he kneels and prays
and weeps.

This angelic ideal of woman was probably more generally accepted in Germany and Scandinavia than among the Latins, who are more practically inclined. Goldschmidt relates in a letter from Paris his astonishment that there a young suitor did not look upon his beloved as a heavenly creation and adds, "Not that our young Scandinavian suitor always or unconditionally views his beloved as such a creation—but we assume he does." It is plain that a guardian angel is surrounded by a mystical aura, and where she is envisaged in long white garments, hovering, it would certainly be profane or actually precluded to direct attention to her legs.

The housewife—whether she is the mistress of a castle or of a manse or is a farmer's wife—is naturally more tangible. But she nevertheless wears decent long garments. In the nineteenth century—in any case in the country, for I believe in the cities things were somewhat different—the religion and poetry of everyday existence belonged to woman's domain. Though the children and servants in the household would risk a strong reprimand if they made fun of the master of the house, that did not mean they were lost souls. But to scoff at the mother or mistress of the household was a sacrilege. "Invisible," wrote Jonas Lie, "invisible yet ever present like the good spirit of the house—isn't that the best thing one can say about a woman?" The housewife didn't have legs either.

An anecdote will serve to throw light on the relationship. At the end of the nineteenth century in Jutland there was a local prefect who had a wife of the unadulterated housewife type and also a gardener named Larsen. One day Larsen came to the prefect's house and asked to speak to him in private. "I feel I must tell the prefect something," he said. "I dreamed

last night that I saw the prefect's wife in the nude."
The prefect was just as embarrassed to receive this
confession as Larsen was to make it. What he replied
is not known for certain, but the story goes that he
said, "It is quite proper of you, Larsen, to tell me
about this. But it must not happen again." If one
imagines one's self in the position of the prefect, one
will understand it would have been easier if the prefect's wife had been more of a guardian angel or bayadère type.

And now the bayadère. Yes, she did have legs to be
sure, and this fact gave her almost her greatest significance. But the fact in no way negates the holy
taboo; in reality it reinforces it: it is the same taboo
expressed in a different mode.

Here the taboo may be defined in figures, and in
figures which will seem incomprehensibly large to
your time. One might say that in this matter the true
gentleman's loyalty vis-à-vis the dignity of woman
found expression in the sums he was willing to pay to
see the bayadère's legs.

My old friend Mr. Bulpett, who with a clear conscience had ruined himself for the sake of a
bayadère—La Belle Otéro—has many times told me
about the grand courtesans who played a rôle in
France during the Second Empire and up to the turn
of the century. Millions passed through their hands
every year. Like Zola's Nana, they drove to the races
in a four-in-hand; their jewels outshone those of the
guardian angel as well as those of the housewife.
Gaby Deslys, he said, had been the last of the really
great courtesans. When I asked him the reasons they
were no longer in the picture, he answered after reflection, "There are too many amateurs these days."
In his capacity as a real sporting man, he was inciden-

tally displeased to see the borderline erased between amateurs and professionals. I remember I once told him something I had read in a fashion journal from home, that the fan was about to make a comeback. He was so pleased by this piece of news that he rubbed his hands together, and when I asked the reason for his satisfaction he answered, somewhat surprised at my ignorance, that it was perfectly clear. A fan was the only gift, save for a bouquet of flowers, which a gentleman could allow himself to give a lady *comme il faut*. For that matter it could be very expensive. "It will," he said, "fill a long-felt need, since you women have not used fans for a long time."

The guardian angel and the housewife could not possibly sanction the existence of the bayadère. Nevertheless there must have been a certain satisfaction for them to have, in the bayadère, on paper and in definite figures, so to speak, a kind of proof of what their own womanly stake was worth.

In reality it was worth more than could be put on paper, for the bayadère, with her four-in-hand and her jewels, was an outcast of society—if not also of Paradise.

I have said that the men of the nineteenth century viewed their women from these points of view, or in three groups, officially. I use the word "officially" because in reality they had in their consciousness still another type of woman which for all of them was very much alive and present but was not mentioned or recognized by the light of day.

The guardian angel, the housewife, and the bayadère—each had her calling, her justification, and her importance in relationship to man. They saved and guided him, or they took care of his well-being and reputation, or they enraptured and transported him. Eve was created from Adam's rib; it was for man's sake that woman existed and Søren Kierkegaard defined a woman's being as "existence for something else."

But there was a woman who, long before the words "emancipation of women" came into use, existed independently of a man and had her own center of gravity. She was the witch.

The witch has played a greater or lesser rôle in various eras but she has never entirely disappeared. One may suppose that for most men the explanation is, that a woman who can exist without a man certainly also can exist without God, or that a woman who does not want to be possessed by a man necessarily must be possessed by the devil. The witch had absolutely no scruples about showing her legs; she sat quite unconstrained astride her broomstick and took off.

And still—despite all the sinister atmosphere and abandon which surrounded her—the witch cannot be said to have renounced or to have betrayed the dignity of woman. She confirmed—in demonic fashion but with gravity—the fundamental dogma that the secret of woman's power is suggestion.

The judges at the witch trials who used every means to procure the witch's confession that on the island of Samsö she had worked magic which kept Princess Anne from her journey to her bridegroom, James VI of Scotland, refrained from acquiring the magic recipe itself from her.

In Africa it is assumed that all old women can practice sorcery. More than that: that they turn into hyenas at night and run around, laughing, on the veldt looking for corpses. I once saw this quite seriously expounded in a book by an important English traveler. I told my brother, who had been on a safari in Somaliland, about it. He grew silent, but told me later that one night—in order to chase hyenas away from the "kill" on which he hoped to shoot a lion or leopard—he had fired a couple of shots and unwittingly hit a hyena. It could not be found in the morning; he could follow the trail of its blood for a way, but then the trail ceased. When he went home to the Somali village, he heard weeping and wailing from far off. A respected old lady, a grandmother and a great-grandmother, had inexplicably lost her life during the night.

I once—also in Africa—had a conversation on this subject with a French-born friend. She expressed her unshakeable conviction that all men without exception believed in witches. They only differed in the degree they feared them. "The more a man is a man, my dear," she said, "the more openly will he admit to believing in witches, but he will correspondingly hate or fear them less. Sailors are willing to admit they have made the acquaintance of more than one witch in their lifetime, but towards them they are rather kindly disposed, and will even admit from time to time that they owe them a debt of gratitude. Men of learning are not ready to admit the existence of witches, but the fear of a witch is in their blood. And those men who themselves dress in long robes—the clergy—they hate and fear a witch more than they hate and fear her lord and master."

"Even though the witch is a lonely figure," said my friend, "she has a good relationship with her sister witches. She is a black guardian angel, a bat on a dark night filled with Northern lights as a flickering reflection from the time that Lucifer was the morning star. She is a housewife to the hilt: fire and fireplace are precious to her and the cauldron is indispensable. She is a bayadère and a seductress even as a Sibyl or a mummy:

> black from Phoebus's pinch of love
> and wrinkled deep by time . . .

And if the learned gentlemen feel their masculine dignity is affronted by the thought that she prefers the devil to a man, then the layman and outdoorsman find some compensation in another remark: the basis, indeed the prerequisite for the witch's entire activity is the circumstance that the devil is masculine."

The old lady continued, "We women, my child, are often very simple. But that any female would lack reason to such a degree that she would start reasoning with a man—that is beyond my comprehension! She has lost the battle, my dear child, she has lost the battle before it began! No, if a woman will have her way with a man she must look him square in the eye and say something of which it is impossible for him to make any sense whatsoever and to which he is at a loss to reply. He is defeated at once."

She supported her theory with examples from history. Englishwomen, she said, had for a long time tried to obtain the franchise, and their arguments and rationalism had failed to budge the resistance of the English MP's. Then around the turn of the century the "suffragettes" began their maneuvers illegally and quite irrationally—they climbed up on rooftops, stretched ropes across highways, and threw themselves in front of the winning horse at the Derby—then the gentlemen in Parliament were overcome by fright; their old convictions began to creak at the joints. And a short time later women had the franchise.

"And I can assure you," said Lady Colville, "that women's societies and women's organizations could achieve far more, indeed would make shortcuts directly to their goals if, instead of forming committees, making speeches, and writing articles—all tame and simple imitations of men—they would let it be known the country over that they would meet on the heath and on the commons under a waning moon."

My young female listeners who have had the patience to follow me to this point will perhaps turn towards me and declare, "But we don't want to be mysterious at all. We are and want to be part of reality. We renounce all our secret power!"

I have already said that the views which I am presenting here are not my own, and that I cannot be held responsible for them. I myself—many years ago, in Africa—had my reservations about Lady Colville's creed.

But when my old friend and teacher in the art of witchcraft had reflected upon my protest, she replied,

"It is of course up to you, *ma jolie,* to make your own choice. I wish only in this connection to tell you a little story.

"As a young girl, my sister returned home from a trip to Italy and declared at a family gathering, 'I wouldn't give five francs for all the paintings in the Uffizi.' My half-grown brother cried out at once, 'For heaven's sakes, Marie-Louise, keep your opinion to yourself; you reveal a complete lack of business acumen!'"

Yes, all that is in a way a continuation of the talk which fifty years ago was carried on by five girls at Katholm one summer night. It is an attempt to answer the scandalized question: "What does uncle think he is? What sort of a right does he think he has?"

That is the first daguerreotype from my drawer.

II

The second daguerreotype which I shall show you this evening is older than the first. The event which it records must have taken place before I was born. Nevertheless, the greater remoteness in time has not lessened, but on the contrary has increased, its pertinence. I believe it has made a great impression on me because I can imagine how deep an impression it made on those who personally experienced it.

I do not say the event took place exactly as I describe it. My youthful fantasy played with it until it acquired its present form. I tell it now as a little story.

A young aunt of mine had recently married the owner of an estate in Jutland. On the neighboring estate, which I shall call Vindinge, she had a good friend named Margrethe who, like herself, was young and newly wed. One day Margrethe drove over to my aunt's in considerable distress in order to tell her of a problem which had recently arisen and to seek advice and, if possible, help from her. My aunt was able neither to advise nor to help her, but the two young women discussed the matter and my aunt then passed it on unresolved to her sisters, through whom it reached me.

They were to have a hunt at Vindinge. Nowadays

one can scarcely imagine what a rôle the great autumnal *battues* played in the life of an estate; they
were the year's grandest and most sacred festivals.
The young mistress of the house was planning the
menus for the hunting dinners with the trusted and
honored housekeeper. Miss Sejlstrup paused, looked
at the mistress of the house, and asked her, "Would
Madam please tell me, why must the servants have
less choice food than the family?" The pause after this
question grew very long. The mistress of the house
was unprepared for the question; it silenced her.
After a time the discussion of the menus was re-
newed as if the question had not been put.

But it had been asked, and from that moment on it
could not be evaded by the person to whom it had
been put. In her mind it resurfaced again and again.
She was, as I have said, very young and she was used
to seeking help among older people for those problems she herself could not solve.

After some time, when she understood that by
herself she could make no progress, she went to her
mother-in-law, who lived at the dowager's house on
the estate, and laid the matter before her. Her
mother-in-law said, "Well, good Miss Sejlstrup has
been too long in service—or I must believe she has a
screw loose! You must ask to be spared such imperti-
nent questions in the future!" As her daughter-in-law
turned this decision over and over in her mind, it did
not seem to her really to be an answer to Miss
Sejlstrup's question.

She then wrote home to her mother, "Miss
Sejlstrup asked me, when we were looking through
the menus for the hunt, why the servants should
have less choice food than the family, and I was unable to answer her. Will you write and let me know

how you would have answered the question?" Her mother wrote back, "I am distressed to hear that good Miss Sejlstrup has complained about the food in your house. Our own house has always had the reputation of providing a good and abundant diet in the servants' quarters. I think that in this case you should have inquired whether she had anything in particular to complain about in the servants' food at Vindinge and, should that prove to have been the case, you should have discussed the conditions with her in detail and have attempted to eradicate the flaws." Her daughter read the letter through many times, and could not explain to herself why it did not seem to provide the answer to Miss Sejlstrup's question. She had really taken pains to see that the servants at Vindinge lived quite as well and as amply as they had in her childhood home. The difference about which Miss Sejlstrup had inquired existed in one house as well as in the other.

Some days later she went to her husband, whom she ordinarily did not like to trouble with household matters. "Frederik," she said, "Miss Sejlstrup asked me the other day why the servants here should have less choice food than the family, and I could think of nothing to answer her. What do you think I should have said?" Her husband laughed at her—or to her. "My dear girl," he said, "I hope you never have to answer a more difficult question than that! 'Well, my sweet Miss Sejlstrup,' you should have said, 'it is because the family is sitting on the money bags and decides how the money is to be used.'" She asked him no further questions, but shortly afterwards when the question arose again in her mind, she felt he had not given her the answer, either.

Some time passed in which she avoided Miss

Sejlstrup's glance. Then she went to her husband's somewhat shabby tutor, who lived on the estate during the winter in order to be able to write in peace a treatise about Erik Glipping. He was well informed about almost everything, and was kindly disposed to explain almost anything to her.

"Doctor," she said to him, "Miss Sejlstrup asked me why the servants here should have food of lower quality than the family and I have not been able to find anything to reply to her. What should I have said?" The old man put his pen down, smiled at the serious young face before him and said, "Little Mrs. Margrethe! You can tell Miss Sejlstrup from me that she is living not a little better than King Erik Glipping did in his time. His table was depressingly simple. Coffee—as I understand it, Miss Sejlstrup drinks not a few cups of coffee during the day—was known at the Court of that time just as little as tea or chocolate, and there was very little sugar. Rice, sago, raisins, prunes, and lemons were seldom seen, and Columbus had not yet discovered potatoes. There was beer soup, cabbage, and salted meat which regularly found its way to the royal table. And with regard to lighting and heating, Miss Sejlstrup reaps such fruits of our civilization as the king could never have imagined!"

"Yes," thought Margrethe, "that was interesting to hear about, and it was too bad about Erik Glipping, although he didn't deserve better after his affair with Lady Ingeborg in *Erik Menved's Childhood*. But was it an answer to Miss Sejlstrup's question? No, it wasn't, after all."

When she was about to leave, the old tutor turned towards her clear-eyed and lifted his index finger. "We must not forget," he said, "and we must not forget, Lady Margrethe, that Erik Glipping was king by the grace of God!" This the lady either did not hear or did not understand; she went away quite as uncertain in her mind as she had come.

And as she had now sought counsel from all those who should be better informed than herself, in the simplicity of her heart she tried to imagine what she herself might have said, had she the fluency and the courage, to answer Miss Sejlstrup. She had had no practice in argumentation; she would have to speak practically. And this is what she imagined she would have said:

"Good heavens, Miss Sejlstrup, I am a Christian! It's no more than four years ago since I was confirmed. And I know very well that when someone asks for your coat you give him your cloak as well, and that it is more difficult for a rich man to enter the kingdom of Heaven than it is for a camel to pass through the eye of a needle. My home is meant to be a Christian home. But how can we arrange that in everyday housekeeping, Miss Sejlstrup?

"Let us go through the household accounts together, as we so frequently have done. The family table here costs in cold cash ten crowns each person each day, and there are only two of us in the family. In the servants' quarters downstairs it costs in cash one crown a day for each person each day, and there are ten of you. I have learned both addition and division and I am also able to reckon *per cent*—we could put the sums together and divide the result by twelve. Then it would look something like this:

2 persons at 10 crowns = 20 crowns
10 persons at 1 crown = 10 crowns
_____
30 crowns ÷ 12 = 2.50 crowns

"So the servants would go up by 150% while the family went down by 75%, and that may seem all well and good.

"But you can see for yourself that our way of life on the estate would have to be changed radically. Many things would have to be given up and would disappear. The first of these—yes, it would have to be you, Miss Sejlstrup. You were apprenticed in the king's kitchen and you are very proficient in preparing French food. But if we all are to have meatballs and pancakes, we shall have no use for anything which you have learned. Stine, the kitchen help, can easily take care of all the cooking. It would be no sort of task to require of you, and I am not even certain you would be content with it.

"And then you can understand that the master and I would not be able to continue social life on the estate. We could not offer sago soup and fried calf's liver here to people from neighboring estates where we had enjoyed turtle soup and paté de foie gras. There would be no hunting dinners and no more hunts—and the next persons to become superfluous would be the butler and the gamekeeper. The hothouses and the flower decorations would also be superfluous, so the gardener and his helper could leave. And if I were no longer inviting guests here, I would not be able to go out myself, so I could do without the chambermaid, Madsen. We would not have to fetch guests from the station, either, or even drive out on visits, so the master would let Jens the coachman go!

"I must say, Miss Sejlstrup, I would not be at all unhappy to take part in such an arrangement. The master and I could lead a cozy life together. But many persons would take offense at us and say that we behaved ourselves in a dreadfully incorrect fashion. I am not sure that the very first of these would not be you yourself, Miss Sejlstrup."

Margrethe was quite surprised that she could compose such a long and reasonable address to Miss Sejlstrup! But was it really an answer to the fateful question? She did not know.

You see this was, as I told you, a story. But it is more than a story: it is history.

When in the pantry at Vindinge Miss Sejlstrup turned towards the mistress of the estate and put her question, the hour struck. One has said something significant when one says the hour has struck for a human being or for a period.

We who this evening have taken out the old daguerreotype in order to inspect it, must now ask those people of another age, "Why could none of you, neither those of the conventional persuasion, or the unthinking, nor those endowed with conscientiously searching minds, answer Miss Sejlstrup's question?" It is tempting—and it is for us the easiest solution—to maintain that the people of that time could very well have answered the question, but that they *would* not. It is tempting—and it is for us the easiest solution—to maintain that the few who at that time possessed many worldly goods, in their own consciences knew very well they were doing an injustice to the many who had few possessions; that they elected to stop their ears to the voice of conscience and to be satisfied with an injustice of which they themselves enjoyed the benefits. " 'Now we're all well placed,' said the cat as it sat on the bacon."

I myself do not believe that explanation. Those people of another era of the sort who inhabited Vindinge, and whom I personally knew, were quite as honest as those who today stand up for principles and ideas. There was actually at that time, if one is to make a comparison at all, a somewhat higher standard of what one calls honesty or integrity.

And now that we've begun talking about conscience I should like to add a few words upon the matter.

I know from experience it is surprisingly easy to arouse a feeling of guilt in people, to give them what we call a guilty conscience. But there must, nevertheless, be a certain relationship between what a human being's conscience requires him to do and what his reason, experience, and fantasy allow him to recognize as things capable of execution.

Let us now imagine—for one can imagine what one will—that the demand for equality has been extended to embrace such boons of life as beauty, intelligence, and talent.

Then relatives and friends would say to the pretty young girl, "How can you let Aunt Maren sit there with the figure she has, or the wife of General Løvenhielm with the nose she has, while you yourself enjoy your own nose and your own figure? What does your conscience say about that?" The teacher would come to the father of his pupil and say, "Your son easily solves equations of the third degree and here sits little Peter Købke next to him who cannot get an equation of the first degree into his head. What does your conscience say about that?"

And the critic would come to the writer and say, "Every month, yes, every week, you write a lovely poem. But next door to you there lives a poet who never advances beyond mediocrity. What does your conscience say about that?" It's quite possible that after the question had been put to her, the pretty young girl would avoid looking at herself in the mirror. It is quite possible the father would look through his son's report card, no longer with pride but with a heavy heart. And it's also possible the writer would reject the next poem that formed itself in his mind. Various problems which in themselves have nothing to do with our subject would announce themselves in this connection. I will name them, because they may arise among my listeners. One of you might ask, perhaps, "How much should there be to each person?" And another, "Would I be happy—and well served—to have several shelves more of mediocre literary works instead of a single, perfect, beautiful poem?" Perhaps the young listener will burst out, "Should I never again see a really beautiful girl?" I shall leave these reflections aside, since a discussion would lead us too far astray.

But a single problem must unavoidably be put by the conscience-stricken—the pretty girl as well as the proud father or the writer—to him who made the claim of absolute equality. They would have to ask him, "But can this indeed be carried out? If it can, how?"

With a certain amount of suspicion and indignation we today seek to find out how it could have been that the conscience of a past era could accept an uneven distribution of worldly goods. We note, with some self-consciousness, that the last century has revised the conscience of society. But let us think it possible to find the explanation where we have not sought it before. Let us imagine—and one can imagine anything—that the change has taken place not with the concept "conscience" but with the concept "worldly goods." Let us imagine—and one can imagine what one will—that a past era, in reality and by their very nature, viewed things correctly and that its own worldly goods, in reality and by their very nature, could not be distributed evenly.

For a new godhead—which was not unknown in Miss Sejlstrup's time but then had a much more modest place among the forces which determine human existence—has since asserted itself, achieved the first place among the powers, overthrown some values and established others and switched human striving from one track to another. The name of this godhead is Comfort, which is known in all languages but which in Danish can be best expressed by words like *Velvære*—physical well-being—or *Bekvemmelighed*—convenience.

Aldous Huxley says, in his essay *Comfort:*

French hotel-keepers call it *le confort moderne*, and they are right. For comfort is a thing of recent growth, younger than steam, a child when telegraphy was born, only a generation older than radio. The invention of the means of being comfortable and the pursuit of comfort as a desirable end—one of the most desirable that human beings can propose to themselves—are modern phenomena, unparalleled in history since the time of the Romans. Like all phenomena with which we are extremely familiar, we take them for granted, as a fish takes the water in which it lives, not realizing the novelty and oddity of them, not bothering to consider their significance. The padded chair, the well-sprung bed, the sofa, central heating, and the regular hot bath—these and a host of other comforts enter into the daily lives of even the most moderately prosperous of the Anglo-Saxon bourgeoisie. Three hundred years ago they were unknown to the greatest kings.

He continues:

> The first thing that strikes one about the discomfort
> in which our ancestors lived is that it was mainly
> voluntary. Some of the apparatus of modern com-
> fort is of purely modern invention; people could
> not put rubber tyres on their carriages before the
> discovery of South America and the rubber plant.
> But for the most part there is nothing new about
> the material basis of *le confort moderne*.

This circumstance struck me when I visited the old
Norwegian farms and houses in the Sandvig Outdoor
Museum in Lillehammer. People in Norway three
hundred years ago were able to create manifold beautiful and artistic objects: jewelry, drinking vessels,
fine carvings in wood, finely woven carpets. But from
the time they entered the world until they left it,
these same people thought nothing of sitting or lying
in ways which according to our concepts were un-
comfortable. And nevertheless it must at all times
have been possible to make a chair the back of which,
unlike the old Norwegian chairs, was not completely
vertical and the seat of which from back to front
measured something more than twenty centimeters.
What really was important or attractive about a
chair or a bed must for these older inhabitants of
Norway have been the decorations upon which they
were ready to sacrifice almost unlimited time and
thought. Comfort came much later.

Huxley writes, further:

> But the nobleman, the prince, the king, and the
> cardinal inhabited palaces of a grandeur corre-
> sponding with their social position. In order to
> prove that they were greater than other men, they
> had to live in surroundings considerably more than

life-size. They received their guests in vast halls like roller-skating rinks; they marched in solemn processions along galleries as long and as draughty as Alpine tunnels, up and down triumphal staircases that looked like the cataracts of the Nile frozen into marble.

Driving in the environs of Chicago [he continues], I was shown the house of a man who was reputed to be one of the richest and most influential in the city. It was a medium-sized house of perhaps fifteen or twenty smallish rooms. I looked at it in astonishment, thinking of the vast palaces in which I myself have lived in Italy (for considerably less rent than one would have to pay for garaging a Ford in Chicago). I remembered the rows of bedrooms as big as ordinary ballrooms, the drawing-rooms like railway stations, the staircase on which you could drive a couple of limousines abreast. Noble *palazzi*, where one has room to feel oneself a superman! But remembering also those terrible winds that blow in February from the Apennines, I was inclined to think that the rich man of Chicago had done well in sacrificing the magnificence on which his counterpart in another age and country would have spent his riches.

He had done well. Here it is a matter of a choice which those persons most fortunately placed in society must make according to their taste—for wealth or power was the condition in the one case as well as the other. The American millionaire's generation, when free to do so, makes the same choice he did. Why, we must ask ourselves, did people three hundred years ago, who actually were completely free to make a choice, everywhere and unreservedly choose the other part?

In his essay Huxley believes he can provide us with the explanation.

Indeed, he says, physical well-being and comfort were without actual significance for past ages. It was rank—precedence; it was dignity, majesty, and pomp which were for them life's greatest values. "Grandiosity" Huxley calls it—arrogance. We can perhaps gather all these concepts in the French word, *prestige*.

In order clearly to demonstrate that they were superior human beings, kings, princes, and cardinals had to spend their lives in superhuman surroundings. In order to preserve their own dignity they had to form their existence like a series of processions and ballets. And for them it was all worth the effort. The need for physical well-being and comfort was in their eyes a weakness which they owed it to themselves to overcome.

It is obvious that those persons who believe in and fight for an equal distribution of worldly goods must unknowingly look upon these worldly goods as identical with physical well-being.

We can imagine and we can look forward to a fortunate state of affairs where every human being lies in a good bed, sits on a comfortable chair, has heat in his room and sufficient good food; has the possibility of entertainment, and of being transported quickly and securely from one place to another.

But if every human being sits on a throne, the value of a throne is diminished or disappears entirely. Every human being could be transported to a goal in an automobile or an airplane, but not every human being could arrive first. Rank—precedence—cannot be distributed equally without the concept itself being liquidated. Not every human being can excel, and it is unthinkable that every human being can impress every other human being.

> You are more than your own power,
> And it is my solace, that you signify . . . .
> (Sophus Claussen)

In his essay Aldous Huxley says that comfort is "an end in itself." It has no symbolic significance, for it is what it is; it is tangible. His opinion is not completely valid. Very few people love *das Ding an sich,* as he presumes, and in many cases large automobiles have their greatest value simply as symbols: they are tokens of success. But the era of comfort has, more than any other time, regularly denied symbols and rituals. Earlier times have carried on wars to achieve the right to put three crowns in a coat-of-arms. The time of comfort is of the opinion that the national flag is in reality a composite of so-and-so many pieces of cloth of various colors.

Who is closest to reality—he who, seeing the tricolor, exclaims "There is France," or he who exclaims, "There are five meters of red, blue, and white cloth?" To me personally it seems as if human intelligence never has taken a more decisive step than when, instead of counting the concrete numbers one, two, three, four, it began operating with abstract quantities—a and b, x and y. The concrete sums one can count up—they are what they are, they are tangible "to take hold and feel"; the symbols are universally valid, and they elevate mathematics into a science.

In contrast to the time when comfort repudiates symbols stands the time when prestige has faith in them. In their purest and clearest form, privileges —those worldly goods which according to their very nature cannot be distributed equally—are of symbolic nature.

A privilege is intrinsically a favor. And what concrete expression the favor finds is of less importance. In its purest form privilege is never personal property; it is only administered by him who holds it. It can be forfeited but it cannot be bestowed. Crown jewels, the golden monstrances and chasubles of the church, fiefs and entailed estates cannot be translated into money by their administrators. In its purest form privilege is disassociated from physical well-being or comfort.

Hara-kiri—that is, ritual suicide by cutting into one's bowels, an act which erases an insult and gives the unjustly accused man satisfaction—was the privilege of Japanese nobility. The old noble families had special, ritual knives lying ready to make use of their privilege. Whether hara-kiri is a comfortable way of leaving this life was never taken into consideration. Among the Somali tribes, all of whom have much family pride and keep careful account of their antecedents, it is the privilege of very old families to use a particular kind of stirrup of ancient vintage. It consists, quite simply, of a ring through which the rider puts his big toe. I myself tried these old stirrups and nobody could get me to ride very far in them. Farah, my major-domo, told me that a young man of lesser birth once, when wooing, had used such stirrups. The old families had sat in council and decided to chop off both big toes of the impudent young rider so that he should not again infringe upon a legitimate prerogative. Contrary to custom, the old women had had a place in this council.

A grandee of Spain had the right to keep his hat on in the presence of his king. I do not know whether this right has ever been exercised, except in Victor Hugo's tragedy *Hernani*. If, with the honest intention of creating equality, one gave everybody the right to keep their hats on in the presence of the king, just as they now have the right to keep on their shoes, one would rob the élite of a favor without in any way enriching the many. A royal grandee of Spain goes through the streets of kingless Madrid today, sees the powerful automobiles of the new men of wealth pass by, and is not at all affected by the sight. For he knows that if there were a king of Spain today in whose presence he might come, he would have the right—which he would never use—to keep his hat on. And he would not exchange this boon for any automobile.

In Italy it was the privilege of the nobility in the eighteenth century to dress in black, and this somber negation of color stood out against the sartorial rainbow as the mark of the élite. At courts in the time of powdered perukes it looked as if the chosen had covered their heads with ashes.

When horse-drawn carriages were still being used in Copenhagen, it was the privilege of the Danish nobility to have a "blinker"—a little mirror—on the horse's headgear. As a child I heard old people seriously discussing the encroachment upon this privilege by some *nouveaux riches*. By the same token it was the privilege of noble ladies to place "snip"—a piece of crêpe—on the hats they wore during mourning; and at the death of Christian IX, in any case, it was still of great importance which ladies could permit themselves to "mourn with *snip*."

In the olden days—in the days of Miss Sejlstrup— one spoke of an estate's "luxuries." I remember that when a young man in the family had bought an estate, my old uncle immediately inquired, "Are there any luxuries?" The luxuries of these estates were not tangible nor could they be translated into money. They could be a view from which one could count eleven churches, or a row of warrior's barrows, or a copse of very old oak trees which must not be felled. They could have to do with the hunt, they could be red deer or wild boar or a particular kind of game bird which was not to be found on neighboring estates. It could even be a legend connected with the estate, or finally, perhaps, a ghost, a "white woman."

I remember an estate in Jutland which was called "the estate with seven times seven luxuries."

I have said that Miss Sejlstrup's question was put at a decisive time. The powerful new concept, comfort, had just begun to penetrate the preserves of ritual and privilege. Those who possessed the old privileges grew uncertain under the pressure of the spirit of the times and contemplated selling their firstborn rights for a mess of pottage.

At the moment when the question was put, the relationships of the inhabitants of Vindinge were also uncertain—for Miss Sejlstrup, who with hesitation asked the question, as well as for the mistress of the estate, who was troubled because she could think of no reply. Face to face they were balanced, in the pantry, each with one foot in a different age.

It can also be said that Miss Sejlstrup's question struck the point of intersection of the two ages. For it was a matter of food—one of the good things in life, but also a necessity.

The era of prestige could have taken as its motto Voltaire's old maxim: *"C'est le superflu qui est le nécessaire"*—'It is the superfluous which is a necessity.' But here the word "superfluous" must have meant not an excess of the necessary but a contradistinction to it. There must have been a difference not in degree but in kind between the two concepts.

Privilege is sinful if it makes a claim on a necessity of life, sinful not only with regard to human justice but with regard to its own being. Ritual can adopt bread as its highest symbol, but only in its simplest, in its oldest, form. With the Danish open-faced sandwich, ritual can have no communion.

The relationship was the clearer, and the idea of ritual and symbols was more clearly expressed, when—several hundred years before the incident in the pantry—people stressed the magnificent decoration of the table, gold and silver plates, the livery and chains of the staff of servants, and invested large sums in show dishes that were not eaten.

The relationship was also clearer when, a few generations after the episode in the pantry, people in the time of comfort itself—perhaps in a phase of surfeit, perhaps surprised and impressed by the mighty scenes of the First World War—became enamored of renunciation and gave up luxury of all kinds. They limited women's clothing to the least possible, had them cut their hair short, and demanded that their dress should adopt vertical lines. When in 1920, on the way from Africa to Denmark, I was in Paris and tried to familiarize myself with the newest fashions and rules of good manners, a French friend of mine said that one no longer saw a real lady in a *pâtisserie*. "And if we are invited out to dinner," she said, "we have a cup of consommé and three pieces of asparagus. I also know," she said, and she was profoundly serious, "more than one person who has died of hunger." These real ladies were unmercifully devoted to eternal hunger. If they felt a temptation and had a biscuit with their afternoon tea, then at dinner they had to give up their asparagus. It was not only thousands or tens of thousands but hundreds of thousands of women who kept these rules.

A fashion always has some meaning. The fashion, or style, of renunciation really meant something then. It was inspired by the war, or it ran parallel to the war, and could not have been conceived without the war. It was, so to speak, the time of comfort in reverse. In art it became Cubism. It stood for the same thing as Rupert Brooke's poem, *Now God be thanked who matched me with this hour!* in which the fair, fêted poet in exaltation casts away everything that life hitherto had offered him. It stood for the will to sacrifice—if the unlimited will to throw away can be called the will to sacrifice. It was arrogant and elegantly cynical—because it is arrogant and elegantly cynical when the symbol of the élite becomes hunger. The superfluous here threw away the necessary quite simply. In its inner essence it was the disdain of death. It was with those soldiers who, with the odor of powder in their nostrils, came in from Zeebrügge and the next morning were off to battlefields in Flanders, that the young short-haired female skeletons danced the night through. But as the content of life was volatilized, the disdain of death became senile. The great war of liberation which had inspired the fashion was—or became—"the great war for civilization." And civilization was—or had come to mean—generally accessible physical well-being. The fashion, or the style, of renunciation came to mean very little.

The relationship was, as aforementioned, uncertain for Miss Sejlstrup herself. Did she in her heart comprehend that it was well-being, or the prestige of those above her, which she desired? If we imagine that a right-thinking daughter in the age of comfort twenty-five years later had had the choice between being in the shoes of the mistress of the manor or in those of Miss Sejlstrup, we must imagine that, for the sake of her physical well-being and comfort, she would have chosen Miss Sejlstrup's.

Clothing has always been an area in human existence where ritual has a predilection for expression. Priests change their clothes before the altar, and during a coronation kings are dressed and undressed many times by the highest ecclesiastics of the realm. Polonius says to Laertes:

Costly thy habit as thy purse can buy,
But not express'd in fancy; rich not gaudy,
For the apparel oft proclaims the man,
And they in France of the best rank and station
Are of a most select and generous chief in that.

The dress of the old upper class was honest and consistently ritualistic—the superfluous there was never a superabundance of the necessary. The dress of the privileged was in no way warmer or more practical than that of the common people; any superfluity which characterized it was symbolic.

The corsets which the ladies of that time wore, and which reached to the armpits, were really as much instruments of torture as the bound feet of the old Chinese women, and like them were an accepted symbol of true, fine femininity. Just as little as a knight could get into his armor without the help of his squire, could a lady get into her corset without the help of a strong chambermaid who pulled its laces to the breaking point. No real lady could at any moment from the time she stood up until she went to bed move at all freely. Other distinctions belonged to the female cultural uniform: French heels, collars stiffened with whalebone, and trains. And while the ritual which gentlemen had to submit to in their dress was somewhat less severe than that of the women, it did not sanction ease or comfort either. At no time did it accept soft collars, soft cuffs, or soft hats, and that garment which we call the dinner jacket did not appear until after the turn of the century.

The English politician Gladstone visited his old university town of Oxford when he was advanced in years and looked with amazement and perhaps with pity upon the students of the new era. He recalled that in his own time every self-respecting student owned a pair of trousers in which he never sat down—the more fortunate had two or three such pairs and were envied by the less fortunate.

The ritual also determined in other ways the daily existence of a lady or a gentleman. No lady could sit with her legs crossed. A gentleman making a visit left his cane in the *entré* but brought his hat and gloves into the parlor and had to learn to maneuver with these on his knees and a teacup in his hand. The ceremonial included going to church, making obligatory visits, and court mourning, right down to the ways of expressing oneself orally.

This relationship was obviously unclear to the mistress of the estate, who with the help of addition and division tried distributing equally the food and the prestige.

Still, in this time of transition there was an important moment of prestige involved in the meals. When the long menus were composed, it was the honor of Vindinge that was at stake.

The master of the estate himself, who valued highly the pleasures of the table, would have preferred to relinquish one meal a day rather than the custom that every pedestrian took his hat off when the carriage from Vindinge passed. His mother, the old widow of the court chamberlain, would have relinquished her morning chocolate as well as her afternoon tea before ceasing to require that she be addressed in the third person. And the host and hostess at the long table in the dining room would have preferred, had it been possible to do so with dignity, personally to abstain from enjoying each of the courses of the dinner rather than see the honor of Vindinge lessened by the omission of a single course.

And let us here return to the menu itself which engendered Miss Sejlstrup's historical and pertinent question.

I have an old cookbook from the year 1875, that is to say almost exactly Miss Sejlstrup's time. I shall not discuss the menus for the grand dinners, the *soupers*, or the balls, but the book includes towards its close a series of menus for daily use. The author writes, "We hope that in any case our lady readers will here be able to find one idea or another for dishes which will win the approval of their husbands, who not infrequently make quiet but rather excessive culinary demands." I shall reproduce a couple of these menus.

I	II
Puréed game	Turtle soup
Oysters on the half shell	Cod with oyster sauce
Salmon cutlets à la genevoise	Sweetbread pies
Saddle of mutton with macaroni	Saddle of venison with gelé and browned potatoes
Chicken with truffles	Chicken à la Marengo
	Artichokes

Celery au jus	Roast goose with com-
Roast plover with	pote and salad
compote and salad	Nesselrode pudding
Plum pudding	Fruit
Ices	

It seems to me clear that the people who sat down with satisfaction to such a meal must have had some sense for ritual, in any case. Miss Sejlstrup could as the evening wore on—at the very moment when, upstairs, people were engaged upon the roast plover with compote and salad—warm up her little room, loosen her corset, put on a pair of slippers, lean back in her chair with a serialized story, and drink coffee from a saucer.

But the mistress of the estate upstairs in the dining room—where it could be hot next to the tall old tile stove, but where it was always cold at the ends of the tables—was the priestess of a secret world-order. It was not only a matter of the order of Vindinge; it was over the grand temple of human dignity that she stood watch.

And, like Samson, Miss Sejlstrup seized the two central pillars upon which the house stood, bent forward with all her strength, and the house crashed down upon the princes and all the people who were in it. And she, like Samson, was crushed in the fall.

> Other times, other birds,
> other birds, other songs,
> and I would doubtless love them too
> if I had but other ears.
>
> (Heine)

Aldous Huxley concludes his essay by prophesying that the whole world will someday be transformed

into a gigantic and gigantically comfortable eider-
down blanket, under which the human spirit will be
suffocated—just as Desdemona was in her time.
But today Huxley's essay is twenty-five years old.
These are already new times—and I feel I am able to
distinguish the delicate whistling, the still-weak
sounds of another, approaching flock of new birds.
Last summer I took a trip to Paris. I traveled very
comfortably in an airplane and I lived very comfortably in a hotel with chairs as broad as beds and
beds as broad as state coaches. My French friends
invited me out on trips in enormous cushioned automobiles.

But—how was it? Didn't everything begin to have a
touch of the superseded, the worn? Weren't the dinners at Maxim's today chiefly imitations of the dinners at Maxim's before the First World War? Weren't
the grand triumphs of the period of comfort beginning to acquire a feeble fragrance of seventeen-
hundred-and-something?

I have a young nephew who is in the next to last
form in school, and he also this past summer, together with a friend, made a trip to Paris—partially, I
must admit, by thumbing rides—upon a very small
amount of cash. He returned ecstatic and impressed.
"It was marvelous," he said. "We slept under the
bridges. We bought all our food on the street; there
you can get everything in the world. We danced in
the street; it was great. You know—it's magnificent in
Paris!" The two friends continued via Geneva to Milan
by hitching rides on a truck, by helping with loading
and unloading. "And you certainly can see the Alps
marvelously when you drive through the passes that
way. It's too bad for you that you never went from

Switzerland to Italy any other way than through a tunnel. And probably in a sleeper to boot!"

He hopes when he has taken the matriculation examination for the university to make a trip around the world with his friend by hitching rides and taking incidental jobs on freighters. I wanted to do something for him which would help and support him on his trip, so I have given him a course in tattooing.

A whistling can be heard about us on all sides and it is pleasant to listen to. Does it mean anything? Yes, the grand equinoctial game of bird migration above our heads means something. It argues the approach of a new season. Can we also in these easy new trills recognize a motif—can they, as they increase, be gathered into a melody?

"No, the chirping means nothing," I was told. "This is the time of comfort in reverse. That's music from a recording which no more has the key to nature and reality than the name which the musicians have borrowed from a questionable card-file: *Vandre-fugle*—wandering birds—a word without meaning, for there are no birds that wander. It is only the fashion."

But a fashion always has some meaning.

The nephew of the master of the estate could not have traveled to Paris as my young travelers did. Or if he'd had the thought for some reason or other, he would have felt oppressed by it and would not have spoken much about it with his friends or his aunt. Nor would Miss Sejlstrup, if one of her nephews had taken such a trip, have made much of it in the circle of her acquaintance.

Let us imagine—for one can imagine what one

will—that the mistress of the estate and Miss Sejlstrup, in heaven, where the two good women must be assumed now to reside, are speaking of the matter and are equally puzzled.

"To be sure," says Miss Sejlstrup suddenly, "I had an old uncle who had been a journeyman worker in Germany. He could tell about his travels, I assure you! The traveling journeymen then had a special name for themselves; they had their own customs and manners. They depended on their craft, and such a journey meant something! They were well received by people wherever they went. My old uncle had tattooed on his arm, R.V.G.G. That was German, it meant 'Traveler by the grace of God.' "

Margrethe became attentive. "By the grace of God," she repeated slowly; in her ears the words sounded like an echo, but she could not remember whence they came.

"Yes, that was also an expression they had," explained Miss Sejlstrup.

Margrethe, who did not think as quickly as Miss Sejlstrup, had to reflect. A little later she said, "Yes, an expression! Do you know, Miss Sejlstrup, when I reflect upon it, I really think I once believed I was mistress of Vindinge by the grace of God. And it was probably what was wrong with me!"

"Madame should not say that with such certainty," said Miss Sejlstrup, "I myself have reflected on many things recently after having had more to do with the grace of God. I can tell Madame something—I believe I then forgot I was Miss Sejlstrup at Vindinge by the grace of God!"

Margrethe reflected again and said, "My husband's tutor was the cleverest of us all, Miss Sejlstrup."

I put my faith in the art of tattooing. It is a ritual art, a cult. It has come to us from the medicine men of the Indians. When on my nephew's behalf I sought more detailed information about its practitioners, they turned out to be a mysterious guild, a kind of freemasonry. Its most important clientele comprised seamen and kings, people who still to this very day must have some sense of ritual. It has its own profoundly traditional and mystic motifs. In the animal world its most venerable symbol is the snake, rather ominously represented—but then we can think of Chingachgook, the great snake, the father of the last of the Mohicans. Still, the art highly respects the ancient, simple, and triple symbol for faith, hope and charity. And at this I put my last daguerreotype back into the drawer of the chest.

Oration at a Bonfire,
Fourteen Years Late

*W*hat I shall talk about this evening I have already spoken about to the pupils at Zahle's Seminary. I was then able—in a way—to bring them a greeting from Nathalie Zahle herself.

My connection with Miss Zahle is unusual in nature and has roots that go back more than a hundred years. In her first position Miss Zahle was a teacher in the family of a miller named Van de Merwede at Bjerre Mill in Jutland. Bjerre Mill belonged to the estate called Matrup, twenty miles west of Horsens, which was my mother's childhood home, and for a long time a friendly relationship was kept up between the families on the estate and at the mill. When I was a child, old Miss Ida Merwede came every summer to Zealand for a month's visit. And Aunt Ida Merwede, as I called her, had been the young Nathalie's very first pupil; she remembered her clearly, she told us children, as if she were still moved by the stories from the Bible and the sagas, from Homer and the history of Denmark, which the nascent great pedagogue once

The original publication of this essay was as "En Baaltale med 14 Aars Forsinkelse," in *Det danske Magasin* (1953), 1:64–82. Also separately published, Copenhagen, 1953.

told her, in the small rooms of the mill, in the year 1843.

When I was asked to speak at Miss Zahle's own seminary, it seemed to me that I was obligated to fulfill the request, and I wished to speak of something which had a connection with Miss Zahle as she was a hundred and ten years ago, something which I could imagine the young, enthusiastic, and ambitious girl had considered important and grappled with in her thoughts on the Jutland roads and paths which I know so well. I hoped that, had she been present, she would not entirely have disapproved or rejected my views on a matter which was close to her heart all her life—a matter which is called feminism.

But in speaking about feminism I must begin by saying it is a matter which I do not understand, and which I have never concerned myself with of my own volition.

If you then exclaim, "Well, nobody asked you to talk about it!" I must reply, Yes, that is precisely what happened. I was asked to speak about it by women who understand feminism and who have concerned themselves with it all their lives. And although the invitation presumably was given upon mistaken assumptions, nevertheless the women may have evoked from me something of which they may make use. The words of an uninhibited and honest layman are worth hearing by learned theologians, from time to time.

In the summer of 1939 there was a large international women's congress in Copenhagen. Leading feminists from all countries spoke one after the other about the development of feminism and its problems. If I had heard those lectures, to which I was invited, I would be wiser than I am today. But it happened that the English actor John Gielgud, who is an old friend of mine, was playing Hamlet at Kronborg Castle on those very days. Instead of going to the enlightening lectures, I spent a week, day and night, in the theater and backstage with the English players—in a Shakespearean world, and when I heard it proclaimed, "Frailty, they name is woman!" it didn't occur to me to protest; I accepted it as a matter of course. Nevertheless the committee of the congress, represented by the leading feminist, Estrid Hein, graciously offered me the honor of giving the bonfire oration at the final meeting of the congress. I thanked Mrs. Hein warmly but said, "I cannot accept this assignment, for I am not a feminist." "Are you against feminism?" asked Mrs. Hein. "No," I said, "I can't say that I'm that, either." "How do you stand upon feminism?" asked Mrs. Hein again. "Well, I never thought of it," I answered. "Well, think of it now," said Mrs. Hein.

That was a good bit of advice, which I followed, even though things did not go so quickly that I got around to giving the oration.

But it is, so to speak, the result of Mrs. Hein's injunction—the reflections without postulates and without bias which I have made—that I here in all modesty for the first time present to a public.

No doubt after the passage of fourteen years they appear more ordinary than they would once have seemed, and they may in consequence have lost any interest for other people. For myself, there is a satisfaction in imagining that the thought of our time has developed in parallel with my own.

When I endeavor to untangle the whole matter for myself I usually begin at the bottom and ask, "Why are there two sexes?"

Or—to put it in another way—"Why is it that, when in nature there are species in which every individual can reproduce itself by budding, with most species the division into two sexes is either a prerequisite or a result of higher development?"

Well, on this point a scientist could give you an explanation, and a much better one than I. But, as I have said, in my opinion the value of my reflections—if they have any value at all—is to be found in the fact that I "don't understand" the matter. So I have imagined various possibilities.

The first is this: in a race which for generations has been procreated through single individuals, the individuals must in the course of time—without any possibility of renewal from without—become dreadfully one-sided and the contrasts between them unpleasantly pronounced. The entire society would necessarily become a frightfully uncongenial collection of loners who could end up by killing each other.

In bisexual reproduction there are at any given time two individuals to create a third, but in the course of ten generations there are a thousand to perform the task; in the course of a couple of millennia there are millions. We are now today in Europe all of the same blood.

But as I reflect—or feel my way forward, as it were—on the matter, this explanation does not seem to be satisfactory.

I have thought of another explanation: gradually, as the various species develop, as we put it, the difficulty of preserving and continuing the mere species grows to an extraordinary degree.

Fishes and crustaceans deposit their eggs in water, on a stone, or in the sand, and let that be enough. In contrast, the birds have more work to do and

must give more of their time to it, make prepara-
tions by building nests, stay on the eggs during incu-
bation, and take care of their offspring for a time after
they have hatched. With regard to the mammals, the
difficulty increases. Rabbits and mice multiply several
hundred times during their lifetimes; a lioness does
not have a litter every year and no more than two or
three in each litter. When we come to man and to the
highly developed human being, conscious of responsibility, we find that a litter rarely consists of more
than a single offspring.

Because of these conditions it could be necessary
that one half of the race should devote itself to preservation and procreation while the other half took on
the task of development and progress.

It would also appear that this has been the attitude
of various past eras in the matter, for in the course of
time the woman's mission expanded from childbed
and nursery to include the entire love-life, on which
depends the entire procreation of the race.

Old Kaiser Wilhelm, as we know, identified woman's function in life by three K's: *Kirche, Kinder,
Küche*—the church, the children, and the kitchen. Personally I would say that, were this seriously meant, it
would be an offer worth considering. But it never *was*
seriously meant. Had the church really been a woman's field of endeavor we must naturally have had
woman   priests   and   bishops   and   also   woman
popes—but about such one knows only of Pope Joan,
who is unfortunately said not to have been a favor-
able representative of her sex and has been sadly re-
duced by later, skeptical times to a legendary figure.
The officials of the church have always been exclusively male and the woman's role has been limited to
that of the churchgoer—which nobody could very

well refuse her. Had *Kinder* been put into the hands of women, had schools and the educational system been their domain, the world would probably look rather different than what Kaiser Wilhelm imagined or wished it to be. For him the concept was presumably most nearly associated with cradles and diapers, a realm for which there has never been any zealous male competition. As far as the third K, the kitchen, is concerned—the area where women can be assumed to have been more or less sovereign—they seem to have displayed an admirable unselfishness. It is the male taste which dominates both the family table and the restaurant—when women eat together and can themselves decide the menu, it has quite a different, lighter, and more varied character. Here I may interpose the remark that Negro and Somali women are clever about poisoning their men by the dishes which they put before them, and that as a consequence they enjoy quite peculiar respect.

But even if a good deal could be said for the Kaiser's program on the whole, I do not believe that it has acquired validity as a law of nature—as a basis for or as a symptom of the higher development of the species.

If I here must give my own interpretation of the expediency of the division into two sexes, I will return to my old belief in the significance of interaction, and to my conviction regarding the opulent and unlimited possibilities which arise from the fellowship and interplay of two different individuals.

I have spoken elsewhere about the same matter in connection with master and servant and in connection with old and young. But no reciprocity—if one except the reciprocity between God and man—has had such decisive significance as the reciprocity be-

tween man and woman. The old English clergyman
Robertson said, "Two things decide the worth and
fate of a human being: his relationship to God and his
relationship to the other sex." I myself look upon
inspiration as the greatest human blessing. And inspiration always requires two elements. I think that the
mutual inspiration of man and woman has been the
most powerful force in the history of the race, and
above all has created what is characteristic of our aristocracy: courageous exploits, poetry, the arts, and the
refinement of taste. I think that one of the ways in
which human beings have elevated themselves above
animals is this: human beings mate the year round—a
society in which the attraction of the two sexes to one
another was limited to a distinct, brief period, must
become notably blunted. Yes, I think that the more
strongly the mutual inspiration functions, the richer
and more animated a society will develop.

I will not attempt to determine—and I do not think
that it can be determined, at all—which degree of
difference between the sexes most powerfully con-
tributes to inspiration.

If one seeks an analogy in the relationship between
master and servant, one understands that the interaction is most productive when the two parties are
rather close to one another; in the comedy by Holberg
there is more of such an interaction between Leander
and Henrik than between Leander and Arv. But I
have lived among warrior tribes like the Masai and
Somali where the lives of men and women took on
completely different forms and where the mutual attraction was certainly the decisive factor in life. I remember that in a museum on the island of Fanø I
attempted to imagine how life must have been lived
in a society where, so to speak, all the men went to

sea and sailed around the earth while very few—if any—of the women left Fanø during their lifetimes. The distant blue of the heavens arched over them, to be sure, and the roar of distant oceans resounded for the girls and the younger and older women on Fanø who spun in their low parlors with strange conch shells on their dressers, or who fetched home the sheep in the stiff west wind. And for the widely traveled men there was perhaps a peculiar inspiration to be obtained from the women—dressed in orthodox Fanø costumes, with kerchiefed heads—to whom they returned after their journeys and who lent half an ear to their reports of shipwrecks, cannibals, and sea monsters but were eager to tell them that the clergyman's cow had thrown two motley calves. And I understand that life on Fanø was harmonious and happy at the time when society was basically dependent upon seafaring. Something of the same must have held true for all the maritime nations, and I am of the opinion that life within them was generally rich and flourishing—yes, even inspired in its own way, as it was in Venice, Holland, and England in those times when the rank of a nation, and rank among nations, was determined by its proficiency in sailing.

Quite personally I can say that, in my view of the male half of the human race, I agree with Mussolini who said, *"Non amo i sedentari!"*—'I don't like people who sit down.'

And in any case, I believe that in daily life, and under the conditions of daily life, competition between man and woman is a sterile and disagreeable phenomenon. There are exceptions, and Atalanta and Gefion are two delightful figures, but in general such competition in life itself is just an unreasonable and pointless as it would be in a stadium.

There is no joy for a woman in putting a man in his place; it is no humiliation for a man to kneel before a woman. But it is humiliating for the women of a society not to be able to respect their men; it is humiliating for the men of a society not to be able to venerate their women.

In one of his novels about a sterile and painful relationship, Aldous Huxley uses the expression, "the love of the parallels"—that hopeless love between two parallel lines which stretch out simultaneously but can never meet.

Very well, reciprocity. And very well, inspiration. Viewed most profoundly, where is that difference in substance between the sexes which most exuberantly determines interaction and most powerfully awakens inspiration?

In the course of time, each of the sexes—with equal conviction and eloquence—had praised and celebrated, or condemned and attacked, the other. Woman is nobler than man, more evil than man. The Danish poet Johannes Ewald unites both points of view by proclaiming that a man can never rise as high or sink as deep as a woman: she is more stupid than a man, she is cleverer (or wiser) than he. She is more faithful, more perfidious—in folk ballads it is alternately the young men's and the young women's faithfulness which is likened to a bridge weakened by dry rot. And Søren Kierkegaard says that it would be interesting to have some literary hack calculate how frequently in the course of time the man has betrayed the woman, or the woman the man, in world literature. She is weaker and she is stronger; she is farther removed from elevated spirits, she is nearer the angels. On this point everyone must judge for him-

physician, the clergyman, and the judge to be dependent upon certain given examinations and to be part
and parcel of certain given uniforms. The Lord has
not proclaimed that the achievements of human beings in these areas must be a *series of results*; he can be
thought to look benignly on His woman servants
when they quietly infuse into the elevated institutions of society their own being and so identify themselves with them.

There has been much contention about the ordination of women as clergymen. The women can now
say, "We've come into the church disguised as
theological candidates. But do not make such serious
faces at the thought of our deficient capacity—or of
our possible competition. Under the disguise we are
what we are, and what we have been throughout
time. With complete loyalty towards our female being
and in complete accord with our female dignity we
have for thousands of years been abbesses, authoritative leaders of large religious societies, wielding
power and influence beyond the country's borders.
And we have been clergymen's wives." While the
clergyman preached, christened, married, and
buried, the clergyman's wife was present in the
parish, and many times there was a brighter Christian
light shining from the kitchen of the manse than from
the pulpit.

In order to penetrate the walls of the medical faculty, women have successfully refuted some traditional medical cynicism and shown that they could
endure seeing blood. Today they are so firmly entrenched that they can say openly, "Fear us not. We
have not come to steal your laurels from you. We are
willing to believe that the great medical and surgical
deeds belong to you. We ourselves—we wish to be

physicians. We will expand our beings to embrace hospitals and laboratories, the precincts of sickness and health. Cannot you on the inside recognize us as those we have always been? For we have been nurses, sisters of mercy, blessed by those who suffer. We have been midwives—with the Danish word there is associated something particularly decisive, dauntless, and agreeable: when a carriage was sent for the midwife, the horses—it was known—could not fall no matter how wild the ride. And we have been clairvoyants! The clairvoyants looked long at each of those persons who asked them for advice, immersed themselves in the individual's life and background, and gathered together experiences from all sides of his life. In any case, some of the patients in our hospitals would be glad to know that the person in the white coat of the chief of service, making his rounds with retinue in all his power and glory, is a clairvoyant."

It is probably the law which in the popular consciousness most strictly demands a change in woman's being—perhaps she for her part could be thought to wish a change in the being of the law as it has hitherto been understood. To explain what I mean I will take a figure not from history but from the world of poetry and fantasy, since the *salto mortale* in thought itself requires fantasy, and I shall speak of Portia in *The Merchant of Venice*. And I shall ask you to forgive me if I speak somewhat longer about her than my subject requires—it is as you know difficult for admirers of Shakespeare to restrain themselves once they have begun to speak of him.

In the performances of *The Merchant of Venice* which I have seen, Portia has, according to my view, been played incorrectly. In the court scene she has been all self; it does not seem possible to establish a definite conclusion.

If, from my own personal point of view, I have to define this profoundly inspirational difference between the two sexes of mankind, then I can phrase my opinion best by saying, "A man's center of gravity, the substance of his being, consists in what he has executed and performed in life; the woman's, in what she is."

If one talks with a man about his parents, he will generally relate what his father has *done* in the world. "My father built the Storstrøm bridge; my father wrote this or that book; my father started this or that great business." And if one then asks about his mother, he replies, "Mother *was* lovely."

And even if this is valid more for my own generation than for the newest, I believe that even he who has had a chief surgeon or a minister of justice as a mother, before he characterizes her by mentioning that fact, will tell us that his mother has *been* an unusually gifted, upright, spirited, or lovely person.

That is to say, the man creates something by himself but outside of himself and often, when it is finished, abandons it and pushes it out of his consciousness in order to start on something else. The woman's function is to expand her own being. Though it can spread out like the crown of a tall tree, it still has its root in her ego. A man who has accomplished nothing and created nothing is not held in much esteem. But I have known many women—perhaps chiefly in the generation that preceded my own—who had no achievement to display, but who had possessed much power and exercised decisive influence and left their imprint on everything that surrounded them. I am thinking of my old nurse, to whom one really could not ascribe any particular competence, but whose personality pervaded our house and our family with a quiet but irresistibly magnetic force by which, so to speak, everything was changed. I think that the great women of history, queens and saints, possessed the same magnetism. Neither Maria Theresa nor Elizabeth I nor Victoria of England can be said to have executed any significant deed, perhaps scarcely to have advanced a great original idea, but through their power each expanded her being until it embraced a kingdom and an empire—in an age which bears her name.

There is an old English love poem in which the lover says to his beloved,

Where'er you walk, cool gales shall fan the glade,
Trees where you sit shall crowd into a shade . . . .

Where you walk, new thoughts and experiences course through life. About you evolves a home, a circle of friends, a happy world.

A man can assert himself in his lifetime and in history by a single deed. Columbus discovered America—I do not know very much else about him in any case—and became immortal as a consequence. If in history we were told about a woman who had discovered America, we would probably exclaim, "What a madwoman! Why did she want to discover America?" No; was she pretty, was she amiable, of what significance was she for the people about her?

Our greatest, or actually our only, strategical genius is often identified, not by a single deed or accomplishment—neither as the victor of Patay nor the kingmaker of Rheims—but by what she *was*, simply and passively: "the maid of Orleans."

And if we go still higher to the woman who, in the course of the history of the world, has meant most of all; who has inspired the largest number of works of art, who has touched and moved souls, and most forcefully changed minds and customs, to the Virgin Mary—whether one now supposes she really existed or not—the same holds true. She possesses her power as a result of what she *is*. God created Heaven and Earth; Christ redeemed the human race. The Virgin Mary performed no great deed save this: quite passively to bear Christ, to offer up her complete being so that God might become Man. Human beings neither expect nor wish anything else of her. From my journeys in southern Europe I have gained the impression that in our time the Virgin Mary is the only heavenly creature who is really beloved by millions. But I believe these millions would be uncomprehending and perhaps even offended if I were to tell them that the Virgin Mary had made a significant discovery, solved difficult mathematical problems, or masterfully organized and administered an association of housewives in Nazareth. No, she has simply to *be* there. The Queen of Heaven expands her being to include the entire human race and the entire earth; she does not fly to the moon; she stands upon it.

Surroundings play a far greater role for a woman than for a man, since for her they are not incidental, things independent of her; they are an extension of her own being. If a man can devote himself undisturbed to the work which is on his mind, he can, as far as I have observed, completely ignore his surroundings—they disappear for him; he can sit in filth and disorder, draught and cold, and be completely happy. For most women it is insufferable to sit in a room if the color scheme displeases them. In the same way, clothes play a greater role for a woman than for a man. It is said that women adorn themselves for men or that they adorn themselves for one another, but I think that neither is quite true. A woman's clothes are for her an extension of her own being.

Needlework can be said to be a special sign or symbol of this relationship. Decorative needlework has never been viewed as actual work or a separate activity, but as an accompaniment to a woman's real work or, in one sense, her coquetry. Though women have created many beautiful and lasting things in needlework, the actual value of needlework lies deeper, insofar as the most active and significant women could very well engage in darning stockings—yes, Penelope unravelled the day's work every night, and nevertheless, or perhaps for that very reason, Penelope's weaving became the world's most famous. Needlework was an activity pursued while far greater work was being prepared, continued, or completed—while the woman who was embroidering or darning stockings listened to confidential messages, entertained and encouraged intelligent friends, intrigued, or told stories to and taught the younger generation.

There is now talk about instructing boys in needlework—it is of course good and useful if a young man can sew on a button or darn a sock. But in reality one *cannot* teach a boy needlework—in his hands the work changes character and rushes on towards a goal. A little boy can be eager to paste together a farmyard out of cardboard, and in so doing he will spread paste over himself and the whole room, but it is *facit* which interests him. An activity which does not lead to any *facit* seems strange to him. A little girl dresses and undresses her dolls; there is no visible result of the activity, but she has lived and lived intensely.

Here I must interpose a special observation. I think artists—poets, sculptors, and composers—in a way have a different relationship to their work than men in general; and here they approach the female *modus vivendi*. Art is an extension of the artist's own being and his work does not really lie beyond him but *is* himself.

A peculiar relationship exists between artists and women. Goethe said that a woman's nature is closely bound up with art and it is certainly true that the average woman is more of an artist than the average man. But few women have been great artists save in those areas where they do not *create* a work of art but can themselves be said to *become* works of art—that is, as actresses, singers, or dancers. These have strongly inspired their public in a way a woman painter or woman writer cannot do. I think that, as far as I'm concerned, were I a man, it would be out of the question for me to fall in love with a woman writer; indeed, I think that if I had met and felt myself powerfully attracted to a woman, the information that she was a writer would cool my ardor. I know that it isn't always that way. There has rarely been a greater man-eater than George Sand; but in those mutually artistic love stories—since most of her lovers where themselves artists—there is an element of something "contrary to nature."

And women in general certainly feel an ecstatic attraction towards great artists, a mystic belief in an understanding which they do not find elsewhere. Yet

in general it is a misfortune for a woman to love an
artist—she is usually better served by Captain
Carlsen.

In East Africa, which in my time was pioneer country, the woman's activity about which I have spoken
became an extension of her own being, valued to
such a degree that we here at home would find it difficult to imagine. A flower garden or a bouquet was, I
believe, felt by those men who came in from hard
work in the fields or from expeditions to be a gift, yes,
a blessing. They asked us, have you been able to
grow lavender? In my time, no man out there under-
took to plant a flower garden. In reality I believe that
there the existence of a flower garden had for men its
real value in that it expressed or represented our presence. In recompense we valued the interplay between us, the work and deeds of man, far higher than
women in Europe could or do. When my men friends
were to come on a visit I looked forward with great
pleasure to their being able to busy themselves and
repair machines in my factory—which they always
did with apparent satisfaction. A French officer who
was investigating conditions in our military barracks
exclaimed, "*Comment donc!* You decorate your barracks with charming colors, hang pictures on the
walls, put flowers in the windows! You fill your
young soldiers' minds with expectation, hope, solace,
inspiration! And then—then there are no women!"

If those women who thirteen years ago asked me to
give their oration had been present today and had
listened to me until now, they would perhaps interrupt at this point and say, "Yes, thank you, we need

hear no more. We understand that, despite all your assurances of disinterestedness at the beginning, you are in reality *against* feminism."

Well, it might be that even old Miss Zahle—although I certainly believe she in many ways would see in me a co-believer—would shake her head a little and say, "The women in the generation which preceded mine opposed me, even in the person of the great actress Madame Heiberg. Must I now endure that the women of the third and fourth generation after me try to tear down what I built up?"

I should be sorry if things followed that course. I would have to protest immediately and say, "I know in what debt I stand to the older women of the women's movement now in their graves. When I myself in my lifetime have been able to study what I wished and where I wished, when I have been able to travel around the world alone, when I have been able to put my ideas freely into print, yea, when I today can stand here at the lectern, it is because of these women and of a few people whom I honor and respect still more. I know that in order to achieve such advantages for unborn generations of women, in their lives they had to go through much and sacrifice more, that they had to endure scandal and ridicule, and that without cessation they had to struggle against prejudice and suspicion. It is edifying for us today to think of the sense of justice, the courage, and the unshakeable loyalty with which they stood fast on their redoubts. But today it is over a hundred years since the concept of feminism first arose and since the grand old women struck the first blow for us. I wonder whether they would not themselves look upon it as a triumph, as a demonstration of the victory they have won, that we today can lay down the weapons they took up?"

The early women of the women's movement were not only just, courageous, and unswervingly loyal— they were also sly! When they were repulsed from the ancient citadels of males, the strongholds of the church, science, and law, they adapted themselves as in their time the Achaeans did in Troy, by going within the walls in a wooden horse. That is, they made their entry in disguise, in a costume which intellectually or psychologically represented a male. A hundred years ago it was impossible to imagine a clergyman, a physician, or a judge who lacked the accepted, recognized masculine insignia. So these just, courageous, loyal, and sly women adopted these same insignia and showed the world that they could pass an examination, defend a doctoral dissertation, and perform an operation just as well as any male candidate aspiring to a high post. They learned the most dignified ecclesiastical, medical, and legal jargons and demonstrated to what a large degree they were qualified for high office by adopting collars, neckties, and cigars. Had they at the same time been able to acquire beards, it would have made their way even easier towards the pulpit, the laboratory, and the bench.

But today, woman has sprung out from the wooden horse and walks within the walls of the citadels. And she has certainly such a firm footing in the old strongholds that she can confidently open her visor and show the world that she is a woman and no disguised rogue.

She can today maintain against the whole world that our Lord did not proclaim the function of the physician, the clergyman, and the judge to be dependent upon certain given examinations and to be part and parcel of certain given uniforms. The Lord has not proclaimed that the achievements of human beings in these areas must be a *series of results*; he can be thought to look benignly on His woman servants when they quietly infuse into the elevated institutions of society their own being and so identify themselves with them.

There has been much contention about the ordination of women as clergymen. The women can now say, "We've come into the church disguised as theological candidates. But do not make such serious faces at the thought of our deficient capacity—or of our possible competition. Under the disguise we are what we are, and what we have been throughout time. With complete loyalty towards our female being and in complete accord with our female dignity we have for thousands of years been abbesses, authoritative leaders of large religious societies, wielding power and influence beyond the country's borders. And we have been clergymen's wives." While the clergyman preached, christened, married, and buried, the clergyman's wife was present in the parish, and many times there was a brighter Christian light shining from the kitchen of the manse than from the pulpit.

In order to penetrate the walls of the medical faculty, women have successfully refuted some traditional medical cynicism and shown that they could endure seeing blood. Today they are so firmly entrenched that they can say openly, "Fear us not. We have not come to steal your laurels from you. We are willing to believe that the great medical and surgical deeds belong to you. We ourselves—we wish to *be* physicians. We will expand our beings to embrace hospitals and laboratories, the precincts of sickness and health. Cannot you on the inside recognize us as those we have always been? For we have been nurses, sisters of mercy, blessed by those who suffer. We have been midwives—with the Danish word there is associated something particularly decisive, dauntless, and agreeable: when a carriage was sent for the midwife, the horses—it was known—could not fall no matter how wild the ride. And we have been clairvoyants! The clairvoyants looked long at each of those persons who asked them for advice, immersed themselves in the individual's life and background, and gathered together experiences from all sides of his life. In any case, some of the patients in our hospitals would be glad to know that the person in the white coat of the chief of service, making his rounds with retinue in all his power and glory, is a clairvoyant."

It is probably the law which in the popular consciousness most strictly demands a change in woman's being—perhaps she for her part could be thought to wish a change in the being of the law as it has hitherto been understood. To explain what I mean I will take a figure not from history but from the world of poetry and fantasy, since the *salto mortale* in thought itself requires fantasy, and I shall speak of Portia in *The Merchant of Venice*. And I shall ask you to forgive me if I speak somewhat longer about her than my subject requires—it is as you know difficult for admirers of Shakespeare to restrain themselves once they have begun to speak of him.

In the performances of *The Merchant of Venice* which I have seen, Portia has, according to my view, been played incorrectly. In the court scene she has been all too solemn and doctrinaire—that is to say, all too forensic. Just as she sparkles in the entire comedy, gentle and quick to laughter, she should also, I think, sparkle in the closed, severely masculine world of the court. She has been called in to clarify an orthodox matter impervious to reason, which the learned have given up in despair. And her magic lies precisely in her duplicity, the pretended deep respect for the paragraphs of the law which overlies her kind heart and her quite fearless heresy. In her very first statement in the role of the learned young judge Balthasar, she reveals them both:

> Of a strange nature is the suit you follow;
> Yet in such rule that the Venetian law
> Cannot impugn you as you do proceed.

Her own suggestion is that the Jew shall be merciful. Shylock replies scornfully, "On what compulsion must I?" And one can see the glances of the men learned in the law turn towards her: "No, who would be able to compel him?" But her reply comes at once. No one can force you, she says, but I can assure you that it would be the best course for yourself. In her long speech about the nature of mercy—which is no sermon but an inspired human interpolation—she grows zealous and says, "In the course of justice, none of us should see salvation," in the same spirit as her subsequent remark, "It is not so expressed: but what of that?" She comes here dangerously near to revealing herself, but she regains control. She says,

> It must not be; there is no power in Venice
> Can alter a decree establishèd.

And after she has thus in vain attempted to arouse the spirit of the law, she demonstrates that she can manipulate its letter as well as any scholar, and by the help of some still more unreasonable, orthodox paragraphs of the law she takes a cruel revenge on the cruel avenger. Still, *The Merchant of Venice* is a comedy; Portia returns to her own place, Belmont, the world where "trees crowd into a shade," where every one of the persons in the comedy is ennobled upon arrival, and music and moonlight can conclude the entire play. In harmony with this, the heroine of the comedy in the court scene—although in a more elevated style than our own master Holberg, and as if with the spear of Athena herself in her hand—has in reality said, "Go forth and be reconciled, ye hypocrites."

And now back to my actual subject. Even if I cannot list names of famous woman jurists, I would nevertheless claim that most disputes and matters of dissent in homes and within families have, in the course of time, been laid before woman judges and have been settled by them. Here again I must think of my old nursemaid and how in the world of the nursery my pugnacious brothers gave in to her orders, which were perhaps not so much purely moral judgments as a kind of mystic decision. Above the righteous judgments of Odin stood the decisions of the Norns.

For those who have believed that femininity would grate in the pulpit and on the bench, it is worth observing that the male experts who have, as a matter of course, taken their places there have, driven as it were by a special instinct, willingly changed their appearance somewhat towards the womanly. Our clergyman's robe with its white ruff is a beautiful and noble woman's costume; the physician's and housemother's white coats have much in common; high-ranking judges wear flowing robes when on the bench and in some countries enhance their dignity with long, curly wigs.

Perhaps the orthodox believers in the women's movement might insist that one expresses contempt for a woman in assuming—so to speak, agreeing— that she cannot execute as much as a man, cannot perform such great deeds, cannot produce such concrete results as he.

In conclusion, I would cite a person wiser than myself by quoting an observation made by Meïr Goldschmidt: "Scholars assume that what for a man is an ideal is for a woman a natural thing. Woman is in many ways more perfect than man. Seeing her, one does not ask her name, class, or profession, for she is herself woman and has within herself all that is essential. Let a man step forth, on the other hand, even the most excellent—the more excellent he is, the more we must ask, in what does he excel?"

And out of deep personal conviction I wish to add that precisely our small society—in which human beings have achieved so much in what they are able to do and in the concrete results they can show— needs people who *are*. Indeed, our own time can be said to need a revision of its ambition from *doing* to *being*.

There is an idea that I have meditated on for some time and which has much occupied me, though I have not been able to explain it clearly to others. It concerns the identity between *being* and *force*.

An acorn can become an oak tree with a heavy trunk and a broad crown; that is an achievement of force and energy of the highest kind—but here force and being are one. Force and energy express themselves by taking form as wood and bark, branches and foliage, and new acorns. It cannot be unhitched and set to some other task; it is completely faithful to its own being, and this peculiar method of expressing force and energy one calls—growth.

But a motor can be made either to produce warmth and light, or to plow or saw or drive a boat. Here it is an arbitrary matter which form force and energy shall assume.

At times it can seem that our day, proud of its mighty achievements, would claim the superiority of the motor over the oak tree, the machine over growth. But it is also conceivable that in such an evaluation we have been misled by an interpretation of the theory of the survival of the fittest. It is clear that the motor can destroy the oak tree—while the oak tree cannot be thought capable of destroying the motor—but what follows? That which itself has no independent being—or is without any loyalty to such a being—is unable to create. Now I have not meant that women are trees and men are motors, but I wish to insinuate into the minds of the women of our time as well as those of the men, that they should meditate not only upon what they may accomplish but most profoundly upon what they are.

So we need, I think, workmen today who not only can surprise the world by what they can produce but who are artisans—like the old craftsmen of whom Kaj Hoffmann writes:

> Gilded mirror from grandmother's days,
> how fair and proud!
> How deep a pleasure have your ways,
> your art, allowed—
> you who once for wages slight
> this work did do,

you artisan, whose soul was bright
and strong and true.

We would be well served in this country by people
who not only, with the help of tractors and threshing
machines, can produce record results but who *are* ag-
riculturists. Who not only can sail to America in record time but who *are* sailors. Who not only pass
difficult examinations and have the knowledge of the
world at their fingertips but who *are* teachers. Who
not only can write a piece of literature but who *are*
poets.

And Paul la Cour writes, "To be a poet is not to
make a poem, but to find a new way to live."

Well, this is your bonfire oration, my gifted and active
congresswomen of 1939. You invited me to give it
and, finally, with an honest recognition of my unworthiness for the task, I have honored your request. If
you cannot applaud what I have said, pray be indul-
gent towards it.

Letters from a
Land at War

Foreword

*I*n the spring of 1939 I was awarded Tagea Brandt's traveling fellowship and hoped, with its help, to realize an old dream.

I wanted to go with the pilgrims to Mecca, together with Farah Aden, who for twenty years had been my servant in Africa, and with his old mother from Somaliland, whom I had never seen but who was well-known to me through Farah's constant mention of her. Farah and I had for many years looked forward to this pilgrimage. When we became rich, we said, we would travel to Mecca. But we never became rich.

In the course of the summer I received from the Arab Legation in London the promise of a letter of introduction to Ibn Saud, and I thought the journey was more or less assured. Perhaps I could persuade Ibn Saud to give me an escort, and Farah and I would buy Arabian horses and combine the pilgrimage with a trip into Arabia Felix.

But thunderclouds were forming over the whole

This essay was first published as "Breve fra et Land i Krig," in *Heretica* (1948) 1:264–87; 332–55.

world and I came to understand I would not get to Mecca that year, either.

When the war broke out on the first of September, the awareness of being confined in Denmark became insufferable to me. On the third of September I drove into Copenhagen, went to the office of the newspaper *Politiken,* and asked the editor, Mr. Hasager, to give me an assignment as a journalist of any kind at all in any place outside Denmark. Such a task would assure me access to countries of which the doors were otherwise firmly closed.

I told Mr. Hasager that I was in no way a journalist by disposition. I had no insight into politics and no political flair. But I was an honest person, and perhaps an unprejudiced layman's notes from a politically turbulent time would have in the future a certain interest as a *document humain.*

Sometime later, Mr. Hasager wrote to me that *Politiken,* together with one Norwegian and one Swedish newspaper, would commission me to spend a month in London, a month in Paris, and a month in Berlin and to write four feature articles from each city.

That was more than I had dared to hope.

I had friends and acquaintances in the government in London, so there I thought the task would be plain sailing. There were similarly good conditions in Paris.

But I could not speak German and I had no connections in *das dritte Reich.* After some reflection I therefore decided to go to Berlin first of all.

In order to get my passport and papers in order, I had several conversations with the German envoy, Renthe-Finck, and told him that from Berlin I was to go on to London and Paris.

I finally departed on the first of March, 1940, and remained in Berlin until the second of April.

In Berlin a surprising amount of interest was shown in me, as a result of people there knowing my plans for the rest of my trip.

When I entered the Hotel Adlon, from the airport, two *doctores* from the Ministry of Propaganda were waiting for me. They explained that a program had been arranged for my stay in Berlin. Every day I would have one or more of the great works of the Third Reich shown me by well-informed people, and facts and figures had already been gathered for my use. An automobile would be put at my disposal and I would have a Danish-speaking woman, as it were, attached to me.

At the start, this concern was anything but welcome to me; I had hoped to gather impressions on my own. But I became reconciled. It would be worthwhile to learn what there was in Germany that they wanted first and foremost to show a visitor who was on her way to London and Paris.

From morning to evening I was in the hands of the propaganda ministry. When, not realizing that it conflicted with my instructions, I went to Bremen for several days, the irregularity was not at all well received.

I did want to show *Politiken* some results of my journey upon my return home, and each night I wrote about the experiences and impressions of the day. I wrote most often about conversations, which I endeavored to reproduce as accurately as I could.

Very often my companions and teachers concluded a demonstration of some monumental work with the words, "Tell them about this in England."

I came home to Denmark on the second of April

and made a fair copy of my Berlin draft between the second and ninth of the month. I had my ticket to fly to London on the tenth of April.

I let my *Letters from a Land at War* lie for eight years without looking at them.

In reality, I forgot I had written them.

Last spring I brought them out by chance and the thought occurred to me that perhaps they really could have some interest of the kind which I had mentioned to Mr. Hasager in September 1939.

The letters will appear in the journal *Heretica* uncut and without additions. Only in this way can they have any value at all.

Naturally when these letters are read now, they seem very different than they did when they lay written out at the beginning of April 1940. Many things in them, for example, the mention of blackouts and rationing, will seem to readers of 1948 quite superfluous.

The readers will find other things missing. If I had been a real journalist I would have accepted the repeated offers from the Third Reich to allow me to meet some of its great personalities face to face. I now myself wish that I had accepted the offers. Actually, even in March 1940, I understood that by declining them I was delinquent in my duty to the newspapers which had sent me there. A single time I said yes, but later sent my regrets. The thought must in some way have been too repugnant to me.

Perhaps my readers will think that I expressed myself with unreasonable indirection, when I could have been straightforward. They must bear in mind that the letters were written before the Occupation. Denmark was then still neutral and there were matters to be taken into account which later disappeared.

I. An Old Hero in Bremen

At the beginning of my journey to the Third Reich I went to Bremen to visit an old friend, General von Lettow-Vorbeck, whom I had seen for the last time in Mombasa in December 1913. He belonged to the good old times. I have not since met a German from whom I received such a strong impression of what imperial Germany was and stood for:

Let the saga of the past interpret the play of the present,
And that which has gone, and also that which will come.

We planned to go on a safari together in August 1914. "Try to come," he said to me as we were saying goodby in the narrow, fiery street in Mombasa which looks out over the blue Indian Ocean, "Wir kommen nicht wieder so jung zusammen."—"We will not meet again so young." He must have been thinking of me, for he was at that time no longer young and had a distinguished military career behind him. Germany sent out a tried and true man to take over the command of German East Africa in 1913. No, God knows we did not go on safari, and much water has gone over the dam and much blood into the earth since then, and those times have not returned.

When I knew Colonel von Lettow, I did not know he would become a hero whose reputation would live long on two continents. We had become good friends on the ship traveling from Europe to Africa and had sat out on the deck during the starry, clear tropical evenings and chatted together. But later, during the war, I heard him mentioned every day by the English officers who were fighting against him. They spoke of him with great respect, not only as a skillful commander and a brave soldier, but as a chivalrous enemy. Gradually, as the English forces in East Africa were augmented, so that the Germans were cut off from relief or supplies, and while he ran rings about the English in the swamps and woods of Portuguese East Africa, often descending upon them like a tropical storm and withdrawing the same way, von Lettow became a myth. The English developed a sort of love for him, a pure infatuation such as the hunter feels towards a particularly fine piece of game. For me, the war in Africa was a great tragedy because the black people in the carrier corps suffered so much in it. It was nevertheless entertaining to hear about the contest between the united English and South African troops and von Lettow's few men—it generated sparks. When the Armistice came, his enemies mourned his disappearance from their lives; there was "nothing left remarkable beneath the visiting moon."

Von Lettow had, to begin with, only a small force of two hundred and fifty whites and twenty-five hundred natives, Askaris; this army was charged with keeping order in the entire colony. In the case of a European war, the plan was to wage war passively in East Africa: the coast was to be evacuated and the soldiers used only for local defense. But this did not suit the new commandant; he believed in taking the offensive and he did not wait until the English attacked. At the outbreak of war he immediately made several thrusts in the north against the Uganda railway and in the south against Rhodesia and Nyasaland. During the first year and a half, he held all the borders and made numerous attacks upon English territory. When General Smuts arrived and began a concentrated siege of the German colony (by that time von Lettow, by his great energy and organizing ability, had increased his army to three thousand whites and twelve thousand Askaris, but had ninety thousand men against him) General Smuts reported to London that the war in South Africa was over and there was need only for a mopping-up operation. It took time to mop them up. The fighting took place in a terrible terrain, in an impenetrable and fever-stricken land. The German's ammunition, provisions, and medicines ran out—their physicians were using the bark of a certain kind of tree for bandages—and the German forces had shrunk to a little more than a thousand men. "He was hard," they said about von Lettow. Out there, they said, he was harder on the white men than on the Askaris. When it was least expected, he came back from Portuguese East Africa into the old German colony and attacked the English on the west side of Lake Nyasa. There he was overtaken, so to speak, with sword in hand, by the conditions of the Armistice, on the thirteenth of November, that is, two days after the Armistice in Europe.

The other day I heard by chance on the radio, in the series *The Conquest of the Earth,* about von Lettow's campaign in East Africa, which was called the most remarkable episode in German colonial history. One can also read about it in Nis Kock's book about men from southern Jutland who fought to defend East Africa. Kock writes, "I doubt that any army in the world has looked up to its commanding officer with greater faith than the German troops in East Africa looked up to von Lettow-Vorbeck." He adds, to be sure, that "Later our eyes were opened to the unpleasant aspects of this man's efficiency." But he tells a story about a man from southern Jutland, Peter Hansen of Egernsund, who, during the attack on the Kondoa-Irangi, crawled out to the wounded on the battlefield, bandaged them as well as he could, and pulled them back to the line. The medical officer was angry because the bandages had been put on too hurriedly, and he scolded Hansen. The General approached and listened for a time in silence. "Well, I can understand, Colonel," he said finally, "that you are annoyed because this man has put on the bandages so hastily, but what I cannot understand is, why you didn't yourself crawl out to the wounded and put them on better."

With all the laurels about his brow, which is now graying, General von Lettow is a very unobtrusive man. During one's life one does not meet many so-called great men; those whom I have known personally have been reserved people. I thought of another great personality or hero from Africa whom I had had the good fortune to know, the philosopher of religion and physician, missionary, and interpreter of Bach, Albert Schweitzer, who in contrast to von Lettow is a heavy, enormous figure, but personally is as quiet and warm as an old farmer. Chesterton tells about an old English officer, a hero from Afghanistan and the Sudan, who "like all the real builders of the Empire, was a true old maid." I would not describe either von Lettow or Albert Schweitzer in that way, but they have in common in their deportment an unusual modesty and thoughtfulness towards their fellow human beings, and one can scarcely imagine either of them raising his voice. People have had to listen to them, and have listened whenever they have spoken.

Now von Lettow and I were sitting in a wintry Bremen and talking about the old days. I had in a way myself been in the war on the other side of the General; I had for a time provided ox-carts as transport down to the German border for the English government. It could have happened that we met there on the plains. "Yes, it is really too bad that it didn't happen," said von Lettow. I asked him whether he knew to what a high degree the English had admired him. Yes, he knew that all right. He had been in England after the war and had been fêted at a dinner by English officers. "They sang *For He's a Jolly Good Fellow,*" he said, "and that is the equivalent of a Victoria Cross."

He asked me to take his greetings to several old officers in London. "One of them," he said, "told me during the dinner, 'I always shot at your old gray hat, I knew it as well as I knew you. And if the sand had only been somewhat looser in the river bottom where we were fighting that day, I could have seen where my bullets went and then I could have got you.' I had the good fortune," added General von Lettow, "to be in a war of the old kind, where adversaries know each other by sight and name, and one knows what each man is able to do. In the Air Force," he said, "this old form of fighting has come back, in a way. The very best flyers know each other and know what one must watch for in particular from each other." He himself had two sons at the front, one of them an aviator.

"How does it feel," I asked, "to fight against a force so superior that the result is given in advance and one has no hope of victory?" "Well, that is not easy to explain," he said. "Perhaps one should say that in such a certainty there may lie as great an inspiration as in any faith in victory." Here in Germany very little has been printed in the newspapers about the battles in Finland. "Historically seen," I said, "it was a tragic situation for the Third Reich that it should end up ranged against Finland. There if anywhere was blood and soil and a single-minded people. Would it not have seemed, historically—and this can be considered a distillation of all the newspapers—to be a splendid gesture for the Third Reich to have come to the aid of a small people fighting a major power? It is difficult for a great power to keep its historical halo if its enemies are always weaker than itself."

I ate dinner with General and Mrs. von Lettow; among the guests was the painter, Professor Horn, who is Rudolph Hess's father-in-law. Out of deference to me, the entire group spoke English; something comparable could not have happened to me in England.

We spoke of the hunt, General von Lettow without much enthusiasm. During their last half year in East Africa, he and his men had on the whole to live upon what they shot. I had myself from time to time, on a long safari, known this kind of hunt, where one shoots in order to obtain provisions, and I knew it to be a hard job, not a pleasure. I asked him in the course of conversation whether he had ever shot a rhinoceros. "No," he said, "I have only once had an opportunity, during the Battle of Longido. Suddenly a rhinoceros came out of the bushes; it had probably been disturbed during its afternoon nap by the shooting. It had an unusually large horn, and I would have liked to shoot it. But what would the English, what would my own natives, have thought about me if, in the middle of a battle, I had started shooting game? It was out of the question." "No, it was your own German conscience that forbade you," I said. "As far as the English and your own natives were concerned, they would have found it quite in order. You could have made your name immortal in a new way as the only reasonable general who disregarded a battle in order to shoot a rhinoceros."

General von Lettow was elected to the Reichstag in 1928. In the minds of most people he was a representative of Germany's demand for colonies. He had a little twelve-year-old girl with long blonde hair whose name was Mulla, and I asked him whether that was a family name. "No. It happened," he said, "that when I first took my place in the Reichstag, the socialists saw me as such a chauvinist and militarist that they gave me a nickname: they called me 'The Mad Mulla.' When I gave my first speech, they drowned me out by shouting that they did not want to hear The Mad Mulla. Just at that time, my little daughter was born, and we thought the name would fit."

The conversation turned to colonies. I could speak without being partisan, for I do not wish any nation in the world to have colonies. When one goes on a hunting expedition in Africa, one receives a hunting license issued by the Game Department which says that the document gives so-and-so the right to hunt, kill, or capture a certain number of lions, buffaloes, antelopes, or other wild game. I have often looked at the license and wondered by what right the Game Department could give this permission. And that is what happens to primitive people and their country when it is made into a colony. Ordinary people without insight into politics do not understand the great powers' race for colonies. As far as I can understand it, they have invested more money and more human energy in their colonies than they have ever got out of them.

I have tried in speaking with people here to comprehend the true origin of Germany's thirst and longing for colonies. Though I have never been in a German colony, I have been in English and French colonies. The systems are different in the two, particularly as far as the treatment of the indigenous population is concerned, because the two nations have different purposes in their colonization. At the time when religion was what men thought about, the Greeks demanded wisdom and the Jews demanded miracles; today England seeks money and raw materials from her overseas possessions, and must have the indigenous population working to that end, while France demands raw materials of another sort, soldiers, *matériel humain*, one might say, and sets about producing an indigenous population that, when called upon, can and will die for France. What does Germany require? Why does the heart of the German people burn with an inconsumable longing for the inhospitable, merciless lands which they have never seen? I have come to the conclusion that for Germany colonies are a symbol, like a flag. They are a badge of redress, the mark of knighthood among nations, the rainbow over the Third Reich. Does man fight best and most willingly for a reality or for a dream?

General von Lettow showed me around Bremen and, among other things, we saw in a park a huge memorial to the German colonies, a peculiar monument, an elephant built of red bricks. I approached it and looked at it; on its foot there was a medallion with a man's head. "Why, that's you!" I said. "Yes, they put me there," he said.

There the elephant stood in slush, colossal and compact, a fantastic shape. It actually looked all right, as if it belonged to Bremen, with its four thick legs planted in the ground. There were some shivering small boys with their hands in their pockets standing there looking at it and talking about it. They too had a dream in their eyes with something grim and implacable in their expressions because the elephant had been taken from them. What does the elephant symbolize and embody to the boys of Bremen? Distant, warm, and lovely lands; a blue tropical sea with large white steamers on it, and on the steamers heavy-set, determined Germans in pith helmets and sunglasses? Palm trees; perhaps something they had seen on a cigar-box: wild black men with wreaths of feathers on their heads and wreaths of leaves around their waists who kneel and offer bars of gold? There is something special about an elephant, which is an incomparable natural phenomenon, something extraordinarily strange and powerful that one must possess. It is frivolous to ask what one will do with an elephant—it is complete within itself, having a tail both front and rear; it is not a means to anything else, but an achievement, on the highest plane. This is happiness: to own an elephant. I have myself felt that, on an elephant hunt. It must have seemed that way to Christian V when he founded the Order of the Elephant.

In Bremen I saw a blackout for the first time. I tend to believe it was more systematically carried out there than in Berlin, because Wilhelmshafen is so near—the train to Berlin was overflowing with young sailors from Wilhelmshafen going to Berlin on leave. I arrived in Bremen late at night; it was snowing and I had not carried an electric torch, and I was told I must register at the police station in order to get into any hotel. In Bremen, as in every other place in the world, the ordinary people are boundlessly helpful. An old porter helped me, out of a pure spirit of humanity; we walked hand in hand through the dark streets from the train to the hotel, and to the police station, and back again. He told me he had been in the Great War and had two sons at the front. We talked about aerial attacks. "Well, the airplanes," he said, "well, they do come here." He had one habit of my black people in Africa, of making a clicking sound with the tongue like a little kiss, to express regret. The African natives made that sound when the grasshoppers came. It was a patient people's quiet, restrained reaction towards the manifestation of superior force.

Incidentally, Bremen is an agreeable city to visit. The architecture of the cathedral and the old city hall is lovely, and a number of large patrician houses, now used as museums or public buildings, stand as monuments to the profound and vital culture of a widely-traveled citizenry—a solid accomplishment that rests upon commerce and shipping. The seafaring people of Bremen have brought home to their city very beautiful things from the other side of the globe. And there are ships everywhere—paintings and tapestries showing entire vast fleets of merchant ships—and in the great patrician halls, tall, monumental, exactly proportioned models of the ships the families once owned, with every sail and hawser in place. These commercially adept people had their hearts in their ships. In one large family group-portrait of a wedding, a ship is being launched in the background, as if at such festivities the old shipowning families could not really tell whether their ships or their young women were being launched. It was probably Bremen that had as its motto, "Navigare necesse est, vivere non necesse"—which was my own motto when I was young.

I went to church in Bremen on Sunday. In the Liebe-Frau Kirche there is an impressive monument to men who fell in the Great War—a young soldier lies with his left arm under his head and his sword in his right hand. An old verger showed me a collection of weapons from the time of the Crusades. I stood and looked at them and reflected how strange it is indeed that the Crusades—a tremendous movement which got all of Christianity to take up arms and leave home, mobilized Frederick Barbarossa and Richard the Lion-Hearted, and brought new culture to the lands of the West—were carried out for the sake of a grave. And for a grave, presumably the only one in the world, where no one lies buried.

II. Great Undertakings in Berlin

The stranger who comes to acquaint himself with the Third Reich meets a surprising and impressive courtesy here in Germany. The day after my arrival in Berlin, an official from the Ministry of Propaganda paid me a visit to give me advice regarding what I should see during my stay here. He—so to speak—attached to me a young Ph.D. from the Ministry and an amiable, Danish-speaking lady, and placed an automobile at my disposal. I put myself in the hands of my guides—their choice of things for me to see was instructive. "Look freely about for yourself," they said. I am grateful to them for their solicitude and their pains—and therefore I looked out for myself.

In a totalitarian state, I suppose, there must necessarily develop in addition to the body of officials a kind of political clergy, a staff of social and spiritual advisors. Here those in the higher ranks have salaries, but most have only "honorary appointments." They have a power of the same sort as the Catholic church when it was at its most powerful. The private, spiritual welfare of the people, and in particular its education in the proper faith and its continuance in that faith has, to a large extent, been put in their hands, and is felt by them as a responsibility. They are, I believe, recruited from what we call the middle class. It is difficult to imagine that this social clergy can have, to any degree appreciably greater than the Catholic clergy, any private life; for the private life of other people makes up the content of their existence—they assist, direct, guide, and restrain it. From the nature of things, it is this active social, domestic, home-missionary work I have some knowledge of. Its men and women all resemble one another—their faces radiate their faith; they are untiring, zealous unto death, without any doubt or hesitation in their souls. What the great masses of passive people say—"the people to whom things are done"—of that I have no knowledge.

The *Reichsfrauenbund* was the first of the large, voluntary social organizations with which I was made acquainted. The society has fourteen million members, and over all of them stands Frau Scholtz-Klink, who in turn is responsible directly to the Führer. I had the honor of being presented to Frau Scholtz-Klink, an erect, typically German woman with long blond braids around her head and a pair of light-colored eyes. The Reichsfrauenbund's assignment is, first and foremost, the education of German women, old and young. It is divided into branches, according to the same system as other large institutions of the kind, by *Gau, Kreis, Ort, Zelle,* and *Block,* down to the very basis of the population, the individual families. The Block, which is the smallest unit in the system, consists of thirty to forty families who live in a single neighborhood—either in a large complex in the city or in a district of private homes or in a village. For its welfare the Block-guard, the representative of the women's organization, is responsible. She does not expect that those who need it will seek out her help; it is her job to know where there is material or spiritual need and to step in at once. She gets mothers to nurse their children; she places girls as maids in the homes of right-thinking housewives; she sends sickly children out into the country and difficult children to a home; in particular, she admonishes the women in her Block to show "neighborliness," so that each one feels responsible for the others' affairs; and she can order the childless woman in the Block who has a large apartment or a small garden to take on her overworked neighbor's seven children while the latter is expecting her eighth. I never really found out what means the Reichsfrauenbund has up its sleeve to get its way in case someone refuses obedience. The fault was perhaps mine, for I lacked the prerequisites to understand the consequences of such a thing. When I asked about it, they answered, "It never happens," and this answer was perhaps in itself quite as enlightening as any explanation.

I ate dinner in the canteen of the women's organization at one of the long white-scoured tables, together with advocates from all parts of the Reich, lively, sturdy young girls who chattered like a flock of sparrows and work-tanned veterans with something strangely childish in their glance. It struck me that the women who are now governing the entire German femininity are a type which, until the arrival of the Third Reich, had little opportunity to wield power. It is strange to think that the being of a single man, just like a magnet which is dragged past a collection of bits of iron, can regroup and change a society.

The *Volkswohlfahrt* and the *Arbeitsfront* are organized in the same way throughout the nation. This society is not picturesque nor even melodic, but, God knows, it has a structure. Not without reason have they made their greatest aesthetic contribution in architecture. I have seen some of the mighty architectonic works: the Chancellery, the new Reichsbank, the Stadium. The architectural style of the Third Reich, which they call neoclassical, maintains itself in contradistinction to what was built in the years just preceding it, but achieves its effect by its very dimensions. I have also seen a city plan for Berlin, showing what the city will become once the work of demolition and construction, which even during the war is going forward under full steam, has been completed; at least as far as area and mass of materials are concerned, it is an incomparable achievement. All the German handicraft in stone, wood, or iron which I have seen here is beautifully executed.

It is impossible not to be impressed the whole day through by the will and the immeasurable capacity of the nation. "Do you think," they ask in Berlin, "that any other nation would be in a position to produce all this in seven years?" "No," one answers, "and God knows I never would have believed it if I did not have the direct, sure testimony of my own eyes." To me, even after having seen it, it is inexplicable: how has it been possible to create these things in so short a time? And further, why was it important to create them so quickly? It is a superhuman and inhuman tempo. It is not a growth, it is a *tour de force* and there is fear somewhere, one doesn't know where, whether in the viewer or in the architects.

None of these things could have been constructed without the German people's unique ability for organization. Of everything I have observed here, that is the most remarkable. One could almost believe that in this people there is a peculiar sense of life as a mathematical problem which is known to have a solution. We people of other nations may, while we marvel, get an impression of something spectral, as if one could organize a cause so that the entire matter would end like the national economy of Tibet, of which I have read that lamps burning yak-oil are placed on the altars in order to insure good crops, but that the number of lamps has in the course of time been multiplied so many times, and yak-oil has become so expensive, that all of Tibet's annual income must now be used to pay for feeding the lamps.

But so it is with the Germans. When I have sat here together with representatives from the various projects, I have felt as if it were the organization of a cause, as such, of any cause whatsoever, that delighted them; to it they dedicated themselves as in religious worship. They have a pure and unadulterated love for statistics, in which they wallow and compete to surpass each other by large numbers, with which they deal cheerfully and without ulterior motive, as if the concepts to which the statistics refer had departed from their consciousness.

There was a very intelligent young Ph.D. from the

Arbeitsfront who attempted to introduce me to its financial system. All German workers and employers belong to the Arbeitsfront; it has twenty-eight million members. They each pay specific monthly dues, which for none of them is less than twenty-five pfennig or over fifteen marks, and which amounts in sum to an average dues of two marks. I was told that this is fifty percent less than a worker previously paid to his union treasury, but I do not know the relationship of what he got from the one and what he now gets from the other. "Now you can yourself figure out what that is in yearly income," said the young Ph.D. Yes, I could, it would be six hundred and seventy-two million Marks. "And how do you think," he asked me with his serious eyes looking into mine, "one could most reasonably distribute this amount?" For them rationing and restrictions seem to be pervaded by the same harmony and exaltation: the people's hardships are over, they have been recorded on paper, classified, and made divine.

Other nations have interpreted the Germans' sense for system and willingness to permit themselves to be systematized as signs of defective individuality. It is not certain that this is the case. Perhaps the average German has his own source of individuality so deep-seated that he can submit himself to all laws without, as a consequence, suffering in the nature of his being. The average Englishman, who demands a greater latitude in practical life, does not really seem to use any greater effort to form his own opinion about life and the world. Particularly when confronted with the ordinary German woman, the housewife with whom one speaks on the street and in shops and who, on the whole, is a strange and remarkable member of the human race, one has the feeling that she, despite all prohibitions, guards her own life pretty well intact. Perhaps, I reflected, the Germans resemble the sedate, unruffled deep-sea fish about whom I have read in my natural history, who swim along their own paths under many thousand tons of water pressure. If it is true that they explode when they are brought to the surface and the pressure is released, that does not happen because they are empty.

I wonder if there has ever been anything comparable to this Third Reich? Of all the phenomena which I have known personally during my life, the one that approaches it most closely is Islam, the Mohammedan world and its view of life. The word *Islam* means *submission*, which is the same thing that the Third Reich expresses with its upraised arm. Yours in Life and Death.

Of the two, Islam is the more elevated ideal because it is better to serve God than to serve a country or a race. The cry from the minaret, "There is but one God and Mohammed is His prophet," is more nearly eternal than any watchword about a chosen people. The half-moon is a nobler symbol than the swastika (which, for me in any case, possessed something restless and broken, spasmodic, in its movement, unless, as on the towers at the entrance to the Stadium, the hooks are bent so that they create pieces of a periphery, so that they unite the figure and bring it to rest).

The two worlds have many things in common. But we must not think of senescent Islam, as we know it today, long after it found a *modus vivendi* with the other religions of the world. One must go back eleven or twelve centuries to the young Mohammedan movement when it arose and expanded like a flag and went forth to conquer the world. Then the clouds must have been full of lightning and thunder and the neighboring kingdoms must have felt ill at ease. Whence did the people of the desert acquire such power?

The Mohammedan view of the world, like Nazism, generates tremendous pride: the true believer confronts all disbelief; the soul of the true believer is worth more than all the gold in the world. It is intrinsically without a class system, like the Third Reich; one Mohammedan, whether he be a water-carrier or *emir*, is just as good as any other. Islam possesses a mighty solidarity and great helpfulness among the believers—ten percent of your assets you must give to the needy of Islam, and this is not alms but a debt which you pay. In its rituals, Islam resembles the Third Reich: the true believers do not have an opportunity to become strangers towards one another. Some things in *Mein Kampf* resemble chapters in the *Koran*.

Islam was propagated by the sword; this is a charge leveled against it by other religions, though in this matter they do not themselves all have the cleanest conscience. I shall quote, insofar as I can remember it, since one cannot buy English books here in Berlin to look something up, what Carlyle said in his book *Heroes and Hero-Worship*, which, incidentally, shares much of the outlook of the Third Reich: "of the sword," he writes. "Indeed, but where did the prophet get his swords? Every new religion begins as a minority of a single man—he is on one side, all the others are on the other side. It would not help him much to disseminate his faith by his own sword alone. Let him acquire his swords."

Even Islam's representation of Paradise was created as a warrior's fantasy; it is an ideal for an army on the march. "As long as you are marching, you must accept all hardships and maintain yourselves by abstinence, having been tested and made ready for battle. But when the city is taken and we have left our camp, then it will be something quite different." That is a five-year plan of monumental dimensions.

Islam bears the imprint of its desert origins; it has its sandstorms and great mirages. In contrast, I think, the Third Reich has a quite ecstatic respectability, *honnête ambition*, as a matter of life or death, in Heaven as on Earth. Which of the two mentalities is the more dangerous, it is not easy to know.

Verily, as they say in the Koran. Mohammed used the word as a sentence in itself: Verily. But Islam was a belief in God. It could both give and take away; with all its power it would save the entire world, if the world would only receive it. The conquered peoples who accepted Islam became one with it. Through this, Islam went forward carrying and bestowing greater human rights than any other victorious race; through it, Islam and the surrounding world came more easily to terms with one another than the Third Reich and the surrounding world seem able to do. This remark is not to be understood as if I thought it a relief for the conquered peoples that, if need be, they could always accept Islam and save their lives, for I do not suppose any happiness may be gained when one saves his life by giving up his faith. But the conditions of Islam itself were eased, it was regenerated as it went forward. Islam, from Delhi in the east to Granada in the west, had enriched itself on its forward march, had foraged culturally in the land of the enemy and drawn inspiration thence for new advances. The desert people had grown spiritually during its migration and now possessed the cultural values of many countries and races. The muezzin's proclamation harmonized with the landscape in India and Spain. "There is but one God and Mohammed is His prophet."

If Charles the Hammer had not stopped Abd el Rhaman at Poitiers, the teachings of the camel-driver might have become the state religion in London and have adjusted themselves in the ancient North. It has often struck me how much the simple, right-thinking Mohammedan peoples I knew in Africa had in common in their philosophy with the old Icelanders whom I knew from the Sagas.

But the cultivation of race gets nowhere, for even its triumphal progress becomes a vicious circle. It cannot give and cannot receive. Despite all strength and joy, and despite the great hopes for the future which have been praised here, the vista of Nazism has a limited perspective. For this reason, there is a tragic component in the being of the Third Reich; its most celebrated rôles are tragic rôles. The people, or the masses, have risen in a new, surprising, and frightening way. They lour against the heavens like a monumental force; they cast a mighty shadow and none of us knows how far the shadow will extend or over whom. Nevertheless, the viewer thinks that, in the last analysis, this people is standing in its own light.

When for some time one has tried to understand the Third Reich and has heard about its organization, its social undertakings, its art and architecture, its philosophy and ideals, one sometimes stands still on the street and, with a feeling of release, watches the soldiers who are marching westward and who are to deal with people of another kind. Possibly, a race which has its ideal and goal within itself and which in its credo forbids the mixture of bloods, needs in time to conduct a war, to conduct some kind of a war, in order to keep its blood in circulation. It is, after all, a sort of relationship to other people to fight with them. "Nazism is not an article for export," they often explain here—another people cannot "embrace," as one says in English, this people's gospel. Nor does the Third Reich concern itself with the spirited importation of ideas from without. It wishes to be self-sufficient. There is no more respectable ambition; one must take one's hat off to a self-sufficient man; he seems to be on the safe side. But there are some areas in life and in passion where self-sufficiency can get on one's nerves, undermine one's constitution, and lead to hysteria—where it may become fatal.

Amidst all the grand military marches and the noises from workshops and factories which have resounded about me here, I heard a fine little German melody the other day. I had gone out to Potsdam; after a long series of harsh winter days, there was a pale light in the air like a cautious promise. I visited the young Princess Louise, granddaughter of the Danish Princess Louise of Schaumburg-Lippe. The villa, or palace, lay beside a lake which was dully silver in the early spring light; the villa was in itself typical of the earlier generation in Germany and of the generation preceding that, both belonging to a time now definitely ended. It stood there, very dignified and collected, and contained much beautiful German porcelain, lace, embroidery, and large painted portraits from twenty-five and thirty years ago (the Princess's parents on horseback in the woods), as if it did not know what stance it should take towards the times and towards the world around it, but still preserved a fine, hospitable decorum. The very young Princess, quite alone in its rooms, was like a flower from a large old garden which one comes upon where there is no longer really any garden.

> Ich bin die Prinzessin Ilse,
> Und wohne in Ilsenstein . . .

How much sweetness and freshness there is indeed in the old German songs. "Ich hör' ein Bächlein rauschen"—like a current of water that sings its way through a meadow without any fuss, having no purpose. A long train rumbles along the bridge across the brook, and its babbling disappears; one forgets that it is there. But when the noise goes away, one hears the brook again.

> . . . Komm mit nach meinem Schlosse,
> Wir wollen selig sein . . . .

III. Strength and Joy

I have come here at a time when Berlin has lost its luster, like some gorgeous bird in the molting season, for the army is at the front.

Here there is no music in the street, there are no flying flags, no footsteps thousandfold—anything that marches, resounds, or strikes the eye is out of the picture and there is no opportunity to be deceived. I remembered what my friends and acquaintances who attended the Olympics four years ago told me about the storm of victory and exhilaration which the Third Reich exuded and how they lost their own footing—of that I have noticed nothing. I can only say that the city is now a sorry picture. The streets are everywhere dirty beyond description; just enough time has been taken to push the snow to one side, but it has not been removed because trucks are otherwise occupied. People walk cautiously in their last-year's clothes; if I have seen no rags, neither have I seen any elegance. In a large city, more than other places, is "le superflu le nécessaire," and without a cultural élite the city seems insufferably monotonous, like despair itself. When I sit in the lounge of the Hotel Adlon—a typical product of the first decade of the century, with heavy, tactful effects of gold and bronze, marble, mosaic, and glass—I think that the only people who look as if they belong there are the *portier* and the cashiers. The public here makes a totally alien impression and, if other kinds of people didn't exist, it would occur to no one to construct such buildings for them to sit in. The food-ration cards, which one must guard with care and produce when one orders dinner, create an intensely frugal and preordained, anxious impression—this is not the sort of grace that can be said to introduce a festive meal. *La dure nécessité, maîtresse des hommes et des dieux,* seems to hover over Berlin.

But when one has been here for some days, the mood changes imperceptibly. Great works are indeed being continued; hammer-blows resound from immense scaffoldings, and from the ground where mighty roads are being laid. This society has not been plundered but is anxiously practicing self-denial for the sake of a purpose. It acquires a kind of elegance in the second degree, like a man who has an important piece of work to do, who takes off his jacket, rolls up his sleeves, and is now correctly clad for the occasion. The will, the collective, conscious feeling of duty, gives to winter's slushy Berlin an attitude and a bearing.

The first time one experiences it, the blackout

seems frightening in the March evenings. Strangely enough, it seems as if one were sinking, and there are accompanying sensations as if one were drowning. One soon becomes accustomed to moving about in the dark; but for all that, one does not escape an intermittent horror. It is no longer the darkness which is oppressive but the knowledge that about one in all directions are four million people who have determined to be invisible and deathly silent in the night. Their silent singleness of purpose is as clearly expressed as through words.

Everywhere the stranger in Berlin is impressed by tremendous exertions of the will. The force of will is the Third Reich's achievement—there where will suffices, it suffices, and insofar as one believes in the power of the will, one is able to accept its gospel.

About the will and its nature, most of my discussions were with the representatives of the Third Reich.

Here in Germany I have been surprised to discover how freely one can speak without causing offense. From what I had heard at home, I was prepared for something quite different. There is here, I think, more interest in a sinner who can be reformed than in those already saved. The goodwill of my German acquaintances appears particularly in their concern for my soul. Moreover, most of the nation likes to discuss and expound its views methodically, and they are agreeably factual and uncompromising in a discussion. Perhaps some of these conversations may be of interest, and incidental expressions of two of the times' *Weltanschauungen*.

The young Germans had the last word practically every time we talked together. No matter how clearly they presented their arguments, there was always something to which I had to reply, "We foreigners cannot understand that." Then they said, "You will come to understand it. We shall demonstrate it to the world." The difference between us lay very deep, but when we were far enough along in a debate, we struck it.

To take an example, I have here in Berlin heard much talk about honor. At home, we rarely use the word, but here it belongs in every mode of thought. But about the nature of honor we could not agree. "It is for us," said one of the serious young Ph.D.'s to me, "a sign of weakness and frivolity when the democracies punish more severely the criminal who misappropriates a man's wallet than him who assails his honor. He who desecrates honor is the most despicable enemy of society and in the Third Reich the law punishes him hardest of all." "That we cannot understand," I said. "For us, will and honor lie on two different planes. The law—including the moral law—and that which one calls honor are in contrast to one another like an object and its mirror image. Thus, hara-kiri, suicide by the person who has been insulted, can, as we know, erase the deadly insult, but an execution of the guilty party has never been able to do it. If a debt of honor is a debt which, in the first instance, can be collected with the help of the police, then we would no longer know why it was called a debt of honor." He answered, "The law is the will of our foremost leaders and must educate the people. It should not only control their conduct, but transform their souls." To this, I could find nothing to say; so he had the last word.

But on the stairs I thought, "This transformation of the soul by means of the law is a program which has been introduced several times before, without any real success. King Christian VI was able to force people to go to church, even to go several times a day, but he had to have beadles with canes who walked about and wakened the people who had fallen asleep. The Puritans of New England no doubt could make their congregations hew to a purely technical virtue by means of severe fines and punishments for adultery. But it is ghastly to think how the young people of the congregation who were restrained in this fashion felt in their private lives and how they behaved towards their spouses."

I also met a Ph.D. who had a high position within the organization "Kraft durch Freude," which was under the Arbeitsfront. "Doesn't the name of our organization itself sound nice to you?" he asked. "Yes, it sounds nice," I said, "but you will excuse me for saying so, it would sound still better to me if it were Freude durch Kraft. For *Kraft* (strength) considered purely abstractly—whether it is a matter of horsepower or water-power—can always be considered a means to an end. And the Third Reich already has a use for all the power which it produces. The *Freude* (joy) seems to be a goal in itself and it has a tendency to disappear—'Like a lizard within the shade of a trembling leaf'—wherever a suspicion arises that it is about to be made useful." "You speak as you do," he said, "because you do not understand us Germans." "No; perhaps that is true," I said, "and I am sorry, for I would like to get to know you and to understand you. But then, I also know it was a German who said, 'So fühlt man die Absicht, und man wird verstimmt'— 'One senses the motive and feels depressed'." To this he did not answer, so an old German had the last word.

We went into the question at another time, when

we came to speak about art. "You cannot deny," he said, "that your culture in reality has believed in the slogan *'L'Art pour l'Art'* and that has been demoralizing both for art and for the people. We of the Third Reich say, 'L'Art pour la Nation,' and under this motto both art and people will blossom." "Well," I said, "one of the best minds of Danish culture has commented on your program: 'When rightly run, it's fine and fun. There's just one snag. It can't be done!'" "We of the Third Reich," he answered, "don't like to say that something cannot be done. Tell me why we should make an exception here?" "Well, I shall tell you," I said. "There are some things in the world that resist any design, just as (I have been told) there are some atoms about which we cannot know anything since they do not endure being looked at. This holds true, among other things, for art." "And why," he asked as seriously as if he were cross-examining me, "are you and your culture of the opinion that works are created which are not created by design and by the force of the human will?" "Some are created by the grace of God," I said.

"Do you really belong to *l'Ancien Régime* to such a degree," he asked, smiling, "that you believe in *la grace de Dieu?*"

"Doctor," I said, "I can answer you just as a friend of mine, a Swedish actor, answered me when I asked him whether he believed in God. 'I am a great and dreadful skeptic,' he said, 'I don't believe in anything else.' I myself believe that the worst method to try to create a work of art is to *will* to be an artist; or, in order to be loved, to *will* to be loved; or, in order to be a hero, to *will* to be heroic." He reflected a little on this, and it is salutary when, during a discussion, one's adversary thinks about what one has said. "The will," he said, finally, "the German will—that is God's grace towards Germany."

Then I thought, "Nemesis, thou art a mighty goddess and it is awesome to see thy countenance! Thou hast appeared!" The cause of the great difference between Germany and England today, more decisive than any political opposition, is that England had good fortune while Germany suffered unhappiness and injustice. Though it is difficult in this year of the Lord, March 1940, to imagine England subdued by a superior power and forced to accept what to the nation itself necessarily seems an unfair judgment, it is more difficult perhaps to imagine that England, even under such conditions and with all its forces concentrated upon reconstruction, could be made to give up that peculiar faith in the grace of God which is called humor. Here, humor itself is anathema, a heresy directed against the sole means of salvation—that is, belief in the omnipotence of the will. Those who have wind in their sails trust in the grace of God, but those who sit in the galleys at the heavy oars must trust in the will. The united, victorious nations decided twenty-two years ago to divest the Germans of their faith in God's grace towards Germany. And this people which, everywhere one meets it, is marked by the deprivation, has determined to depend upon the will as God's only grace towards it.

"Do not," I thought, "do not take belief in *la grace de Dieu* away from a conquered enemy."

Here one may observe a remarkable and significant phenomenon of our time: propaganda—which to be sure, is not art but an art, and one in the service of the grand design. "Propaganda is the salt of the Third Reich," a young German told me. I believe, however, that the propaganda artists may sometimes, after the fashion of the depraved, democratic nations' motto, *L'Art pour l'Art,* carry on propaganda for propaganda's own sake. It generates something like an obsession; it seems a kind of magic. It is a precarious thing, like a business which is using up its capital and possesses no reserves. For it exists and functions by virtue of a tradition which (one must believe) stretches back to the time when human beings learned to speak, and which is based on the assumption that there is a connection between the word and the thing. In the course of time human beings have taken considerable liberties with this tradition, but officially they have never broken with it. Doctor Coué, who was all the rage twenty years ago, was really the first person who falsified the relationship of words to facts and made a hocus-pocus of it. From ancient times we have had the assurance that things are getting better and better, and in its very wording this phrase had an association with the sense of progress. Doctor Coué experimented by reestablishing relations, so to speak, backwards; and enjoyed some success as long as the relation between fact and word was maintained to a reasonable degree; but he himself undermined it every day and so his forceful language came to lose its force. His capital diminished day by day, it finally was exhausted, and he went bankrupt. But Doctor Coué was a specialist and his field of activity was limited. The propaganda that has here reached such a state of perfection covers all aspects of existence and constantly surprises one by finding new fields of endeavor. But once a new generation has grown up that has wholly emancipated itself from the tradition of a union between word and fact, the substance of the word will have been juggled out of it, and it will be like paper money which is nowhere backed by gold, and the propaganda itself will have lost its savor. And with what shall it be salted? It will no longer be good for anything . . . (*Matthew* 5:13).

The film is an ingenious and powerful tool of propaganda. Here I have seen many brilliant propaganda films. I regret that I do not have a sense for films (because I do not like photography at all and certainly do not see things the ways the camera sees them). In Germany they presumably photograph as well as can be done, and long series of pictures are ably and lavishly created; but the films are apparently directed at a public which either completely lacks fantasy itself or, at least, is not disturbed by the fact that it knows in advance what everything is going to lead to and end with.

I have also been in the UFA ateliers at Babelsberg and walked through its tremendous buildings there. It was an ice-cold day and snow had fallen during the night. I had the honor of greeting Zara Leander and Willy Birgel, who were playing Mary Stuart and Bothwell. We arrived at UFA's open-air stage just as the queen, in a carriage drawn by six horses, was surrounded by Bothwell and his men on horseback. One might suppose it difficult to execute a scene from the Scottish highlands in the middle of Berlin, but the camera was buried deep in the earth so that its horizon was very low, and in the background some sand had been piled up and planted with small fir-trees, all of which, I was told, would look like highland landscape in the film. The horses were having difficulty pulling the carriage through the deep mud and slush and would not rear up as they should when Bothwell's group came galloping; they probably had become accustomed to the surprise attack. While we watched, the scene was taken three or four times. Zara Leander and a young lady of the court who was with her in the carriage complained that they were freezing. Inside the studio, in rooms as high-ceilinged as a cathedral, they were arranging large, magnificent interiors from the eighteenth century, and it was interesting to see how carefully and conscientiously all the details were designed and assembled by UFA's scene-painters and laborers; it was a handsome piece of craftsmanship, though the material was of an ephemeral nature. To my surprise, it was *Jud' Süss* that was to be filmed there. Count Schönfeld from the Ministry of Propaganda, who was with me as my guide, explained to me that not the hero of the novel (by the exiled writer, Feuchtwanger) would be presented, but the historical Süss, and I understood it would be a sort of propaganda film. I do not remember much about the historical Jew Süss; here, it seemed that his life had taken place chiefly in bed, for there were three pompous Louis XV beds in various rooms where the film was to be made—at the foot of Süss' own bed I saw the star of David, the holy Jewish symbol. In other studios they were practicing scenes a half-minute long from a Bavarian peasant comedy and a drama set in a fishing hamlet on the North Sea coast. When we emerged, we saw Mary Stuart once more being stopped and captured by Bothwell.

I stood and watched and thought, "Here I see with my own eyes Dante's hell on earth. No man or men could have thought this up; only the spirit of the time could do it. The poor queen of Scotland once made a fatal mistake, and in that unhappy moment her life was decided—and now here she must, three hundred years later, experience that dread moment in a more dreadful manner. Among tall suburban apartment houses, in the raw and cold Berlin air, she proceeds to a tragic meeting in a carriage with a curtain of painted cardboard through a pile of sand which represents the moors and glens of her native land. Her own beauty, which was her pride and joy, is recreated in hellish fashion with heavy orange-colored makeup and stiff, inch-long eyelashes suitable for a doll; she wears ermine and silk that are not ermine and silk. And yet she must believe—from the evidence of print—that the place is the highway at Dunbar and the day the fateful 28th of March in the year 1566. And when the inescapable moment is reached, when the group of riders springs forth, takes her horses by the bits, and stops the carriage, when swords fly out of their sheaths, when Bothwell, alongside one of the carriage wheels, cries 'Marie!' to her face—then an order comes drily from the black-clothed technician surrounded by machinery down deep in the earth, 'Do it again.' Here we have the twentieth-century's form of justice in judgment, the modern, stylish costume of the goddess Nemesis." Time and again, since I visited Babelsberg, I have, without wishing to do so, seen the heroes of the Third Reich as they would appear in the makeup of film stars, in the wings, at the great moments of their lives and careers. And which moments will the public of the future call the most important and demand be made eternal? Moments that the heroes, on the orders of a director, must repeat again and again? That we cannot know.

At Eastertime I was in some of Berlin's churches and heard much beautiful church music. At home I'd been told the German churches were empty, but during these days they were so filled it was difficult to find a place to sit down. I had also been told that propaganda was making use of divine services and the clergymen were preaching on political texts. I was unable to follow any sermon closely enough to say what actually occupied the mind of the parish. But I did not have the impression that the parishioners were listening intently. It seemed to me as if all these people, old and young, in the pews about me, sat there examining their own thoughts, as if they had come to church in order to do so.

IV. The Stage

In Berlin the theaters are full, which redounds to the honor of the Berlin public, considering the blackout and the slush of the winter months. It is difficult to buy a ticket to any theater, and I would not have got to see much if the Ministry of Propaganda had not kindly obtained seats for me.

There are few modern plays in the repertoire; they play classical things. Many foreigners in Berlin complain about this, and wait impatiently for the new theatrical art which is to be created by the force of the will of the Third Reich. It may be that this dutiful, harshly tried people unconsciously makes its way to the theater in order to be encouraged, strengthened, and kept on the right path for a few hours, and, in order, without any design, to put themselves at the disposal of great spirits:

> And when all else fails,
> there is solace to be drawn
> from tragedy and the sorrows of great men.

Here one hears much talk about popular art. Not a small cultural élite, but the great German people itself will, they say, now create the art of the Third Reich. Very well, and if the great German people could speak for itself, what would it say? I have looked at a number of works of art here that have been described to me as the people's own art. Exhibitions of paintings I have not seen, to be sure, and as far as I know there has been none, but I have had a taste of graphic art in the great decorative works, ceiling paintings and mosaics, in the tremendous new public buildings. All these are pervaded by the gigantic respectability of the Third Reich. The great naked, flat figures are as respectable as they can be; the respectable naked young man, with a hand on a plow or a sword and wide-open blue eyes, has by his side a respectable, heavy-limbed, naked young maiden with a pale, pious face, who in some spaces further along has developed into a physically abundant, happy young mother, respected by all, who exudes milk and honey. It is an heroic idyll, ever-repeated. It is in this way that the people see themselves. I should imagine that the people are secretly a bit embarrassed when they are encouraged to recognize themselves in the figures—for their own sakes, or for the artists'? These are people seen through the eyes of the middle class, or rather, they are the wish and the dream of the middle class: how people should be. They do not resemble the original much more than did the figures in eighteenth-century pastoral poetry, which was a sensitive and witty idyll, an aristocratic culture's picture and dream of the people. Neither the heroic nor the idyllic mood suits the common people. I believe that their own art is or will be satiric—a kind of tragic satire that absorbs in its domain all the misery and horror of life, and laughs piously and caustically. Most of the Negro art that I have seen has embodied such tragic satire, like the fairy tales about *Big Claus and Little Claus* and *The Swineherd,* and like *Tom of*

Bedlam's Song. Common people do not favor hyperbole either as heroic epic or caricature; they are softspoken even in passion. They deemphasize—if one may use the word—on purpose, and say of those human beings to whom they would give the highest praise that such persons are really something, or that they are no fools—which, taken literally, is a reserved recognition.

In order to see what the people of Berlin laughed at, I got Doctor Pagel to accompany me to Carow's *Lachtbühne,* which is a very plebeian music hall where one can drink wine and beer; it was entertaining. Carow, who presumably owns the establishment and about whom I heard that he had been imprisoned a couple of times because he went too far with his jokes, had himself written the piece and played the main role. It was entitled *The Paragraphensnafu,* and was a modern version of Sancho Panza's legal procedure on his island. There were coarse jests, but no insipid ones like those made by the bourgeoisie; there was depth in the people's reflections upon the law and its enforcement. The public was in good spirits, felt at home, and was extremely well-disposed towards the author and actor, for through him they achieved a release from much grief.

They were playing *King Lear* at the Deutsches Theater, and I was glad to have an opportunity to see Shakespeare in Germany. I had last seen the play in London—and the very day I went there, I received a letter forwarded from Denmark, from John Gielgud, who was playing Hamlet at Kronborg that summer, and he promised me much scenic art, including Shakespeare, when I came to England. But they are not playing Schiller in London now.

A century and a half ago the Danish poet Jens

Baggesen saw *King Lear* in Hamburg on his journey southward. "My delight was so great," he wrote, "that I don't believe it could have been higher or lasted longer without diminution." He had high praise for Schröder, an actor who played the king, but added, "The particular source for the tremendous pleasure which swept through me was the harmony of the whole performance, the unity of the dramatic parts in a dramatic whole—something which our own stage still lacks entirely." Baggesen no doubt saw Shakespeare on the stage for the first time in Germany, for the earliest Danish translation, by Peter Foersom, appeared twenty years later. It is to Germany's honor to be the first of all countries, apart from his own, to play and love Shakespeare.

King Lear was not played as well this time in Germany as in 1789. The performance was elaborately enough conceived, but it was in many ways oddly affected. There were a couple of lovely backdrops for the scenes on the heath, but otherwise the decorations and costumes were sometimes so strange that they took one's attention away from the players. I have never seen Lear played without a cloak or a robe, of which the folds accompanied and put life into his grand gestures. Here Balser played the king in white knee-breeches and a long, buttoned-up, white frock-coat similar to those one sees in old Norwegian peasant costumes—which must have made it difficult to play the role, from the first. Balser played Lear as a kind of grand, humane philosopher in the midst of a brutal and deranged world; but one did not understand that he had for long preserved his faith in its value, or that he was finally struck to the ground by its unworthiness. Bruno Hubner played the fool as a very old man—incidentally, he was most eccentric and shapeless in his costume—which was a depressing idea. There were all too many old men on the stage and an atmosphere of senility over Lear's court; the play became, not a tragedy of human life, but a tragedy of old age. In London I have seen the fool played by a sixteen- or seventeen-year-old boy, and there was an impressive, fantastic interplay between the boy's genial relationship to the formidable old man who is driven to madness and his strange, clear-sighted, and bitter devotion until death. The boy had a depraved, tragic attractiveness; he was an *enfant terrible* whose jests spanned the pinnacles and depths of existence. In Berlin, coming from the mouth of the old fool, the mad sayings and bits of songs sounded both macabre and piteous, as if he were in his second childhood. The Berlin fool died out in the hut on the heath, after the line, "And I'll go to bed at noon." This could surprise no one, since from the start he had looked as if he had one foot in the grave. Many students of Shakespeare are of the opinion that at this point the fool, crushed by his sufferings in the night, prophesies his approaching death; and certainly he is not again seen on the stage. But his visible demise at the moment creates a false climax that makes the action falter. Edgar lifted him up and determined he was dead, but both Edgar and the other persons on the stage displayed little human sympathy, and could not do otherwise, since they had no lines for the occasion.

Edgar himself, Gloucester's legitimate son, was well played by Albin Skoda; he shone. The performance moved on a different plane while he was on the stage. In costume and manner he was inordinately refined, shimmering as if made of air, which could be interpreted—and was interpreted by the robust and red-blooded bastard Edmund—as a sign of weakness and degeneracy. He was idiotically naive towards Edmund's wiles because he was himself so far removed from falsehood. But this ethereal youth, a religious mystic in his way, had more good sense than anyone else in the play; indeed, he was so wholesomely reasonable that he came back from having played the flighty, mad "poor Tom" quite unruffled, quite like himself, and at once began talking about affairs of state with Albany. Edgar had less heart than the other noble characters in the play; he was inspiredly helpful rather than actually sympathetic towards his blinded father and the unhappy king. In particular, he was quite without the mighty moral indignation which determines the others' fate. Because of this, he became, to a certain extent, a central figure in the tragedy, as if he were the poet's own voice in it; all things did his bidding as they came, and for him everything was in a way undifferentiated, just as it must have been for Shakespeare himself. The misfortune and the injustice which he suffered gave him far more reason to reflect than to complain. His refinement was vital in the extreme, with the *fond gaillard* which Mirabeau opined was the mark of a true nobleman. When Edgar finally caught Edmund—and gave him a brief sermon on the principle of revenge, to boot—he was again so unfeeling in his mention of their deceased father than one could wish he had refrained; but then it was not alone the victory of good over evil and of legitimacy over the rabble, but of spirit, which stood its ground vis-à-vis mere matter.

At the same time that they were playing *King Lear* at the Deutsches Theater, they were playing Bernard Shaw, Musset, and Ibsen in Berlin. It does not look as if the Third Reich thinks it has anything to fear from those classical works. The Germans indeed appropriate foreign classical art in their own way, like a great power; and a stranger from a little country who sits and listens to them while they talk about the matter can feel a bit ill at ease. Shakespeare, they say, is in reality Germanic, by virtue of his mighty humanity; Shaw is Germanic in his clear understanding of problems; Ibsen is Germanic in his search for truth and bitter idealism. It is not only the dramatic classical art alone that the zealous Germanic hospitality embraces, but the entire history of art and deed. Hans Christian Andersen is invited in; he is of course German in his spirit; Søren Kierkegaard is the same because of his depth of mind; Rembrandt, in his artistic earnestness; and Michaelangelo is Germanic by virtue of his very size. Such a faith can move mountains, and one looks about fearfully—how much will be buried here under the landslide? Behold! Germany carries on a conquest after the manner of Alexander the Great—let them prove to the world that Alexander and the old Greeks were German in spirit and in truth.

"I wonder whether the story about Louis XIV and Tamburini is too well known for me to tell it to you?" I asked. In the year 1663, when the king was twenty-five years old, an Italian ballet dancer named Tamburini came to Paris, and aroused attention through his dancing and his divinely beautiful figure, but particularly because he resembled King Louis, who was the same age, to a T. The entire court went to see Tamburini, and the king eventually heard about him too. He found the situation piquant, and had the Italian come to him and dance for him. "You see, sire," said the tall old court official who stood behind the king's chair, "here we have a living example of how it would have been if your time had permitted you to cultivate the art of the ballet." The king graciously began to converse with the dancer and learned that his mother in her day had been one of Italy's loveliest dancers. "And tell me, my friend," he said with a little smile, "did not your beautiful mother also win laurels in my France? I have been told that in the year 1637 she was a great success here in Paris." "Alas, poor Mother," said Tamburini, delighted by the king's approbation and condescension, "she was only a provincial dancer and never left Italy. No, whoever told Your Majesty that must have been incorrectly informed. The one who in 1637 had the honor of a success in Paris was my father."

At the Staatstheater I saw *Dantons Tod*, which was written a hundred years ago by Georg Büchner. Connoisseurs of literature here have objected that it is not a drama at all but a long series of dialogues and monologues. This is quite true, but why should it not be so when it is, in its way, so effective? It was magnificently played, and magnificently staged by Gründgens, whom I do not know as an actor but who, in any case, is a first-rate producer. The entire play was staged beautifully in dark colors, dark brown and black, so that one afterwards remembered the scenes like a collection of large old mezzotints with a single garish spot of color added here and there.

It is strange in revolutionary times to see in the theater the French Revolution, the classical and eternal revolution. Here they believe it was bold of them to produce a work in which the *Marseillaise* is sung. I thought there were other things in the play which required still more boldness to display at a time when political ideas are being proclaimed like a religion. When he wrote the drama in 1835, Büchner was obsessed by the French Revolution; he wrote about this himself, *"Ich fühle mich wie vernichtet. . . .* I felt myself annihilated under the grisly fatalism of history. I accustomed my eyes to blood. The individual only foam on the wave, the great man a mere accident, the reign of genius a puppet-play!" For dramatic effect he took some liberties with historical persons, but the peculiar volcanic atmosphere of the Revolution, with its thundering capriciousness of the masses and the vicissitudes of fortune, all these are reproduced for us with great earnestness and exactness in the long series of monologues and dialogues that constitute *Dantons Tod.* I had previously studied the history of the French Revolution; but one forgets quickly. Now, after meeting again with Saint-Just, Camille Desmoulins, and Fouquier-Tinville, the time and its people have become so much alive to me that I have purchased German books on the Revolution and have read them here.

In history, it is always the human element that has a chance for eternal life. In the triumvirate of the classical revolution—Robespierre, Danton, Marat—it is Danton about whom one can now write a tragedy.

About Robespierre one may believe he was a god or a superman; he certainly was not a human being, for everything human was alien to him. The ascetic whose course of life was blameless, with the blood of his friends on his hands, while holding a bouquet of wildflowers, said once and for all what he had to say, and fantasy no longer pursues him. The Danish poet N. F. S. Grundtvig tried to write about him in verse:

> Only as a blood-sucking leech, alas,
> Was Robespierre colossal.

In my mind, it is as if his figure were creaking; it

certainly protests against being treated in this way. Within historic consciousness, he is two-dimensional, a paper cutout, an unhappy person. He was once admired and boundlessly powerful; we cannot explain it and do not require that it be explained; nor does it frighten us anymore. The fright which Robespierre instills is a *horror vacui*.

And Marat, on the other side of Danton, has in the course of time grown black as a coal. He was not so much what one calls demonic, the devil incarnate or a troll in a box. He has no presence except an incredible loud mouth; he is incomparable and infallible when he cries out. Time has done Marat an injustice. He was certainly the most original spirit of the Revolution; before the fever of the Revolution and sickness destroyed him, he had life and substance within him. He had an unusual, strangely shaped head, which might have come from a painting by an old Spanish master, and it does mean something when a man looks as if he had been painted by a great artist. He had a clearer vision than any of his contemporaries. He was the only proletarian mentality among all the men of the Third Estate, who—but I have never heard why—was supposed to be everything; a liar but no hypocrite; and the needs of the people concerned him. But this human being, Marat, did not indulge himself in humaneness; he would not eat and would not sleep and would not believe in anybody; he identified himself with a frightful newspaper and became *L'Ami du Peuple*. Historically viewed, Marat has had the good fortune to have Charlotte Corday at his side; she did not permit herself any humaneness either but, like Marat, followed a program leading to death—a severe white lily next to a poisonous plant. About the two of them an epic probably could be written. But during the century he has become too much of a ghost to be the main figure in a work of art or to be seen behind footlights.

About Danton we can, as I did the other evening, still believe he could love, rejoice, and suffer; he fills out all parts of the picture, he breathes with his great lungs, and he is not merely marked with the blood of others; his own blood pulsates within him. One sees him on the stage of the Deutsches Theater at a table sharing a glass with friends, in bed with his young wife, and finally at the guillotine itself. The great, coarse, weak, brave man is close to us when he jests, raves, and doubts; he and we suffer a common fate. "My place of residence," he says to the revolutionary court, "will soon be the great Nothing." At least, as one result of Danton's life, more than a hundred years later human beings can be moved, can hope and mourn, while seeing *Dantons Tod.* *

Yesterday I heard Furtwängler direct a Beethoven concert at the Philharmonic as beautifully as one can imagine it could be done. The Ph.D. from the Ministry of Propaganda who accompanied me said, "The Fifth Symphony: this is the true, the purest expression of the German soul." I then heard the symphony differently than I had ever heard it before.

"Thus fate knocks on the door," Beethoven said. We do not know whether it is a promise or a threat. Berlioz called the fourth movement "The Dance of the Elephants." But Schumann, when as a child he heard the Fifth Symphony, whispered during the first bars of the finale, "I am afraid." And the finale rises, effervesces with power and opulence, suggests infinite resources, and expands its passion to the limit: "Victory? Victory?" it cries, "Finally?" Some evenings before, I had heard *The Magic Flute* quite charmingly, consummately performed at the large opera house and had gone home to Unter den Linden, in a snowstorm, so filled with joy that it had to find expresison in verses from *Gösta Berlings Saga:*

You, whom I love as you taught me to love,
With wings flying into endless space....

This evening, the Fifth Symphony gave me no wings. After I had spent almost a month in the Third Reich, the music brought me echoes of conversations about the will and God's grace. It became for me more superhuman than divine. The salvation which it proclaims is no source of joy; it has great pathos and is a goal that has been accomplished; it is essentially a triumph which has had suffering and struggle as a prerequisite. For a moment I understood the child Schumann and wondered why the presence of the superhuman seemed to crush what the divine was lifting up—and whether I, in order to feel myself secure musically in the Third Reich, had to go all the way back to Haydn! Thus, fate knocks on the door. We do not know whether it means a promise or a threat, and perhaps in the dictionary of Fate there is no difference between them.

Since my guide in Berlin had explained the Fifth Symphony to be the true and highest expression of the soul of Germany, I began to wonder whether in the art of other peoples it would be possible to find a single work which in the same way could symbolize and represent a people's mind and being.

One cannot expect the soul of England to be expressed in music, for England is an unmusical nation, one which hoists its great sails in other waters. Shakespeare's *Henry IV* summons up French horns and violins, flutes and drums from a larger orchestra than any country knew in Shakespeare's time. Perhaps most people could agree that that drama explains politically what we mean when we say: England. Perhaps *A Midsummer Night's Dream* can also explain it, not so much as we now remember the comedy—with Mendelssohn's music which makes it half a ballet—but as we have it from Shakespeare's own hand; in that we marvel how such a high political order can arise from a play which mixes several worlds, and charming, incomparable poetry can be compatible with a cheerful disregard for poetry's most valuable regalia: lovers' faithfulness and love itself.

As for France, I could not find a single artistic symbol: I had to seek a constellation. I finally came to Renoir's pictures and the cathedral at Chartres. But not even the cathedral was what I sought, and my readers must themselves try to discover a more nearly perfect solution.

When in years to come I look back at this winter, I do not think it will be the Great War that particularly characterizes the season for me, nor even the severe weather which at home in Denmark has pushed existence back into the early Middle Ages. Rather, it will be the peculiar position of the planets in the western sky, the unique configuration of the great stars, which evening after evening surprises and almost frightens the viewer. I had seen it early in the winter over the roof at Rungstedlund, when I came home by the Shore Road. And here in Berlin I have lifted my eyes to where it sparkled high above the *Siegessäule,* the Column of Victory. It was in reality the most unusual event of the winter; and in several hundred years, when no one remembers how many

tanks or how much cavalry there was on the Eastern
or the Western Front, wise men from East or West
will remember the configuration of the planets, and
write about it.

Here the gods had come together to announce the
fate of human beings; clear-eyed and silent, the bless-
èd looked down upon the earth.

Highest and farthest towards the south, grave and
invisible to the eye, was Uranus, mate of the earth, as
if ready to jump up and take to flight; beneath
Uranus, Mars waited restlessly with its dull reddish
luster. Lowest on the horizon towards the west
blinked Mercury, which is usually busy elsewhere
and comes so infrequently together with the other
gods that this small planet's presence at the meeting
made it an event in the history of the heavens. Above
Mercury sat, majestically, Jupiter himself, the cloud-
gatherer Zeus, the praiseworthy, the elevated one.
But in the middle of these stars, clear as a diamond in
the heavens, shone Venus, the eternal renewer of
life.

In Africa, my native Mohammedan people pointed
towards Venus when we were out traveling at night
and told me that the prophet had a word for each
planet, an adjective that described one of Allah's at-
tributes. "That star," they said, "It says: Almighty."

> What chariots, what horses
> against us can bide,
> when the stars in their courses
> do fight on our side?

Reunion with England

It is a strange, unreal, and perturbing experience to be asked to send a greeting from England to Denmark via the BBC. When that happened to me yesterday, I thought to myself: I can't do it.

For five years I have sought the voice of the BBC in the ether, waited for it and listened to it—but to employ it myself? It is as if one were being asked to blow the trumpet once at doomsday. But here in London they assured me in a friendly fashion it could be done, and I shall now take them at their word.

Then another question arises: what greeting is worth sending to Denmark from England through the BBC?

In the thirties, I lived in England for a few months every summer, but it is now eight years since I was here.

Day before yesterday I flew from Copenhagen to London in perfectly calm weather through a supernatural interplay of blue and violet colors, with an Alpine landscape of white clouds beneath me. The plane moved as steadily as if we were speeding down a highway in the air.

This essay was first published as "Gensyn med England," in *En engelsk Bog. Tilegnet Kai Friis Møller* (Copenhagen, 1948), pp. 9–14.

Long before, in Africa, I had traveled in this way, and then I thought, "Yes, there *is* surely a highway in the air. Along this way the dreadful roc flew back from Africa to Arabia with an elephant in each claw!" The day before yesterday I thought the same thing: there really is a busy highway in the air, which we are using now. Along this way they came for five years from England to the continent, one great bird following the other with an elephant in each claw. They came steadily, as it says in the Book of Job about the war-horse: "He despiseth fear; above him shall the quiver rattle; chasing and raging, he swalloweth the ground."

Suddenly the clouds parted and far below us was green land: England. It was still here.

I was traveling with my brother who, in the First World War, served as a private in the English army. I turned to him and said, "It's England!" He laughed, and when I saw his face I wanted to ask him, "Why do you look that way?" But he, at the same moment, looked at me, laughed, and said, "Why do you look that way?"

As we flew on over the landscape with great groups of trees, church-towers, and houses beneath us, I asked him, "What does this reunion with England mean to you? What does England signify?" He thought for a moment and replied, "Self-restraint." As for myself, if I had to find a single word for what England signifies to me, it would have to be "freedom." Not merely in a political sense, but freedom to be a human being, to have leeway, to have a margin in life—freedom of movement, even where severe laws and rules must be kept. Would I now, I considered, seeing the country again, find this condition changed?

We have all read and heard about the ruins in England: I shall not describe them here. They are far more extensive than I had thought. On the first evening I was in London, my hosts took me for a tour of the quarter around St. Paul's, and it was terrible to see the destruction with my own eyes. But above the ruins rose St. Paul's Cathedral itself, as tranquil as before.

Aldous Huxley says of the builder of St. Paul's, Sir Christopher Wren, that his

> most characteristic quality is a quality rather moral than aesthetic. Everything that he did was the work of a gentleman; that is the secret of his character. For Wren was a great gentleman: one who valued dignity and restraint, and who, respecting himself, respected also humanity; one who despised meanness and oddity as much as vulgar ostentation, one who admired reason and order, and distrusted extravagance and excess. A gentleman,—the finished product of an old and ordered civilization.

The great gentleman St. Paul's spoke to me and said: "Dignity." It had perhaps been easier for St. Paul's to stand in a way so completely dignified above a wealthy and flourishing city. But it is possible to stand in the same way above ruins.

In these days I have felt and experienced London's history—the history of "an old and ordered civilization"—in its entirety and as a unity. I was not confined to a single isolated period of horror and destruction; I moved freely through England's every age. The Vikings once came over the sea and ravaged the coasts and thus England came into being. The Norman conquerors came a century later in order to conquer the land, but the land absorbed the conquerors and they became one with it and thus England came into being. The very city through the streets of which I now walk was once overcome by the hand of the plague, and fire raged through it; there have been ruins here before today. And thus London came into being.

Under a profound impression of the proximity of the ages, of the unity of past and future, I recall an old Scandinavian proverb: when there is a really dangerous animal on the prowl and the usual weapons fail, then one must cast bullets of the family silver, that is, of silver which has been inherited from father to son and grandson. There have been dangerous animals on the prowl here; some of them are still about. It is time we go to our chests and see what we have left in the way of family silver. How manifold is the centuries' wealth in that London whose blackened ruins are silhouetted on the sky! Without many pence in their pockets, its common people carry it with them. The far-extended, harmonious interrelationship of generations can be sensed everywhere: as it once was expressed in an epitaph for Danes who fell in battle—precisely against these our neighbors—"for they shall be named in times to come, the fathers' worthy sons."

I am now, after the war, visiting the conqueror. But, as dearly purchased as the triumph has been, as strongly as one feels here about the wave after wave of horror and mortal danger which has swept over the country, yet all impressions may be gathered into a single thought: "Victory comes to the man who gains strength from defeat."

On Orthography

I. On Seeing and Hearing

*M*ost of the present demand for reform in Danish orthography seems to come from people who comprehend and remember aurally. I should like to speak a word for those people who understand and remember visually. I myself have difficulty in remembering a sound and, in order to secure a new word in my memory, I must envisage how it looks when written down.

True, the spoken language existed before the written language, and the written word stands for the spoken word; yet the spoken word does not have the rights of a firstborn, for it simply represents the concept, the true original. With numbers we disregard the sound and go directly to the concept. Suppose there on a blackboard is the number 12; we pronounce it "tolv," the English say "twelve," and the French "douze," but visually we are all in complete understanding. It is doubtful whether in working

This essay was originally published as "Om Retskrivning," in the Copenhagen daily, *Politiken*, 23 and 24 March 1938. Also separately published, Copenhagen, 1949.

through a mathematical problem we pronounce the sound of a single number to ourselves. Even the most zealous phonetician would presumably prefer to have a problem in arithmetic presented to him in numbers rather than as "fifty plus forty minus thirty times twenty divided by ten." The list of our kings and the telephone book, if they were systematically written out with letters of the alphabet, would be frightening. The number 12 can also be written as XII, and while this changes neither sound nor meaning, the number visually acquires a different character: it looks as if it were an inscription and signifies a permanently fixed number, rather than one suitable to reckon with.

Today more than in the past we employ signals that are international and say something in all languages and say it through the eye—"instantaneously" communicating what would take some time to express in words. An automobilist who obeys the traffic sign *side road crossing main road* scarcely translates the meaning of the signal into sounds. If the purpose of orthographic reform is to make it easier for a child to learn to read, then I believe an extensive use of hieroglyphs would be more to the point than a phonetically systematized way of spelling. Children are happy to recognize a symbol within a text.

Reading is, on the whole, not a matter of spelling but of recognizing words by their appearance. The symbol COW is to the reader not a phonetic reproduction of the word "cow" but an ideographic hieroglyph, so to speak, an emblem of the cow itself. It is possible that a phonetically devised orthography would make it easier for a child to learn to read. But it would not be of decisive importance, for—if this were done for each European language—it would take an

English or a French child a much longer time to learn to read than a Danish child, since it must be very difficult to explain to an English child phonetically that *el ah yu dji aich* is *laf* (laugh), while *aich you dji aich* is *hew* (Hugh), or to a French child that *asj a y te* and *e a y* are both *o* (haut, eau). As it is, people in England and France read their books and newspapers quite as quickly as we do. They do not consciously spell the words they read: they recognize them pictorially.

Only if the form of the picture is changed is it necessary to spell something out. In a crossword puzzle I do not recognize those words that are printed vertically, but have to spell my way through them. I would have to do the same if I should read a page written from right to left. Even if all the words were spelled phonetically and correctly, the task would take me much longer than usual until, by practice, I had learned to recognize the words in their new form.

Numerous abbreviated words, like *cf.*, *etc.*, *i.e.*, appear in the text without any phonetic existence and the reader scarcely knows, when he has read a line, whether he has seen *etc.* or *and so forth*. The accepted symbols of the language—exclamation marks, question marks, quotation marks—are not read phonetically, either, but are present in the sentence in order to give it a certain character. Some letters of the alphabet have about the same role. The silent Danish *h* before *v* occurs in most cases in the words *hvad, hvem, hvilke, hvis, hver, hvordan*—what, who, which, whether, where—a kind of sign for a question, just as when one in Spanish places a question mark at the beginning of the sentence in order to show the reader immediately what is going on. Those people who comprehend by the eye would wish to preserve the silent *h* in these words, even though they would sadly have to accept its disappearance from other words which do not ask a question like *Hval, Hvalp, Hvede, Hvid, Hvaelving*—whale, whelp, wheat, white, vault.

The pictorial form of the word has for such people not only a practical but, at the same time, an aesthetic significance. I know by experience that I cannot grasp how one of my own sentences sounds before I have seen it in writing. Much old French poetry is almost exclusively visual and many English poems satisfy the eye but not the ear: "O Wind, —if Winter comes can Spring be far behind?" Contrariwise, there is some modern and particularly popular poetry which cannot be grasped by the eye but satisfies the ear when it rhymes *O.K.* with *Nørrebro*. The letter of the alphabet which does not exist for the listener and the form of that letter affect the reader poetically. Writing the Danish word for *woman* as *Quinde* instead of *Kvinde* makes the word sail along more majestically in a sentence because of the similarity with the English word *Queen* and of the rarity of the letter q, while *Kvinde* has associations with *Kvie*—heiffer. Nor can any reader doubt that in this matter the capitalization of substantives has a function. In general, they group the words in the sentence dramatically and make immediately clear to the reader which words play major roles in it.

Albert Engström wrote in an essay about the pictorial beauty of Greek words that the Norwegians in their *Hav* have a pictorially more accurate characterization of the sea than the Swedes in their *Haf*, which was used in his time. Yet the two words are pronounced identically.

II. On Reading and Writing

All schoolchildren learn to write as well as to read and, in general, they probably devote more time in learning to write than in learning to read. But school is not life, and life does not pattern itself after school; school should pattern itself after life. As soon as the young people have left school, there is a different relationship—the art or activity of reading and the other art or activity of writing are divided quite unequally among different people. The Danish man in the street, or at least the Danish woman in the street, writes at most two thousand words a year but reads—if he or she subscribes to a newspaper or a weekly, such as *Hjemmet* or *Familiejournalen*, and gets through four or five books from the library—two or three million words. The only items which are written and read to an equal degree, that is, by one person, are private letters, and these are generally not considered as literature: their value is personal, so that orthography in a letter is of minor importance and a mistaken spelling may even give a letter an added charm in the eyes of its reader.

It should, therefore, be easy to read, for there are millions who read. Everyone must read in order to know the laws and rules accessible in print, and it is to the advantage of a country that the people can read and that they do read.

But it need not be made easy to write, when only a tiny minority practices the art of writing. They are not forced to write; they take on the task voluntarily, and if they don't have the ability for it, or much interest in it, they can let it be. It is no advantage to a people when a very large number of them take up writing.

Any reforms in orthography which make it easier to write but more difficult to read will, except in school, make work easier for a small minority at the expense of the majority. The vast majority, ninety-five out of a hundred schoolchildren, have to pay for this assuagement of their schooling when, later in life, they take their places as readers. If an author who writes in one of the Sunday supplements of our newspapers, one that has two hundred and fifty thousand readers, out of laziness writes a sentence less clearly than he could, so that every one of his readers, in order to understand what the meaning really is, must stop reading and reflect for two seconds, there is sacrificed just as much time as if the author himself had reflected without a break day and night for a week upon what he wanted to say—which he would ordinarily do only in the most unusual cases.

Again, the minority, the five out of a hundred who later in life will find their places as writers or clerks, have to pay for the alleviation in the schooling if they are going to write so that they can be read and understood by their readers. A writer has a use for and may demand all the means that a language can give him in order to express himself and be understood.

The capitalization of substantives, which we have hitherto used in Danish, has no phonetic existence any more than exclamation marks, question marks, or quotation marks, but is present in a sentence in order to clarify its construction. I can read a book without noticing whether or not capitals are being so used, but I have many times discovered that capitalization is helpful and gives an overview when one is reading an unknown text aloud. The fact that the capitalization of substantives is not used in other languages than Danish and German is an argument neither for nor against it. Perhaps the Danish and German languages have here an advantage over others. I have had friends in England who were studying German and who said they envied the Germans—and us—the capitalization of substantives. There are Danish words which do not correspond exactly to any words in other languages, as, for example, *Føre* (the state of the road or the ground, as in good or bad *Føre*, skating *Føre*), *Søskende* (brothers and sisters), *Døgn* (period of twenty-four hours). I have had need of these words when I was speaking or writing English, and I see no reason to get rid of them purely for the sake of parallelism. Other languages have other advantages. If the alternate spellings of the phonetically identical *kunne* and *kunde, skulle* and *skulde, ville* and *vilde* in any way serves to make the language easier to read, then they should be preserved in the orthography for the sake of the majority of readers. It is not a matter here of an arbitrary *tour de force* which schoolchildren need to know. The fact of the matter is that *kunne* and *kunde, skulle* and *skulde, ville* and *vilde* are in reality just as different as *faa* and *fik* (get and got), *staa* and *stod* (stand and stood), *være* and *var* (to be and was). One must be a rabid phonetician to let the sound be more important than the meaning in the comprehension and classification of a word. The alternate spellings of the words in question can cause schoolchildren some difficulty because of the accidental similarity of sound between the two forms of the verbs—as long as they have no understanding of what a verb is or how a sentence is built; but those children who have an inclination to books and language and who presumably will write later in life, will acquire this understanding in their schooldays. It is difficult to imagine that an author who was able to write a book or an article should be so confused by a similarity of sound that he forgets whether he had intended to write something as an infinitive or in the past tense. I have seen the argument advanced against the use of capitalization or against the alternate spellings in *kunne, skulle,* and *ville,* that these subtleties in an unnecessarily unkind way separate those who can write from those who cannot, so that he who cannot is unmasked when he applies in writing for a position and doesn't get it. That is a fantastic argument.

When Ali Baba's slave Morgana saw that the forty thieves had found her master's house and marked it with a cross in order to return and kill him, she took a piece of chalk and marked ninety-nine other houses in the neighborhood with the same sign, so that Ali Baba's house was undistinguishable among them. This was a stroke of genius and as a result Morgana has become immortal—perhaps those people who have had a similar idea concerning orthography will also become immortal. She became justly immortal, for she not only had energy and self-confidence, but she knew what she was doing: her purpose was to confuse.

Morgana had, of course, no interests in common with the forty thieves. But the applicant and the employer in reality have a common interest, namely, that the right man should be in the right place. In these circumstances, as in others, one must be permitted to assume that human beings have what is called intelligence. It is unreasonable to assume that a farmer who needs a herdsman and finds an applicant qualified for the job would turn him away because in his application he has confused *kunne* and *kunde*. But the employer for whom it is of decisive importance to secure a man with a sense for the meaning of words should, on the whole, take the point into consideration. When one has chalked over all indications of which applicants can write in order to make him who cannot invisible among them, one has done them a disservice and the employer a disservice—and one has also done a disservice to him who cannot write, although his welfare has lain at the heart of the whole orthographic reform. For when he gets the job, he will be very soon confronted by assignments he cannot cope with.

III. *On the Possibility of Writing as One Speaks*

It is possible to write Danish phonetically, so that a foreigner is able to read out our spoken language correctly from the printed page. The same foreigner will be completely unable to read the books or newspapers which we ourselves read with ease. Nor will we be able to read the text which the foreigner is using. Effecting a reform for the sake of phonetic spelling will require the acquisition of a new phonetic alphabet.

Danish has many different sounds for each letter of the alphabet and our new school books would have to contain new symbols simply for the sounds of the vowels: for the *a* in *har, Kar, Sal, skal,* and *Skal,* for the *e* in *men* and *Men,* for *i* in *Bil, hil, skil,* and *til,* for *o* in *for* and *fòr,* for *u* in *hun, kun,* and *lun,* for *y* in *nyt* and *Spyt,* for *æ* in *Sjæl* and *Skæl,* for *ø* in *Brøl, føl,* and *Øl.* It will become more difficult to write our language than it is now, although it is conceivable that, for persons with a particular sense for the sound of the language, it could be more interesting. For the vast majority, reading Danish would become almost intolerable.

The attempts which have hitherto been made by writers and journalists who write Danish phonetically and correctly are not convincing and often give the impression of being almost arbitrary. I shall provide some examples.

I have seen the words *det, jeg, til,* and *ved* written *de, je, te, ve;* the word *med* written *mæ;* and the words *hvordan* and *hvorfor* written *vodden* and *voffer.*

But the monosyllables ending in *e,* which already exist in Danish—*Ble, Fe, ske,* and *Ve*—are all pronounced with a glottal stop and do not rhyme with *jeg, til,* or *ved.* If *e* in the new words is supposed to be phonetically correct, then the old orthography in the above-named words cannot be preserved. But the new orthography is not systematically phonetic either, for *e* is not pronounced the same in all the given examples and *til* does not rhyme with *jeg.* There is scarcely a single word in the language which rhymes with *jeg* as that word is pronounced in daily speech. If we really are going to spell phonetically, the word *jeg* must have a special symbol of its own.

Vis-à-vis the letter *æ* in *mæ,* the same holds true. All Danish words which hitherto have ended in *æ*—*Bræ, dræ, Fæ, Knæ, Læ, Træ*—are pronounced with a glottal stop and none of them rhymes with *med.* If one decides the *æ* in *mæ* is phonetically correct, then one must find a new symbol for the *æ* in these words.

The words *hvordan* and *hvorfor* are both sometimes pronounced with stress on the last syllable and then the *a* and *o* of these spellings are clearly heard. If there is still the possibility of pronouncing the words in this way, one would have to write the words two different ways in the phonetically improved orthography—which really would be confusing for the less gifted. But even if we leave this aspect out of consideration, *voffer* and *vodden* are not phonetically acceptable spellings for these words.

In all the Danish words which are written with double *f* after *o*, the *o* is pronounced rounded, as in *Offer*, *Stoffer*, *Kristoffer;* and *voffer* does not rhyme with these words. If this sound is to be represented correctly, it would be better to spell the word with *u* and have it rhyme with *Luffer, puffer,* and *Skuffer.*

Vodden is no better. In all the Danish words with double *d* after *o*, the *o* is pronounced rounded and the *d* is soft, as in *Odden, Skodden,* and—with a glottal stop—*Brodden.* If the sound of *vodden* is accounted phonetically correct for double *d* after *o*, then the old spelling must be changed in these words or the new spelling will be less enlightening than that which we now have. There is no point in trying to spell *votten* with double *t,* for the word rhymes neither with *Rotten* nor *Potten.* The *u* in *Mutter* is perhaps the vowel that most closely resembles the *o* in *hvordan.* But *Mutter* is itself, viewed phonetically, an exception and does not rhyme with either *lutter* or *sutter,* or indeed with any other word in the language, so that it is unreasonable to use *Mutter* as a norm.

In addition, there are many words in our language which are compounded with the commonly used words like *ad, af, jeg, med, til,* and *ved,* but which are not used so frequently and therefore in use have not lost a consonant as the shorter words have. It is difficult to take a position regarding these words, for one would not destroy the relationship of these words, by differing spelling, whereas on the other hand, the way Danish is spoken today, it would not be phonetically correct to spell *Agang* for *Adgang* or *Afgang, Akom, Akomst, Jeform, Mæhustru, tevant* or *vevare* for *Afkom, Ankomst, Jegform, Medhustru, tilvant,* or *vedvare.*

IV. What One Needs

Let us assume that a Danish citizen from the year 1838 rose from the grave, walked again, and entered Ollerup folk-high-school where Niles Bukh was working with one of his classes of young gymnasts—perhaps the situation will be most striking if we imagine that, at the moment, it was a class of girls.

One can imagine that a citizen from the time of Frederik VI would feel himself both disoriented and indignant, and that he finally would say to Niels Bukh, "What you are doing here is completely crazy. Why do you want to waste time teaching young farm girls such impractical things? Teach them how to milk a cow, to churn butter, or to card wool, the sort of thing they have need for. That's the way you would best serve them. Whatever makes you want to teach them the high jump and discus throwing? It's all very well if the young daughters of our aristocracy and civil-servant class receive instruction in plastic gymnastics and posture. But you must yourself know that these farm girls will never need to jump the high jump—and will you tell me why in the world they might ever need to throw a discus?" One can further imagine that Niels Bukh would reply. "We're giving our young women what they have need for in all of life's circumstances, namely, a harmonious and self-controlled body."

When it is a matter of book-learning, many progressive citizens of today take up the same viewpoint as the man of 1838. They are of the opinion that the younger generation is best served by being taught the skills which it needs and can benefit by at once. For all profound knowledge, insight, or cognition, they say, youth today does not have time, nor does youth need it.

But a skill does not in itself have any real human value and confers no human perspective. It is different with insight and cognition: the person who has acquired them becomes different than he was before; he has grown, he has become richer.

If one acquires the skills of milking, churning butter, or carding wool, but does not have an opportunity to apply them, then one is neither worse nor better than one was before. But an all-round physical training has changed the young men and women who have undergone it. It will give them mastery over any work at all with which they may be confronted in life, and make it easier for them.

Book-learning, which does not aim at immediate needs, but which harmoniously develops all human intellectual faculties and potentialities, was, a hundred years ago, the privilege of the upper class. But that does not mean it is an antique weapon, a flint axe or a broadsword which the new times, having discovered gunpowder, can lay away in the grave of the old upper class. It can still be used. Those modern pedagogues who, by relinquishing the development of the whole human being, want to train youth in such skills as they have need for and can use immediately—they are not less barbarian than those parents who, in the old days, enrolled their sons in the choir of St. Peter's in the conviction that they had more need for a sure income with a promise of a pension than for anything else.

From this point of view, the acquisition of languages must also be determined. A child who has learned a language through the ear alone has need of what he has learned when he is together with people who speak that language. If the child does not have an opportunity to practice, but forgets what he has learned, then he is neither better nor worse than if he had never learned the language. But the person who has learned a language grammatically and has understood its construction and inner relationships acquires an understanding and sense for cause and effect; he has learned to reason. He can use this knowledge wherever he finds himself in life, whether he is passing laws or making a budget or playing cards. The grammatical rules, even the intimidating and despised rules about *kunne*, *skulle*, and *ville* are here on the same level with the discus, which Niels Bukh's girls learn to throw.

I had a school for my black people in Africa ten years ago. It played an important role both in their lives and mine. Attendance was not compulsory; the pupils came because they wanted to go to school. They paid for their own slates and books, and after a long day's work, in the evening, they walked several miles with the slates under their arms to the schoolhouse. The subject they most wanted to learn, and which I wanted most that they be taught was arithmetic, a very elementary kind of mathematics. And they were proficient in calculating; they divided three-figure numbers into five-figure numbers and seldom made errors. They were also interested in how much twenty donkeys are worth if two donkeys are worth as much as five sheep and a sheep cost twenty rupees.

I got my black schoolteachers from the French mission, and the head of the mission station, Father Bernhard, who is my good friend, often came over to inspect our school. At these opportunities Father Bernhard and I carried on long discussions about pedagogical principles. As missionaries, the Catholics are, above all, practical people, and Father Bernhard was of the opinion that we wasted our valuable time.

"Let the natives learn something they have need of in their own community," he said. But both he and I overlooked in a grand manner during our discussion what the natives themselves needed and kept to the subject of what could be of value to us in what they did. "Teach them what they have need for. You should teach your people a trade, carpentry work or tanning. Or if you still have such a love for numbers, teach them the multiplication table—they will never have need for anything else. Why do you want to teach them such impractical things?"

"Oh, but Father Bernhard," I said, "I have need of people who can think a little."

The old priest looked at me in a fatherly way and said, "Que vous êtes donc toujours téméraire, Madame,"—'Ah, you are always reckless, Madame.'

Viewed from different sides of the globe, things look different. Seen from my own farm, which lay a little south of the equator, the Big Dipper was upside-down. It is improbable that modern Danish scholars would find my ambitions regarding school to be foolish. But it is probable that they, in Father Bernhard's place, would say to me, "How reactionary you are, Madame!"

H. C. Branner
The Riding Master

When Allah created the horse, he said to it,
Your equal is not to be found.
All the treasures of the earth
lie between your eyes.
My enemies you will tread upon,
but my friends
you will carry on your back.
You will fly without wings,
and conquer without a sword.

The Koran

*E*ven if one should, for the sake of argument,
doubt the great significance of this book as a
work of art, one would nevertheless have to
recognize its significance for cultural history.

Even if one should, for the sake of argument, doubt
that the author had written it in profound earnestness, one would nevertheless feel that a profound
earnestness pervades it.

The Danish readers of 1949—not merely the Danish
literary critics, as it sometimes happens, but the
Danish reading world as a whole—took the book to
their hearts at once, were appalled by it and trans-

This essay was first published as "H. C. Branner: 'Rytteren'," in
Bazar (1950), 1:50–63, 71–94.

ported by it, and felt elevated and edified as by a gospel. In a hundred years a weighty judgment may be passed on the intellectual life of our time in Denmark: "It was in *The Riding Master* that this generation found release for its essential being." The book must be read more than once. Many things in it mean more—mean sometimes something quite different— than they appear to do at first sight. It is full of symbols. The present writer can, in any case, base her claim to discuss it on repeated readings. *The Riding Master*'s action and characters have been discussed and dealt with by shrewd critics, but it seems necessary to discuss and deal with them once more in an effort to clarify the book's idea and message.

Four people, conceived as distinctly modern and, to a marked degree, children of our time—and they are really such children, in their ceaseless introspection and defective or nonexistent self-esteem or self-confidence—have, prior to the beginning of the novel, as in a dark wood, met a centaur with whom they lived in relation for some time. The association was momentous for all of them; the centaur did not survive it.

The book shows how, after this experience, each of the four people, helped or hindered by the others, manages to find a footing in existence and a possible way to continue, or simply to save, his or her life.

We usually speak of the course or sequence of events in a book as the action. In this book very little happens, for it is not through action the characters seek salvation. There are in the novel two attempts at rape and two at suicide, but these remain only attempts. An attempt can, to be sure, have the quite practical result of creating an effect and carrying forward the action, but that does not seem to happen in this book.

Instead, the characters in the book talk together a great deal. The command "Be quiet!" occurs nineteen times in their conversations, but it has nowhere any effect. The characters rise with bloody mouths from a lovers' struggle on a rug, or they are aroused to life from a sleep which was supposed to have been eternal—and take up the discussion where they left off.

They talk about themselves, sometimes about each other, and constantly about the centaur, the Riding Master.

To such a great degree are their dialogues (all the conversations in the novel are dialogues, for the characters are brought on the scene two by two; no scene contains a larger group of people) dominated by the deceased, that the reader must ask himself how they had ever been able to live without him, and whether they would have lived in silence if they had never met him. We learn that two of them met him for the last time ten or twenty years before; yet they constantly mention his name, and whatever it was they experienced with him, that is what they talk about. Whatever has happened to them in the interim they mention in passing or not at all. And only one of them talks about or seems to remember anything which took place before their meeting with the Riding Master.

In the many long conversations about him, only a single remark by the Riding Master himself is quoted, on one of the last pages of the book. Throughout the novel it is said of him, "He almost never spoke"— "They didn't get a word out of him"—"He almost never spoke to me"—"It seems to me as if he never said a word." But more than twenty times it is said by one or another person that "He laughed." And once it is said he wept.

Nevertheless, in the last nocturnal hour—after all the living have spoken and forced each other to speak—we do hear a sentence from the mouth of the Riding Master. And such great weight is laid in the novel upon the unseen, silent figure from whom it takes its title, that his one remark has the function of summarizing and concluding it. I shall return to this point.

The Riding Master's four living characters are two women and two men: Susanne, who was the Riding Master's mistress; her friend Michala; Herman, who is the Riding Master's successor as the owner of his riding school; and Clemens, the physician, who is Susanne's lover at the beginning of the book. The Riding Master's name was Hubert.

Susanne and Clemens are, after the Riding Master himself, the main figures in the book. They divide it between them: the first half is hers; the last, his. Some subordinate figures are introduced and then dismissed in order to make these two stand out in some relief. Michala and Herman have to get along without any retinue.

The mighty passions which, in their dealings with the Riding Master, once engrossed the characters of the book, have now, after his death, been transformed in all of them into an awareness of guilt. On whom this guilt really should rest is not clear. The accusations raised against the Riding Master himself—of swindling in the school, or of rape—are all retracted. The charges which the figures raise against one another or against themselves turn out to be unfounded, or poorly grounded. Even with regard to the Riding Master's death, the truth is uncertain. Herman says to Susanne, "I killed Hubert!" And again, "It was I who killed him." She rejects the notion with disdain and derisive laughter. Clemens says to Susanne, "You killed Hubert." She answers him at first, "That is not true. He killed me." But some pages further on she says to Clemens, "He or I had to die. And it was he. For I was the stronger." All the situations in the book are pervaded by an ineluctable and appalling conviction that injustice has been done.

There is one point about which the four persons in the novel seem to be able to agree. They all bear a grudge against the deceased. Herman says, "I hate Hubert." Michala says, "I hate him. I hate him even if he is dead." Clemens, for whom the feeling of hatred itself is uncharacteristic, says, "In a way, I hated Hubert." And Susanne says, "I hated him so much that I had to stay with him." And again, later, "I loved to hate him."

Nevertheless, the reader understands from the narrative that all of them, while Hubert was alive, sought him out—though he never sought them out; that they had followed him and clung to him as if they loved him. And at that time, they were not deceiving him.

On the basis of all this, one imagines the relationship thus: in himself, the centaur harmoniously united that nature of man and beast. While he was among them, this strange harmony gripped, awed, and moved the four people, without limit. Now that he is gone, the fact seems to them incomprehensible, indeed unbelievable, and—as it often is with the incomprehensible and the unbelievable—outrageous and unbearable. One of them nevertheless attempts to copy the deceased and make himself into a centaur. For the others, it's a matter of a desperate choice between two natures.

The book itself seems to be an expression of the same choice. In the first half of the book, the word *horse* appears more than fifty times and the horse is there formidable and fateful—in the words of the novel, "as big as a church tower and much bigger than houses." In the other half of the book, the words *human being* are repeated again and again.

In this book, as in all books where the really decisive events precede the first page, much must remain, or is placed by the author, in a *clair-obscur*, so that the reader can make his way through the narrative only step by step. The proper reader is more captivated than wearied by the exertions such a meandering requires.

It has been said of *The Riding Master* that, in every scene, Hubert's shadow rests upon each of the speakers. One could advance a contradictory metaphor. In mountainous areas, it can happen that the wanderer meets his own shadow or it rises up behind him, projected in gigantic size upon a wall of fog. Similarly, the people of normal human dimensions in the book move along the stage near the footlights; those farther back move, supernaturally enlarged, upon the background of the centaur's being.

The narrative takes place during eighteen hours divided into "Morning," "Noon," "Afternoon," "Evening," and "Night." According to the author's plan the first chapters are broad, develop slowly, and include details about the surroundings and the ambiance. The last chapter is very short, as if all the evidence were now gathered up and the final judgment ready for deliverance.

Susanne is the important female figure in the book, its heroine. The contents of her day are shown and her movements through the eighteen hours are followed. Twice the line of movement is broken and a part of Clemens's day is inserted in order to expand the basis of the narrative a bit and to give it balance. In the novel's last chapter, of only ten pages, "Night," Susanne and Clemens are together.

Susanne is the character who was closest to the Riding Master; his life and death have affected her existence most deeply. After his death, it is not possible for her to find peace of mind by moving the center of gravity of her life elsewhere. That she herself can even consider the possibility of this—and how— demonstrates how fundamentally the experience has destroyed her being and how close she is to perdition. That the others can imagine such a possibility for her seems strange, at the very least. To be sure, the reader is not told at the start of the narrative how long it has been since Hubert's death. He learns that, since then, Susanne has lived in Clemens's apartment—she says to Clemens, "Can you remember the day you came home and found me here? That day, Hubert was dead"—but not how long she has lived there. It does not seem a matter of years, scarcely of months. On the first page of the book, Susanne looks from her bed at the furniture in the bedroom—"her own French furniture, oppressed by Clemens's massive mahogany"—and thinks, "Lightweight, homeless, accidental, not here to stay." And for the other persons in the book, the arrangement is still surprising; they have in no way accustomed themselves to it. Nevertheless, Clemens plans to celebrate Susanne's birthday by a trip out into the country or dinner at a restaurant, and Susanne and Clemens, the night before the story begins, came home late from a large party. Susanne, the reader thinks, might well have been allowed to sit astride Hubert for a time.

Restless and unhappy, Susanne begins her pilgrimage in the chapter "Afternoon," after a couple of wild and fruitless attempts to find peace of mind with Clemens. She walks out of the apartment onto the street and goes to visit Herman.

As a human being Herman is pitiful, but as a character in a novel he is boldly sketched and reminds one of some of Gogol's figures. He is banality driven to the fantastic, with its inseparable element of the slightly macabre and of something that evokes sympathy.

Herman has been obsessed by Hubert. "If Hubert had said to me," he says to Susanne, "that I should throw myself beneath a horse and be trampled to death—I would have done it." Nor can he give him up now; he has taken over Hubert's house and riding school; he lives in Hubert's rooms. He obviously plans to take up the heritage of Hubert, to recreate himself in Hubert's image and himself to become a centaur.

The reader of the book understands from the beginning that Herman's ambition is hopeless, a dream of pure madness. Herman's human dimensions are so fragile that he cannot be united with anything more substantial than a hobbyhorse without being jolted wildly out of proportion. And in him the weak human personality hates and fears the being, more than animal, with whose nature he is endeavoring to unite himself. "I hate the horses," he says. Herman has no relationship with these horses which, for him, in reality still are Hubert's. If there is any idea involved in his life with them, it is the *idée fixe*: fear. "Think how big a horse is and how strong," Herman says to Susanne. "What would a human being do if the horse knew its strength? Consequently, it must never be allowed to forget its fear for a moment." And when describing for her his work with the horses, he says, "Not to mention the mortal danger!" Later he says, "Hubert wasn't afraid enough. That was his mistake as a rider and caused his death. But I know anything can happen. Any second. It's wearing out every nerve in my body!" Here again, the phenomena of the novel are enlarged before a background of myth. These tremendous, dangerous horses that can trample a man to death belong to real life just as little as Herman's remarks can be imagined coming from the mouth of a real riding master, for it is not dangerous to ride in a riding school. Hubert himself, the riding master, appears again and again mythically enlarged in the stream of words coming from Herman, who is otherwise unimaginative and banal. "He imagined," says Herman, "that he could put himself in the place of the horse. Riding was for Hubert a play with the gods." And Herman's own fear announces itself once more. "The horse," he says, "must fear me like an alien will. An animal of prey hanging with teeth and claws upon its back!" A curious riding master and teacher. A sorry, a grotesque centaur.

Now Susanne and Herman meet in Hubert's rooms.

Susanne is, in a different sense than that which has already been mentioned, the character in the novel who has been closest to the Riding Master: she resembles him. Under his guidance, she has been transformed and has become so much of a female centaur that a love relationship between them has been possible. If Susanne today—since he is gone who harmoniously united nature and humanity and since such a harmony seems to her incomprehensible and unbelievable—if she still could make a choice, she would cast off her human nature: she would be a horse. She thinks of "a time before time, and vast, foggy plains where the horses wander about freely." She has a horse's mane. She is therefore always quite alone among people. She still sees in the act of love the only thinkable means of salvation, but her now deceased mate places himself between her and every possible love. Where is now the force which transformed her? Other men around her try, piteously. She rages to Clemens against them. "Your friends, your enlightened friends who want to free the world. They won't free me. That's because they are petty creative writers. But I have known one who was greater. IIe was so great that he recreated me into the person I am!"

Susanne is desired by those who have loved and hated Hubert—and who still love and hate him. They need her. They have, in their own language, "a use for" her.

Herman says to Susanne, "There is something I lack. I don't quite know what it is. But I know you have it. It is you I have use for. It is you I want!" Susanne's suitors and she are in more profound disagreement than they themselves are aware. It is Hubert that both parties desire in vain, and they stand side by side with their eyes on the same spot, without turning to one another, totally deterred from an embrace. She herself suspects it. When Herman says to her that he has loved her ever since he saw her the first time, she asks him, "Why did I never notice it while Hubert was alive?" "Then you belonged to him, of course," Herman replies with downcast eyes. "You never spoke to me," she says, ridiculing him. "You scarcely looked at me."

Herman tries to take Susanne by force. Had he succeeded, it would perhaps have been a release for the unhappy woman; and that may have been in Clemens's thoughts when he, despite his jealousy, allowed her to be alone with Herman, and when he says to her, "I thought perhaps Herman could help you." But Herman is unable to possess Susanne, unable indeed to keep alive his lust. She challenges him, half-heartedly: "Well, show me you are not afraid," she says to him, "show me that you dare, Herman." In tragic triumph, she sees him collapse. "You are he," he wails wretchedly and grotesquely, "that's why I couldn't take you even if I wished!"

Susanne, who has been desired against her will and rejected against her will, is in her turn without compassion for her unhappy lover. He pleads with her to leave, and she replies, "Why should I leave? I am at home here." She treats him as he treats his horses, who must not forget their fear for a moment. She desires he should feel her ruling him like an alien will, an animal of prey hanging on his back with teeth and claws. She forces him to take from her hand the sugar which is repulsive to him, and hears him crush it between his teeth as he is kneeling before her. It is a bitter and painful moment for him and for her. For Hubert would have taken the sugar from the hand of his mistress as a friendly and cheerful endearment; he would surely have preferred that kind of relation to the hectic conversations to which the circle of his acquaintances now dedicate themselves.

Then Susanne goes out of Herman's room—of Hubert's old room—as she had gone out of Clemens's room. She visits Michala.

In one sense, Michala is the most modern of the modern people in this book; she is the one who occurs most frequently in modern life. If we today walk from Kongens Nytorv—the King's Newmarket—to the City Hall Square, we cannot avoid meeting her. She is the unnatural woman; in her own jargon, "emancipated" from nature—torn away from it, robbed of it.

Fortunately we do not meet every day, on the way from the King's New Market to the City Hall Square, a Michala as worn and exhausted as this secondary female figure in *The Riding Master*. A great misfortune has overwhelmed her. As a child, or in her youth, Michala met Hubert and stood face to face with myth in the figure of a centaur. The more nearly intact the human being who meets myth has preserved his own nature, the richer the meeting will be. But what defenses did poor Michala have? No instinct, no temperament, no real faith. She is quite simply crushed by the meeting, as in a collision. Now, little Michala is living "on chemicals." In the story, Michala arouses the reader's sympathy, as Herman never does: She is an almost immaterial creature, a graceful moth that has been stepped on and is half-dead. We find we are surprised that the destruction of such a minimal existence still can cause so much pain. Nevertheless, this weightless Michala, like all the figures in the novel, is enlarged against the background of the myth of a centaur. An era—a world? The poverty of all mankind when emancipated from nature?

So, Michala has also met Hubert and the meeting is mirrored in her consciousness as in a concave mirror. She raises a false accusation against him. This must happen; in their relationship she is forced to lie, for she does not have within her the strength of character with which to speak the truth about a myth. She "hates him, even if he is dead." And, at the same time, she is scarcely able to recognize his existence. And time and again she rejects the thought of him. "Is it he again? Can we never finish with him? A ridiculous, foolish person, the stupid. . . ." It is an annihilated person's sad attempt to annihilate. "But I have one thing to thank him for," she says. "He took faith away from me." Here, the author turns the concave mirror just a bit, so that a glint strikes the reader's eyes, and his heart.

Now, Michala longs for the time before she knew the Riding Master, for her childhood. The word *child* occurs many times in her conversation with Susanne. "It's the child that is important—the child before fear. The child that creates its own world." On her wall, she has a picture of a naked rider drawn by a seven-year-old child. In this way, she can recognize and acknowledge him and be reconciled with him. "See how victoriously he comes! Laughing! Guiltless!"

Michala desires Susanne just as Herman has done. "It's you I need," she says to her, "you are the one who must help me. You have something within you that you yourself do not know. Something original: life, mystery. You can help me to see things again, to feel things again." And in perfect accord with the myth in the novel, she now asks Susanne, first of all, to teach her to ride. Michala reaches for Susanne as wildly as Herman, but in a nobler fashion, not out of personal vanity but for the sake of life—the bit of life she has left. And Susanne does not punish Michala as she has punished Herman. Without compassion, she rejects her untruth and, without compassion, disengages herself from her embrace, which is as convulsive as that of a drowning person. When Michala asks her, "Do you hate me now?" she answers, "No, I do not hate you." And she remains seated until Michala falls asleep. Then Susanne leaves Michala's room, restless and homeless, as she has left Clemens's and Herman's rooms. She goes back to Clemens and the great drama between them, the strongest in the novel, can begin.

Gigantic old motifs resound through this interplay. Not written in imitation, but reproduced in a modern style and spirit.

Here are now the first harps in the air, or at least a single harp, and where does it come from? From the folk ballad, the ballad about the maiden transformed into a hind.

The knight is hunting in the woods and sees the transformed maiden. He follows her for a long time, but she turns herself into a falcon and sits high up in a tree, and the knight under the tree feels he will die of grief if he does not capture the bird. He is advised to lure the falcon with "tame flesh"—flesh and blood from his own breast. He takes the advice:

> The blood ran and the breast burned;
>   he hung it on a linden bough.
> She fluttered her wings, for well she knew
>   she must not lose the flesh.
>
> Down from her perch flew the falcon wild;

> she tasted the bloody flesh,
> At once she became the fairest maid
> who walked upon the earth.

In his book on the magic ballads of Scandinavia, Axel Olrik writes of this ballad, "There is an impressive seriousness in the description of the falcon which, cleaving to its nature as a bird of prey, seeks the redeeming flesh—not by virtue of being human and knowing the way to redemption, no, by virtue of the transformation itself, by its nature as a bird of prey, fluttering with happiness when the blood-dripping flesh is hung upon the linden twig."

We hear in a lyrical arrangement the theme, which, in *The Riding Master*, grates on the ear as it announces its presence and wrestles with itself. In the same way, Clemens puts out his own heart for Susanne, and during three of the novel's five parts she pecks and pulls at it, just as wildly and ferociously as the falcon of the folk-ballad does at the knight's flesh. We can imagine this as the idea or direction of their life together: that he, with love's intuition, lures the bewitched woman through the very nature of her bewitchment until she is saved and becomes a human being. Still greater and older motifs are heard, so powerful and ancient I cannot name the instruments on which they were originally played.

The promise of salvation through blood recurs in untold ages of man and among innumerable peoples. And deep in the mind of manifold ages of man and peoples has lain the faith and the expectation of the miracle: the solitary figure who is able to redeem everyman by himself assuming the guilt of everyman. If, prior to the autumn of 1949, and while he was planning his novel, the author of *The Riding Master* had expounded his sketch for the reviewer who, in all humility, is writing this, that reviewer would have allowed herself to say to him:

"Take care; at this moment you are in danger. Keep this old theme, with its divine and human associations, out of your work. It will destroy your own means of expression. Do not try to combine mystery and myth in a work of imaginative literature, for that is unseemly."

The author would no doubt have answered, "Wait and see!"

And the author of *The Riding Master* would then have undertaken with care and with the help of a very old book to which he had referred from time to time, to depict the miracle: the salvation of many through an individual.

> He is despised and rejected of men; a man of sorrows; and acquainted with grief; and we hid as it were our faces from him; he was despised, and we esteemed him not. . . .
>
> But he was wounded for our transgressions, he was bruised for our iniquities: the chastisement of our peace was upon him. . . .
>
> He was oppressed, and he was afflicted, yet he opened not his mouth: he is brought as a lamb to the slaughter, and as a sheep before her shearers is dumb, so he openeth not his mouth.
>
> Isaiah 53: 3, 5, 7

Clemens is a small man, a little too fat, in a new suit which is meant to make him seem thinner. "A man," he says about himself, "who is ashamed because he is too fat and nevertheless cannot resist eating too much." When he grows excited, he forgets to pull in

172

his stomach. He wears glasses that do not flatter him and, conscious of this, he constantly takes them off and puts them on. He tends to sweat lightly. He is overtired from his day's work as a physician and is found by his mistress asleep in his chair, pale, with relaxed features and his glasses far down his nose. He has difficulty in starting his automobile and thinks, "I should not be permitted to drive an automobile." When, to please his beloved, he tries to learn to ride, he is afraid and the horses notice it and throw him off "constantly"—and the other people in the riding academy laugh.

Clemens takes upon himself everyone's guilt. In one passage, despite a policeman's testimony, he assumes the street-hawker's guilt. Hubert, who has been his school chum, had been expelled from school —"But the guilt," says Clemens, "was mine." He says to Susanne, "In a way, I am guilty of Hubert's death." When Susanne complains, "I am no longer really alive and it's your fault!" he replies, "Yes, it is my fault." He explains to her that, vis-à-vis people he knows or has known, he always feels a sense of guilt, and when she asks him whether this is also true about the dead, he answers, "Primarily and mainly, about the dead. It is as if it were my fault when they die." He tells Susanne that his mother died when she gave birth to him and adds, "So, I was directly responsible for her death," and rejects Susanne's attempt to deny the idea. "Whatever you say does not help me," he explains. "My feelings tell me that I am guilty of her death. And if I were not guilty of it and yet had to bear the responsibility for it, everything would be meaningless."

Then at Christmastime in 1949 the author of *The Riding Master* would have approached the present reviewer and exclaimed, "Wasn't I right? I have written my book and the Danish reading world has received it with delight and dismay and has felt itself elevated and edified as if by a new gospel! From many sides I have been told, 'The gospel of *The Riding Master* will save us!' And Clemens is the great, luminous figure in my book, the personification of the good, the suffering, and the victorious Savior. From all sides, he has been recognized and acclaimed —Hosanna!—as the Savior our time has needed and has awaited!"

"Yes," the reviewer replies. "The Danish readers are delighted and dismayed by *The Riding Master*. Many readers have assured me of this themselves. An intelligent woman told me some days ago that she had read the book aloud to her mother-in-law— herself a famous authoress—and that when she had read the last page, both of them burst into tears at the thought they now must be separated from the world and the characters of the book. They could find solace only in picking up the novel, opening it to the first page, and beginning to read it again. From all sides, it has been proclaimed that the gospel of *The Riding Master* will save our time. In a hundred years, there will be a valuable observation regarding the spiritual life of our time in Denmark, in that people will say, 'It was in *The Riding Master* that that generation found the liberation of its own being.'

"But I myself, who have read *The Riding Master* many times, have found in the book a confirmation of what I said to you a half-year ago, 'It is unseemly to combine mystery with myth. When these two meet in a work of art, myth is victorious. It gives to mystery a life of its own life and blood of its own blood—and dehumanizes it.'"

We hear today from all sides that our time has rediscovered the existence of evil. Today, evil seems to be defined as that which "hurts." Against this image of evil, the time pits its image of the good human being. And the good human being is interpreted consistently as he who does good, the do-gooder. This is new. Past times have believed just as little that the human soul could succumb to what hurts it as they have that a mother's soul could be saved by charity.

The new evangelists, the latter-day saints, make capital of the old evangelists, or they make capital of Christ himself, and He is introduced into their prophecy disguised in His own person. But in the ancient sacred books, there is no authority for this. Christ was not charitable. In his labor of salvation, He did not employ the modern prophets' automatic salvation, which has the character of redemption by anesthesia and does not presuppose any contribution or cooperation on the part of the person who is to be saved and does not require any demand or will to be saved. He willingly gave credit to him who had been saved: "Your faith has saved you." Only about a single one of his miracles, the feeding of the multitude in the desert, does it happen that there is no mention of a request for help, and this miracle can, best of them all, be categorized under the heading of charity. And here it was not a matter of a chance collection of hungry people who should be fed, but of people who—doubtless at some personal risk, directly after the execution of John the Baptist—had followed Christ to a barren spot in order to hear him. What an impressive admission the suffering and dying thief on the cross makes when he recognizes that "we are indeed here justly, for we receive the due rewards of our deeds," and exclaims, "Jesus, remember me when thou comest into thy kingdom!"

In the new gospel of *The Riding Master*, Clemens is the Savior, the personification of the good, and he saves through charity. As long as he practices this automatic salvation in the book, without cooperation from those he saves, he redeems them less than he demeans them.

He demeans the drunken old street-hawker by assuming his guilt before the crowd gathered around the automobile accident, and gives him alms before leaving. He demeans the woman already demeaned, whom he visits in his practice of medicine, in that he lets the despairing woman display her misery to him, threaten suicide, and lie about her husband or lover, who, as far as one can understand, is fairly innocent. Clemens demeans her by solacing her, "It will not hurt when you bear your child. And afterwards, you will get to live in a castle. And you should not think of the child now." Try to put these words in the mouth of Christ and hear how they would sound.

Insofar as it might have been possible, in Clemens's and Hubert's school years, to demean Hubert, Clemens would have demeaned him. He tries now to do so after he has assumed Hubert's guilt, by begging his forgiveness for doing so. Down long-deserted roads with rain and wind and withered leaves beating against his face, he bicycles, standing up on the pedals, to the strangely threatening house where Hubert lives. Clemens now remembers nothing of his conversation with Hubert—"Only the windy darkness and the trees." But he remembers that Hubert laughed.

Consistent with his role as savior, Clemens demeans most deeply the person he loves the most: Susanne. Susanne has come to Clemens on Hubert's death-day. She herself says about this, "I didn't know how I got here. When I awoke, I was simply here, with you. Do you remember how we lay next to one another and you held my hand? We said nothing, we simply lay there quietly and looked up at the ceiling. Like brother and sister." But when the novel begins, Clemens is her lover.

When we read the novel the first time, we stop here, and put it down and ask, "How is this possible?"

We ask ourselves and the author, "How could Susanne permit this disgrace? She has loved Hubert. She has lain with him in the stall among the horses—and there was no bed, only an outspread horse-blanket and, about them, the large, sleeping horses. She has dreamed about a time before time, and about vast foggy plains where the horses wandered freely. She has desired to bear her lover a horse-child, a horse-god. How did she arrive in Clemens's bed, amidst his heirloom furniture?

And, we ask further, does Clemens's zeal as a savior—as a demeaner—go so far that he, in achieving his ends, makes use of his mistress's loathing of his own person?

We receive no answer. Since, in the first chapter of the book, we are introduced into Clemens's and Susanne's common apartment without any preparation, we must accept the love relationship between them as a *fait accompli*. But in our mind, we recoil from imagining their first embrace.

In their daily life together in this apartment, Clemens demeans Susanne further from one hour to the next. He demeans her by holding her to a bourgeois existence—as already mentioned, by a birthday dinner at a restaurant—while at the same time encouraging her to give up the dead lover about whom she had wept blood, for the sake of a current lover to whom she is averse. He demeans her in letting their life together become a series of painful scenes where she, time after time, must offend him—even palpably—and, time and again, must ask him for forgiveness.

Thus far into the novel—and until the last quarter of the book—its good person cuts a sorry figure. We are supposed to imagine that he can save his surroundings; we are supposed to imagine that he can save our own time and us too. But that is a sad supposition.

Nevertheless, as the story advances, the relationship between Clemens and Susanne changes. One can say that, in the last two chapters, Clemens grows line by line. It can also be said that he is luminous, although not with any pleasant light. When we close the book, Clemens has become its most important character.

He has acquired power over his surroundings and the other persons in the book. He has acquired so much power over the reader that we consider the possibility of seeing in him the Savior. He has grown so remarkably that he seems to have acquired the power from some higher instance in the work—but I shall return to this point presently.

How has this happened? It has happened because Clemens, line for line, has become more and more inwardly united with the centaur and has been superimposed upon the centaur's being. The good human being, the evangelist, allies himself with the mythical figure, and the mythical figure enlarges him tremendously, gives him life of its life and blood of its blood. And makes him inhuman.

Or—is this actually the situation?

The inhuman is not acceptable to the people in Denmark, and the author of *The Riding Master* is a Danish author and a human being. If we think that he appears like a lion, then it is both sad and shameful; no, he is not that sort of person at all; he is a human being like other human beings. We do not need to tremble, he will give his life for ours.

In this review of *The Riding Master*, I have mentioned harps and other ancient instruments, bassoons, the sacred horns of Israel.

But he who listens carefully in the last part of the novel will hear the tones of still another instrument which is less strange and less solemn and disturbing—the sound of which almost has the ability of calming the listener so that he, to be sure, is horrified, touched, and moved, but is horrified, touched, and moved, so to speak, in a harmless way and, without too much pain, accepts the violent movements about him. This is the sound of the folk tale.

What the name of the instrument is that makes this sound or these sounds, I am not sure. In old ballads and verse, there is mention of "playing on the lyre." If I look up the word *lyre* in a dictionary, I discover that the lyre is an old, popular stringed instrument going back to the Middle Ages, with three to six strings on which a tone is produced by a wheel that, turned by hand, touches the strings. It can also be called a revolving lyre and must be assumed to have a relationship with the Greek lyre—the classical instrument in myth—even if it must be assumed to have a brace in the sounding box.

Farther north, it is called a cithern. The lyre itself I have, as far as I know, never seen, but I recognize its tone when I hear it. The lyre has been played for dancing and presumably also at burials. It seems quite understandable that the lyre comes from the Middle Ages, for the Middle Ages created the legend which, within its own mode, united mystery and myth—"When our Lord and St. Peter walked upon earth"—and is closely related to the folk tale. The gargoyles of the Middle Ages are to be found on the roofs of the cathedrals, evil and yet compatible in a harmless way.

The folk tale arose among people who had lived under harsh conditions and can itself seem harsh and cruel. In the folk tale, the end always justifies the means, and it never recoils from salvation accomplished by superior force. But the harshly tried people did not take their harsh conditions too seriously and its own particular instrument avoided the severe pathos of myth and the infinitely painful profundity of mystery.

In the folk tale, the King Dragon is forced to shed his nine skins, and his naked, bloody body, groaning and wailing, is then flogged with twigs which have been dipped in lye. But at daybreak everything is all right, for then the King Dragon is saved.

In Hans Christian Andersen's tale, *The Traveling Companion*, Johannes—the good person—finds out how he, on his marriage night, may release the bewitched princess. When he crawls into the bridal bed, he pushes her into a large tub of water which he has put in front of it, and immerses her three times in it. The princess cries pitifully and squirms in his arms, but when she comes up for the third time, all is well, for she is saved.

When the grand theme of salvation and redemption is played upon the lyre, the tone changes. We are in complete and heartfelt understanding with Johannes when he forces the shrieking princess down under the water to "pray piously to our Lord."

In the chapters "Evening" and "Night," Clemens acts like Johannes in *The Traveling Companion* and immerses the shrieking and squirming Susanne three times.

He immerses her the first time during the long conversation between them in the next-to-last chapter. She comes home to his apartment deathly tired—which we do not find strange when we reflect on the afternoon she has spent. Clemens warns her with strange, with fantastic authority that he "has something to say to her," and forces her to listen to him. With increasing fear and finally in mortal dread she tries to escape from him. She tries every means to get away; she promises to serve him, she tries to lure him to her bed, she finally crawls on her knees before him. But he commands her, "Stand up." "Yes," she says and collapses, "if you will stop saying that." "I must say it," he replies. She begs him, "Then say it now while I am lying here." "I cannot," he answers her again. "You must get up." She hides her head in her arms and tries to make herself heavy, but he is stronger than she thought; he lifts her up and holds her pressed against him and finally her glance meets his.

"Susanne," he says, "you have killed Hubert."

At this point in the novel, the readers squirm a bit in the author's hands.

All the chatter among the characters in *The Riding Master* about which of them has killed Hubert—that, in the last analysis, gives the book the nature of a murder mystery with the title *Who Killed Hubert?*—is incomprehensible to the reader until he learns to treat it like a folk tale.

Hubert has not been murdered and no circumstances pertaining to his death create suspicion directed at anyone. While he rides in his manège, with a single spectator in the balcony, he falls—or is thrown—from the horse, and his head is crushed, either by the horse's hoof or against the barrier—which is not quite clear. The event is rather improbable, since it happens to a "superb horseman." But it is still less probable that the horseman's death could have been caused by another person. With derisive laughter, Susanne rejects Herman's confession that he had secretly caused Hubert's death when Hubert was not home, by whipping his horse, kicking it, and pushing a needle into its groin, to insure that the horse would throw Hubert sooner or later. It is obvious that she is justified in ridiculing Herman, for the horse would have known the difference between Herman and Hubert, and a horseman of Hubert's skill would have noticed the nervousness of the horse when he got into the saddle and would have avoided the catastrophe. How Susanne herself, from the gallery in the manège, would have been able to kill Hubert, cannot be explained, nor is there any effort on the part of the author to explain it.

That there is another, secret circumstance to Hubert's death, which only Susanne knows and which can only come to light through Clemens's accusation of her, is something that Clemens cannot know by any natural means. Clemens's steadfastness in this scene is of the same nature as Johannes's steadfastness when the pious youth follows the traveling companion's orders, that is to say, it is quite in the spirit of the folk tale.

Clemens immerses Susanne a second time, in the suicide which she attempts in the same chapter, without success.

The unsuccessful attempt at suicide is one of Clemens's ways to redemption, his particular means of grace, a most profound debasement—perhaps I can here permit myself an expression borrowed from Thorkild Bjørnvig's book about Martin A. Hansen, and speak in the spirit of *The Riding Master* of a *sacral* debasement. The two women whom he has decided to save must both experience it.

I write here "attempted suicide," not because the two attempts in the book are unsuccessful, factually speaking, but because they are foreordained to fail and, under Clemens's supervision, necessarily must fail.

The woman in the book who first attempts it, Clemens's patient, has in advance threatened to die by gas, and Clemens knows almost to the minute when she will carry out her threat. He has asked the other inhabitants of the building to watch out, and he has warned the wife of the superintendent to keep an eye on his patient and to keep in touch with him by telephone. A specialist in poisons and a chief of service, Dr. Kjærgaard, writes in his book *Common Symptoms*, "Gas poisoning is most frequently prevented before it is too late, when inhabitants of the building smell gas and break in." These remarks pertain to cases that are not expected and where no preventive measures have been taken. Clemens himself explains that he only missed by a hair being guilty of the disconsolate woman's death. But that is incorrect. He was guilty only in that she was unable to die.

Susanne, the other woman in the book who unsuccessfully attempts suicide, desires to die and determines to die and, in the moving final pages of the chapter "Evening," really experiences suicide. But she does not die and it was quite as impossible for her as for her companion in suffering to die under Clemens's surveillance.

Here, in the book's next-to-the-last chapter, Clemens is most active as a savior through suicide.

During the conversation with Susanne, he expects every moment a telephone call regarding the woman who has decided to die by gas. And the telephone rings according to plan, some minutes after Clemens has forced Susanne to listen to the accusation that drives her to an extreme. He leaves her quite ready to attempt suicide. We understand by his deportment when they part that he expects it. Clemens rushes zealously away to save the one woman from whom he has demanded an attempted suicide after having prepared the other's attempt—and salvation.

In the last analysis, Susanne's salvation is also planned. In the very first chapter of the book, Clemens and Susanne are talking about the box of sleeping tablets which she has. He asks her, "Do you know that ten of them are enough to..." and, at the same moment, allows her to take the bottle out of his hand. He clearly mentions a lesser number than is necessary for her purpose—a much lesser number.

Nobody is in a position to speak, explain, and reason a few hours after anything approaching a mortal dose of sleeping tablets. Dr. Kjærgaard—again in his book, *Common Symptoms*—has a statistical table on instances of poisoning by sleeping tablets. Those patients who have been rescued from actual danger have lain in a coma for two or three days and have been brought back to life by radical treatments—among other things, by blood transfusions. Susanne, in *The Riding Master*, is fully conscious until four o'clock in the morning after she has taken her sleeping tablets late at night, and there is no mention of any medical treatment. Nevertheless, Susanne herself believes, presumably like the woman who attempted to die by gas, that Clemens has saved her life at the last moment. And he lets her retain this belief.

At this point in the book, Clemens's figure has grown so powerfully and he has acquired so much strength that we follow him without protest. It is once more the folk tale's "King Dragon's casting off a skin!"

Clemens has proclaimed to Susanne that she never can escape him. He has told her that she is his entire life and when she has asked him what he wants to do with his life, he has replied, "Change it. To love is to change." Susanne must not die, but the animalistic nature in her, the horse within her, must be killed before she again can stand upright like a human being. The redemption can be carried out, like a cure, without—even against—the will of the distressed party.

This power over Susanne and over the reader Clemens has obtained, page by page, by identifying himself more and more with the centaur. In the conversation with Susanne in the section "Evening," he has succeeded in making Hubert's case his own and making a stand against her as his avenger.

Clemens immerses Susanne a third time, in the chapter "Night."

He has just called her back to life and she is weak and confused and not always able to understand what he is saying to her. "I'll sleep a little longer," she says. But he resumes the conversation—or conversations—with unyielding energy. He speaks, first about his own sense of guilt, which he reviews more thoroughly than before, this time in anger; after that, he speaks of her guilt *vis-à-vis* Hubert. Finally, he falls silent and waits.

Then, in the final hour, she admits to him that she hitherto has not told the truth about Hubert's death. He did not die laughing. He died calling out Clemens's name. "He asked for water," says Susanne. "But when I wanted to give it to him, he struck my hand. 'Who are you?' he said. 'I don't know you. Clemens must come. Clemens....'" The book's single statement from the Riding Master's own mouth is meant to summarize and conclude the whole work. And the reader feels, after the tremendous strain which has led up to it, that it must be so. Here the tremendously magnified Clemens celebrates his triumph, not only over Susanne, but over us, the readers of *The Riding Master*. We no longer have any objection. We accept and approve Hubert's conversion—which takes place not after the classical model "between the saddle and the ground," but in the very dust; we accept and approve that there has been time for Susanne to come down from the balcony and fetch water for him, and for him, with crushed and shattered head, to strike her hand and to speak. "Who are you? I don't know you. Go away. Clemens must come. Clemens . . . ."

When we read *The Riding Master* the second or third time, we stop at this point, reflect, and see before us a new and most remarkable solution, the accumulation and conclusion of all the conflicts that have moved us. Isn't the situation really this, we ask ourselves, that the spirit of the folk tale in the figure of the fantastically magnified Clemens, has triumphed and taken the power, not only from the other figures in the book and from us, but from the highest instance of the poetic work itself, the author? Has the creator of *The Riding Master*, the psychologist and realist, imagined—and wanted—it to be that way?

Hubert's single statement can, to be sure, explain some things in the novel. It can explain why Susanne went to Clemens after Hubert's death—she did not go voluntarily; Hubert himself sent her there. But can this explain why she, time and again, in her life with Clemens, must relive Hubert's death, and each time according to her own false account of it? "He laughed when he died." "He continued laughing, although his crushed face was completely black with blood and dirt." Does this explain why, after one of these accounts, she adds, "When I think of it, it is just as if that moment were the most important I experienced with him." Does it explain why she, in her conversation with the wretched Herman, who tries in vain to measure up to Hubert, laughs in the unfortunate man's face, "Did you really think you could kill him with your needles? No, Herman, that was wishful thinking. He died his own death, not your little fearful death. And you will never escape him. He is still here. He looks at you through the eyes of the horses."

In *The Riding Master*'s first chapter, "Morning," Susanne is alone and once more, as often before, reviews for herself Hubert's death. She sees the reddish-brown mare approach, dragging Hubert in the stirrups. "But it was just like a game to him and he laughed continuously and very loudly. He laughed even when he was struck by a hoof and then struck his head against the wall, and it was strange there was almost no sound, but it was enough that his face was crushed and black with blood and dirt, but he laughed anyway, he laughed with his crushed face, he laughed without his face, he laughed, he laughed." Susanne's memories went no farther then, in her profound solitude.

Such a treatment of the reader by a serious psychological author would scarcely be called honest. Where there is a long and careful spiritual accounting, conscientiously carried out, it is not permissible to withhold a single cipher from the first column of numbers or to keep it secret. But, in a magic formula, it can be withheld to the last minute, and even the one who uses it cannot know its effect in advance. But when it is used, it alters the entire tale from its very beginning.

> And nine is one
> And ten is none.
> This is the witch's one-times-one.

The harsh, cruel, and coarse folk tale—has a happy ending. The folk ballad can conclude in pain; the tone of the harp trembles and dies away with a sigh, and the lyric narrators of a later time have absorbed its tone in their melodies and let the tale end in sadness. But the old orthodox folk tale puts a trump on the table after all the misfortune and horror.

The folk tale's orthodox conclusion is, "They were married and lived happily ever after."

We are to believe that *The Riding Master* ends happily. Susanne and Clemens look long at one another in the dawn after the misfortune and horror of the night. "Why are you smiling?" he says. "I am not smiling." "You are smiling." And we assume that their fortune corresponds to the form of the old folk tale and that they are married and live happily ever after. Berta, the good person in the novel, has, on one of the first pages, a single wish: that the young lady marry the doctor. "That would change everything." And now that, clearly, everything has to be changed, why should not kind Berta's wish be fulfilled?

The reader's task would be easier here if the author had kept strictly to the folk tale's orthodox "Amen" or "The curtain falls." He makes it even more difficult for us to believe and to feel ourselves secure by letting the two happy characters, on the last pages of the book, discuss how they will arrange their future.

A problem looms before us. Can Clemens—especially in his relation to Susanne—retain his dimensions after the two of them, as we have been led to believe in the last chapter, have finished with the Riding Master himself?

We see that Clemens himself does not believe it. Susanne suggests to him that he and she should escape from their relation to Hubert "in a way which is as old as the earth! By forgetting him!" But Clemens answers her with a frightened expression and pulls back the hand she has been holding. "You don't mean to say that you could ever think of forgetting him?" After walking quickly back and forth several times, he announces, "Some things are necessary. And it is necessary that we give him a new life. A life as a human being. Like a human being within us."

We understand well that this is necessary for Clemens. Clemens has grown while he was following—or pursuing—Hubert, and has clung to him. Clemens has finally won the complete upper hand when, for a single moment, he has made Hubert turn to him. But how painful this pursuit beyond death is to read about.

The wild animal—when free—always has his honor intact. We comprehend here, on the last page of the book, the centaur's infinite solitude among these human beings without honor. And we feel that we now would not have begrudged him liberation.

Very well, Clemens has triumphed after the fashion of the folk tale. He has released his beloved from an animal form; he has separated her from the body of a horse. Why is it that the reader cannot shake off a depressing little doubt as to how far the ever-helpful, organizing, arranging—but never creative—Clemens will be able to make her into a whole human being? Will she, in his hands, ever be anything but the legless lady? And let me finally return to that with which I began. Or to him with whom I began: to the reader of *The Riding Master*.

In a hundred years, the spiritual life of Denmark in our times will be explained by pointing out that the Danish reader took *The Riding Master* to his heart upon publication, and was enraptured by it.

What is it that one has explained? It could be this:

The Riding Master

The average Danish reader who, for more than three-quarters of a century has been satiated by the depiction of reality, has,—like the thirsty hart in a dry land that smells and senses a running spring far away—suspected and sensed myth and adventure far away in *The Riding Master*—the spring, the fountain, the well; and has run towards them. The skilled writer has himself not known with what tones he has attracted people, but people have pricked up their ears and recognized them.

Has not one said the same that Jens Peter Jacobsen said in a posthumous poem,

> Tired of speech is the king's ear,
> It thirsts for song.

And has not one called him, who will answer as in the poem,

> A lay, liege king,
> A lay thou shalt have!

Danish poets of the year of Our Lord 1949! Press the grape of myth or adventure into the empty goblet of the thirsting people!.

Do not give them bread when they ask for stones—a rune stone or the old black stone from the Kaaba; don't give them a fish, or five small fish, or anything in the sign of the fish, when they ask for a serpent.

December 1949

Contradictory Postscript to "H. C. Branner, The Riding Master"

I wrote this review of *The Riding Master* in the fall of 1949. When today I read it through, it strikes me how strange—in more than one sense, strange—that my cry, or sigh, to the young Danish poets, although it never appeared in print, was heard and followed. Frank Jæger's *Everyday Stories;* Leif E. Christensen's "Beyond All Borders"; Svend Aage Clausen's "Hatchet Blow and Flora," and other stories of the same sort, are they not our young writers' attempts to bring back myth or the folk tale?

The reviewer who wrote the above essay feels odd in 1952—in more than one sense, odd—like the sorcerer's apprentice, *der Zauberlehrling.* She feels, as presumably the *Zauberlehrling* felt in his time, to a certain degree proud, to a greater degree humiliated, but above all full of scruples. (*En passant* she might wish to remark that, when she invoked the serpent three years ago, she did not envisage it in the form of a tapeworm or some other kind of intestinal worm, as seems to be the case to such a marked degree with the young poets.) While the waters are rising about her, and before the master, who too long has been absent, presents himself with the supreme magical word, she feels a kind of obligation to warn the zealous young apprentices of the year 1952.

One can arrive at the number seventy in two ways. One can add one to one until the entire sum is reached. Much of the time the old naturalistic novel proceeded in this fashion; and the author of the naturalistic novel proclaimed: that is the way life is.

One can also create the sum of seventy with one single motion by writing it collected and complete: 70. This is how the storyteller does it when he proclaims: this is the way art is! That is myth, which itself is an *Eventyr,* that is magic!

The present unworthy disciple of many great mas-

ters quietly offers you—for whatever use you will
make of it—insights that from time to time have been
granted her by the highest grace and that she from
time to time has bought at the highest price.
First, that the number 70 is not a flourish acciden-
tally produced by giving freedom to the hand. It is a
symbol, and its importance lies in what it signifies. It
is many centuries old; within a culture it is common
property and can be interpreted by simple folk. If, in
place of this symbol one used a code number comprehensible only to a small initiated circle, or a
number comprehensible only to a single person, viz.,
he who writes it, then the master would erase it
angrily. "This is not magic."
Next, your accounting must really denote seventy.
If it does not, you are not loyal disciples of the master
but prestidigitators. Not only must your readers be
absolutely convinced that all seventy units are to be
found in your sum, but you must yourselves insure it
with your being and your honor. The number is a *facit*
of honest reckoning.

That honorable artist Jakob Knudsen has said that
art is the control of fantasy. Coming together directly
from *The Riding Master,* we can in a discussion of art
and fantasy continue to employ metaphors from horseback riding. A school of riding and the art of riding
are subject to controls—but letting one's horse run
wild is not art.

And verily, the sorcerer's humble apprentice says
unto you: no art has more severe laws than magic; no
artist is more severely bound by his laws than the
magician.

(Here's the only way to fix
all the world's Magician's Tricks:

The Riding Master

Put a rabbit in the hat—
later pull this out of that.

Training for the magic habit,
fail not to insert the rabbit.

Piet Hein)

Rungstedlund

A Radio Address

*G*ood evening, listeners! It is a long time since
you last gave me the pleasure of welcoming
you to Rungstedlund.

For most of that time, I thought we should
never meet again. I have been hospitalized for more
than a year and have undergone more than one operation. Before the last, I convinced myself I would not
survive. They told me how I would feel when I awak-
ened after anesthesia and I thought, "Is there any
point in talking about that? I know I am not going to
wake up again." By chance I heard later that one of
the physicians had said, "If she survives this operation, it will be the greatest *coup* of her life," so I can't
imagine there was really much confidence in the undertaking from the medical point of view.

The day before the operation I was completely certain I should get the radio to send its truck out to the
hospital, so I could record on tape what I believed
would be my last message to listeners in Denmark. I
thought I would say to them, "It isn't bad to die; it is

This essay was first published as "Rungstedlund," in *Hilsen til
Otto Gelsted* (Copenhagen, 1958), pp. 18–41.

good. In my time I have seen many people die; many African natives have died, so to speak, in my arms, and I have never seen any of them afraid. I myself feel that death is not an interruption of life, but a rounding off." But I did not have enough strength to realize my plan. And then I didn't die, either, so the point of it was lost.

This evening I want to tell you something else, namely, that I think there has been a happy and agreeable relation between you and me, and that I am grateful to you for it. I feel the same gratitude towards my readers; yet there has always been something about paper and ink which is distasteful to me. When as a twenty-year-old I published some stories in the periodical *Tilskueren* [*The Spectator*], and our old critic Valdemar Vedel encouraged me to continue writing, I told him I did not wish to, for I did not want merely to become printed matter. He laughed when he next saw me. "So you don't want to become printed matter—you won't ever, either," he said. Now I wish I had said to him that I wished to sit surrounded by a circle of people and tell stories as the spirit moved me. In Africa I did so, for the natives liked to hear stories and were indifferent as to how carefully they had been thought out. If I began, "Once there was a man who had an elephant with two heads," those who were most interested would interrupt, "Certainly, Msabu, he did indeed. What did he do; did he feed both heads at the same time, or each by itself?" Of the four elements I have always liked air the best, and I should like to be a voice in the ether.

During the last ten years it has been a continually surprising and pleasant experience for me that people in taxicabs, railway compartments, and shops, when

I have asked a question or given an answer, have greeted me with, "Hello, Karen Blixen!" and told me they recognized my voice from the radio. Of course, there was also an angry lady who, in the middle of the escalator at Vesterport Station, turned round to ask, "What sort of rubbish is it you are spreading on the radio?" But that was also an ingathering for me, and rather more personal and human than a reprimand in print. In *The Merchant of Venice*, Lorenzo says at night, at Belmont, listen, Portia has come home! and Portia remarks, "He knows me as the blind man knows the cuckoo, by the bad voice." If, from the time one was a small child, one has stood still in the woods every spring and listened, and called out a sound of one's own, one is even willing to take on the rôle of a cuckoo. It has been as if I had a friendship with an entire people, just as it was in Africa, where, on my safaris, the natives knew me through a sort of instinct wherever I appeared. This adds a richness to life.

Now as we are met again at Rungstedlund, and each of you who has a radio turned on is really sitting opposite me in front of the fire, I think it is time to tell you a little about the house we are in. I have had Rungstedlund on my mind for several years in a particular way. I would like to ask those of you who can, to get a pencil and a piece of paper: before you shut off the radio, I will ask you to write down something particular regarding Rungstedlund.

We are sitting in the old Rungsted Inn, one of the oldest houses—perhaps the oldest house—between Copenhagen and Elsinore.

North Zealand is related to our past during the last five hundred years in a way different from the rest of the country. Unlike Jutland or the island of Funen, the region was not an area of separate large estates and single families; North Zealand was the property of the Crown and was distinguished by the "King's Copenhagen." The woods were royal hunting parks and the broad roads were called the king's highways. Everywhere in North Zealand, when one looks out from a height over the country, one can point out places in Danish history and the history of Danish literature. Here lies Gurre, in a haze of Danish poetry, from the folk ballads to Holger Drachmann. Here, before the attack on Copenhagen, Carl X Gustav's troops bivouacked like birds of prey before a bird's nest, and dramatic events from that time's underground resistance drew a line between Søllerød, Humlebæk, and Kronborg. Here Charles XII debarked at Humlebæk. Here, on the King's Highway between Copenhagen and Elsinore, the unhappy Carolina Mathilda traveled in her carriage as a captive to Kronborg, and from here one could see the flaming red heavens over Copenhagen during the bombardment of 1807. Here the hills from Dyrehaven, the animal park, appear with their romantic and cheerful tones from Oehlenschlæger's *Midsummer Night's Play*. Here, along the entire shore road, from Copenhagen to Elsinore, Jews sought refuge in private homes and row-houses, fifteen years ago, and were helped aboard fishing boats to be carried to Sweden. Mr. Juul, here in Rungsted—and he was put in the Frøslev concentration camp for it—and the other local truckers telephoned from house to house, "Tonight we will try to use a boat from Snekkersten. Tomorrow there will be a chance at Skovshoved." One may find unexpected reminders from a far, far more distant time, in which one does not know the names of individuals. When the shore road next to Rungsted-lund was straightened, I moved an old stone fence, and my old coachman, Alfred Petersen, who has been at Rungstedlund for sixty-five years, took me down to show me a stone which had hitherto lain with its flat side turned down, for he thought on it there "was something." It seemed doubtful to me, but Alfred stuck to his guns until I telephoned Professor Brøndsted at the National Museum and said that I had found a stone "with something on it"—an arm and a hand; a line that developed into five, then was single again, like a thumb at a right angle to the four fingers. "I'll be right out," said Professor Brøndsted. He wanted the stone for the National Museum, but I thought it should stay here, where once a man sat and worked on it. The professor borrowed it, and included photographs of it in a scientific article. He told me the picture on the stone was between 2,500 and 3,000 years old; he said the symbol really was a hand, a divine hand and a symbol of protection. "It's strange," I said, "to judge by the position of the thumb, it is a left hand." "No, it is not a left hand," said the professor. "It is a right hand seen from the side of the palm. The god is inside the stone." The stone now lies under a large tree in the garden. Archaeologists have come from Norway and Sweden to look at it.

Even "the coast" has changed in the course of time, and has become tame and well behaved. From being a stretch of windblown land covered with willow trees and heather, with the shore road as a sandy, uncertain path along the beach, and with the thatched houses of the fishing hamlets with net-drying grounds, it has become an almost unbroken series of neat houses and gardens for people who have their businesses in Copenhagen.

However, the waters look today as they did in the oldest times. It is the Sound, "Denmark's highway, the portal of the North." In my life I have seen various waters—the Straits of Gibraltar and Bab-el-Mandeb—but when I have seen the Sound again, I have always thought, "You can be distinguished from them all, for you have your own blue, open glance." It is a privilege to live along the Sound.

Rungsted Inn lay approximately midway between Copenhagen and Elsinore and was presumably, from the beginning, a place where wagons and private carriages could be unhitched for a rest. It was an inn with royal privileges as early as the reign of Christian II, and Christian IV gave Villum Carram a charter for "the new Runsti Inn, with all the acreage and meadows belonging to it, together with one hundred wagon-loads of wood to be picked up from the ground and free feeding in the forest for his own swine, on the condition that he keep a hostel for Danes and foreigners, so that traveling men have nothing to complain about." Later, Queen Sophie Amalie gave her chambermaid Philix "Rungstedte Wirtshause" on the condition that she pay annually two and one-half barrels of codfish in manorial dues. The stock of fish on the property itself was estimated at 4,500 carp and 18,000 crucian carp—I don't know what they wanted with the crucian carp; the ponds in the garden are still full of them, but eating them is like trying to eat cotton with pins in it.

A learned French traveler on his way to Sweden wrote in the year 1700 that Rungsted Inn was the most attractive on the entire route. He praised the dog kennels, so we must believe dogs then enjoyed a particular position here. Behind the house, he says, there was a large, unusually beautiful garden with a knoll.

The Inn was privileged to distill brandy—during the pestilence of 1710, when all villages were closed, the innkeeper, Mattias Frigast, was permitted to sell beer and brandy on the shore road next the Inn. In the course of time he took such advantage of the privilege that the master of the guild of distillers in Hørsholm appeared one day with his functionaries and sealed up Frigast's apparatus. Later the innkeeper got his privilege back, however. There have doubtless been racy jests and songs fired off here, and many a pewter cup of brandy—and pert barmaids—have been swung through the air; rough-and-tumble fights have taken place; and difficult, shouting guests have been thrown out. And it is pleasant to think of tired freight-horses recognizing the last bit of road before Rungstedlund, where they knew they would turn in through the gate, and be taken to the water-trough and the crib. At that time the Inn did its own farming, and the stalls for the horses and cows, the pigsties and the barn, lay in an irregular rectangle about the building which now stands there, alone; its wings and walls are the same as they were in the year 1600. Rungstedlund's farm buildings burned down one summer night in 1898; I saw them burn. As a child I rode the estate's horses between the farm buildings down to a watering-place.

The house itself was probably never planned or designed by any architect; it simply grew by itself and was improved according to the changing taste of successive generations. It is constantly falling down on my head and I am constantly having it shored up. Professor Steen Eiler Rasmussen, who is my neighbor in Rungsted, has explained to me that this or that detail dates from the year 1800 or 1850. When an attic suddenly collapsed and revealed a peculiarly primitive construction, the professor told me that this was the way people built in the years following the state bankruptcy of 1813. It was easy for me to imagine. According to present ideas, the house is extremely impractical, with as much "no-man's-land"—halls and stairs and pantries—as living space.

But Rungstedlund must have preserved some of its hundred summers' sweetness and winters' comfort. Many times people from abroad who have visited here have written to me about my "unforgettable house." An American intelligence officer, who, after the Liberation in 1945, was my first guest from the outside world, wrote, "I had been in your country for three weeks without having obtained any real impression of it. But when you showed me your house and garden, you gave me the key to Denmark."

Rungstedlund comprises about forty acres of gardens, woods, and meadows, all of which—among the well-kept gardens of the shore road—seems something like a wilderness. Around the pond and the canal in the garden there is a whole woods of the same sort of broad-leaved dock that Hans Christian Andersen's "happy family" lived beneath. There is a large peaceful field, protected from the wind, where horses and cows wander about. There are many old trees, and under them a particularly rich woodland floor with anemones, primroses, and violets. In a corner to the northwest, towards which the entire property rises, lies Ewald's Knoll.

A fire was first lighted in the common room of Rungsted Inn more than four hundred years ago, and it has since burned out and been rekindled many times. It has always cast light and shadow around the room in the same way. It has shone upon many kinds of people who have sat here and talked of many kinds of things.

Hørsholm's local historian, Rosted, has a strange tale about some conversations which took place here. Kirstine Munk, Christian IV's morganatic wife, knew the king suspected that not he, but the Rhinegrave, was the father of the child she was carrying. She arranged to meet the Swedish resident, Johann Fegræus, here at Rungsted Inn several times, in order to tell him about her difficulties with her royal husband, indeed to suggest she was ready to tell what she knew about the king's secret plans against Sweden if she could, in this way, ingratiate herself with the Swedish court. The light from the fire played over the brocade dress of the beautiful, scheming woman, and the attentive face of the Swedish diplomat.

There is a dark, stiff, thin figure which I seem to have seen in front of the fireplace from time to time. He has scarcely spoken, for he was one of the most lonesome figures in the history of the world and probably looked silently into the embers. The eighteen-year-old Charles XII of Sweden—he who, according to Frans G. Bengtsson, "was made in the factory, now closed, where kings were made"—had attacked Denmark in his very first eagle's flight, and had his headquarters at Rungsted Inn. Did he see in the embers mighty pictures of that victorious march through Europe which was to "make Sweden the central point of the universe"? He probably did not see in them the dreadful White Russian winter, and imprisonment in Turkey. Did he see his lonely, wild "kingly ride" home to an impoverished country which, for fourteen years, had been without a king, and on to his lonely, questionable death near Frederikssten?

Then there happened, a hundred and eighty-five years ago, without the house itself knowing anything about it, the most significant thing in the whole life of the Inn and something which should extend its lifetime into the coming centuries.

On an early spring day a fragile young man arrived at the Inn, no doubt with one of the freight-wagons from Copenhagen, and moved in as a lodger with the master-fisherman Ole Jacobsen and his wife. There must have been some previous arrangement with his family, who sent him out here, and the Jacobsens understood their lodger to be something of a black sheep in the family—when scarcely more than a boy he had run away from home in order to enter a foreign army, and he reappeared in Copenhagen as a vagrant, poet, and toper. It was the Jacobsens' task to wean him from brandy—in this they were never really successful. But they were good people with open minds who came to like their guest. His name was Johannes Ewald. At Rungsted Inn, he says, he associated with "the common people, seamen and fishermen," the class of people which, in a certain sense, is called the lowest but which, in another sense, and no doubt a more truthful one, is called the highest. The fishermen at Rungsted and their wives and children became well acquainted with his young fragile figure when he wandered along the shore in the spring breeze, looked searchingly seaward among the ships and recognized strange flags or, whole summer days through, sat on the bench on the knoll in the Inn's garden, or followed the reapers' work and song in the fields. They saw or suspected that in him there was something they had not previously met in human beings: immortality. And the ability to immortalize the landscape, birdsong and roses, the glittering or dark-rolling ocean, and the fisherfolk along with it. Poor, sick, lonesome, and unhappy in love, he had within him, in addition to the immortality which he imparted to everything, the ability to catch in a phrase one of the Danish language's most ecstatic words: *Lyksalighed*—bliss: *Rungsted's Lyksaligheder*—the joys of Rungsted. Most of my listeners certainly know something of this poem, which begins so gently and freely, like a bird's song in the tree, "where the songstress builds, and chirping reveals her nest," and which rises like a threatening storm over the landscape, and then, in its final stanza, ends with incomparable grace and fervor in its appeal to an individual. He lodged at Rungsted Inn for three years; my study to the east is called Ewald's Room. He parted with sorrow from Rungsted Inn; it seems today one might well meet him in the fields or hear his steps within the house.

Time passed over the old Inn. A hundred years later, another young man came from foreign lands and established himself at Rungstedlund. He was Wilhelm Dinesen, my father, who as a seventeen-year-old lieutenant had been at Danevirke and Dybbøl; then as a French officer had served in the Franco-Prussian War and who, during the Paris Commune, had seen barricades built and French blood flow in French streets. He had turned away from Europe and its civilization and for three years had lived among the Indians in North America without seeing another white man. He had been a competent and fortunate hunter of pelts, but the money he earned he spent on his Indian friends. The Indians called him *Boganis.* Under that name he wrote his *Letters from the Hunt* here at Rungstedlund—a hunter's diary full of love for nature, the seasons, animals and birds, battle, solitude, and women. He married the lovely young Ingeborg Westenholtz, my mother, from the Matrup Estate near Horsens, and Mother told me that when they returned from their honeymoon and walked beneath the trees in through the fields, he said to her, "Whatever may happen in the future, please remember we came here on the last day of May and it was beautiful and you were happy."

I was ten years old when Father died. His death was for me a great sorrow, of a kind which probably only children feel. I think I was his favorite child, and I know he thought I resembled him. He took me with him when he walked over the fields, when he troated for a roebuck in the woods, or searched through the marsh for snipe with his two French griffon hounds, Osceola and Matchitabano, which were named for two old Indian chiefs among his friends. I remember clearly how he taught me to distinguish among the various kinds of birds and told me about migratory birds—and his quick, happy reaction at the sight of a rare bird, the kite with a notched tail, like other people's happiness over a glass of good wine. A whole world was opened to me when I heard about the bird migrations, that mighty net which is spun around the earth as a result of some inexplicable call, for which life itself is wagered. I recall how I wondered when he told me that, among the storks, the male leaves the tropics for Denmark eight days before the female, and then she follows him to their old nest. "If a lady," I thought, "were to follow her husband, she would certainly ask him to write down what train she should take, and where she should change trains. How do the two find each other on a straw roof on the island of Funen?" Since then I have myself seen the storks in large flocks on the African plains, leading a bachelor existence during the wintry half of the year.

The nightingale arrives at Rungstedlund almost exactly on the eighth of May. How full of anticipation we children were as we awaited its arrival, and nevertheless how unexpected were its golden tones, coming from a tree in the woods, suddenly. We had a kind of law among us: each year we had to see a nightingale while it sang. Every year I have been in Denmark, I have waded through the long wet grass and nettles, and while there was still barely any light caught sight of a very thin little bird's silhouette on a branch above a bit of pond—for nightingales like underbrush and nettles and moist places and prefer gardens not too well-kept. What incredible power lies in the little vibrating throat! If a human being had such a powerful voice in proportion to its weight, the popular singers Nina and Frederik, when they sang at the City Hall Square, could be heard in Amsterdam, Prague, and Oslo.

So throughout May and the first half of June, Rungstedlund's garden resounds with the song of the nightingale; one bird answers another; it is a long ecstatic festival of song.

Now I want to tell you a strange and true story about a nightingale.

During the third year of the First World War, I was to go back to Africa after a visit to Denmark. It had been difficult enough to get to Denmark; the ship upon which I had traveled from Mombasa to Marseilles was torpedoed on its return voyage. When in the autumn I was to go back, there was no passenger traffic at all in the Mediterranean, because of the submarines, and we had to travel south around the Cape of Good Hope and then back north along the East Coast of Africa to our harbor, Mombasa, below the equator. The tour from Southampton to the Cape took six weeks, because there were also submarines in the Atlantic, and our ship, in order to avoid them, went close to South America. The trip was worth making, for the Cape is as lovely a spot as there is on earth. During the two days we were furthest south, I saw albatrosses with their incredible wingspan and their inexplicable, gliding flight. I sat on deck those two days; the others said to me, "Come down and eat lunch," and I replied, "No, I can always eat lunch, but I shall never again see albatrosses." My good friend the Swedish poet Harry Martinson and I once discussed the ups and downs of our lives, and both of us exclaimed, as if we had discovered an important entry on the credit side, "And we have seen albatrosses!" When at Christmastime we came to Durban, about halfway between the Cape and Mombasa, there were orders for our ship to return to England, and we had to wait for another ship to pick us up and take us further north. I did not like Durban, which is a sort of spa for Johannesburg millionaires; when I had been there for a time I bought a car, traveled into the highlands around Pietermaritsburg and visited old inhabitants on their cattle-farms and had an enjoyable time. While I was still breaking in the car, I went out several times to a place called Amanzimtoti, an hour's drive from Durban, where there was a little wood. One day I went there with some other passengers from the boat, stopped short, and exclaimed, "Listen, there is a nightingale!" The others laughed at me. "Oh yes, certainly it is a nightingale," I said. "You don't suppose I can mistake it? But it is true the birds sing their full stanzas only for us in the North, during the breeding season—the nightingale we hear now is only tuning his instrument." We made a bet on the point, as far as I can remember, a high one, but we couldn't get it decided. Twenty years later I spoke in Denmark with a young ornithologist who, as a boy, had had the run of Rungstedlund garden in order to study bird life, and I asked him how far south the nightingale goes in its migration. "They go south to the equator," he said. "The very first nightingale from Rungstedlund which I ringed, was sighted south of the equator. I don't remember the name of the place, but I have it in my notebook." He took his notebook out of his pocket, leafed in it, and said, "It was called Amanzimtoti."

Now it cannot have been that ringed nightingale which I myself heard sing at Amanzimtoti, but it is possible that one particular nightingale family has its winter residence there and returns to Rungstedlund for the summer on the eighth of May.

I have come to look upon Rungstedlund as belonging particularly to the migratory birds. The seasons here are first and foremost characterized by their arrivals and departures. How many times have I not, in the nights around the spring or autumnal equinox, stood outside the house and listened to their flight high in the heavens above the roof!

The human inhabitants of the house have also been
birds of migration. They traveled far abroad and then
came home. Young Johannes Ewald flew to Germany
and Austria on his very slight wings; he returned to
Rungstedlund—a songbird who sang most beautifully at dusk, and here it was beautiful and he was
happy. The young Wilhelm Dinesen, Boganis, flew
out to the battlefields of Europe and the prairies of
America and came home to Rungstedlund. I myself
left for half a lifetime's stay in the African highlands,
and then came back.

In the years after my return from Africa, as I have
seen greater Copenhagen enclose Rungstedlund
more and more, I have wondered how I could preserve it and keep the old Inn and the Inn's garden
and their little bit of Danish nature and Danish history. It has been as if a great sorrow, a great loss, and
a blank space lay before me when I thought that
everything would be changed completely, indeed
disappear and be gone. In the course of time there
could be an asphalted, suburban road called Boganis
Street just as there is now, in the suburb called Rungsted, an Ewald street, and by these names future
generations could be considered adequately to have
shown their piety towards the past. But where would
be the green vales which gave pleasure to Ewald and
Boganis? Every summer when I have heard the cuckoo in the woods, I have thought, "How can I preserve a large tree in the garden for it to sit and coo
in?"

I had been told it was undemocratic to let an area
big enough for three hundred row-houses lie—as it
was said—useless.

From time to time, I think that Danish "democ-
racy" protects the people who don't need it more

than those who really do; I think it protects automobiles rather than bicyclists. I know very well there
could be much enterprise and family happiness in
those three hundred row-houses. But what about the
landless multitude at that time, those who only on
holidays see something besides paved streets? The
owners of row-houses are zealous defenders of pro-
prietary rights and on their property no trespassers
may come, nor is there much there for anyone to
come to see. If all of North Zealand is finally laid out
in row-houses, the owners will invest in some lilac
and laburnum bushes, in roses and radish beds, but
there will be no more large trees. And the mass of
people who do not themselves own land will move
along the flagstones without ever sensing turf under
their feet or foliage above their heads, and without
anywhere meeting that stillness which once permitted people to "hear birds' songs which could move
the heart."

The great landless masses have a trait which is
pleasant to touch upon, for they are alert people, who
are willing to join in a collaborative venture—they
have agreed with my attitude about the mission of
Rungstedlund. The garden at Rungstedlund has not
been closed for a generation; people have been able to
go in and out freely. Today, there must be many
established *patres familias* who can remember how as
boys during the winter they skated on the pond and
in the summer hid as Indians in caves and under
bushes in the woods, and there must be at least one
couple celebrating their golden wedding anniversary
who remember walking hand in hand along the green
paths in the woods. I have no fence along the shore
road, but my lovely roses and hyacinths, which grow
along the sidewalk, have not been picked; people

have understood they were there for the common pleasure. One Sunday afternoon I came in through the fields and saw a card-table set up under an old oak tree with four happy card-players in shirtsleeves slapping the cards down on the table.

There has been a single frightful incident of abuse, which I shall tell you about. In the garden we have large, edible grapevine snails, which are said to have been introduced by Count Stolberg a hundred and fifty years ago. One day I came to Ewald's Knoll with some English guests to whom I wanted to show the garden. And there had been—I choose the word carefully and say "some boys," for generally only boys can go amok in such a way—who had collected several hundred snails, and had put them on the benches on the Knoll, and had stamped upon them until everything was a mass of shells, slime, and rotten snails. It had apparently happened the day before, because the stench was dreadful around the Knoll. It was an ugly and crude deed, not only because here—even though snails presumably don't feel much—something living had been trampled to death, but because the massacre apparently had been undertaken on the benches with the idea that a loving pair at twilight, or a couple of old, nearsighted ladies, would sit down in the middle of the mess. Indeed, I became so angry, so ashamed before my English guests, and so despairing at the mentality I confronted, that I said to myself, "Now I am going to close the garden and there will be no access for anyone from the outside." This should probably be called the exception which proves the rule.

I would like to think that Rungstedlund in the future could be a breathing space in the middle of a big city.

And because the migratory birds at Rungstedlund have meant so much to me, I have envisaged it as a bird sanctuary, a true paradise for birds which have come here over the oceans of the world.

But hitherto I have not been able to realize my dream. It is costly to preserve property as a monument. First of all, one has to give up the potential income that one could gain by dividing it and selling it, and I have not known whether my finances would be able to permit me that. And an institution like the Ornithological Society cannot accept Rungstedlund simply as a gift from me and from those of my brothers and sisters who are partial owners of the property. Some capital would have to accompany the gift to cover the taxes and upkeep, the fencing, planting, feeding, the construction of birdhouses, and many other things which the task connotes.

I know that I have been particularly successful as an author, but authors do not earn as much as people generally assume. At the time I wrote my first three books, what Danish authors made in America was taxed twice.

This year finally, despite all obstacles, I have succeeded in having my latest book published, and since I hope to have another book out in the fall, I have had the great satisfaction of realizing my plan. *The Rungstedlund Fund* has been established and recognized as a private foundation. The purpose of the Fund is to preserve Rungstedlund as a bird sanctuary under the direction of the Ornithological Society. Rungstedlund will, from now on, be a protected area and lie unchanged, and there will be no interference here except what the bird-life requires.

I have succeeded in doing this in the following way. I have given by deed to the Rungstedlund Fund all the income which presumably will come from the sale of my books from the day of the establishment of the Fund until fifty years after my death, when the copyright lapses. The arrangement also includes film rights and dramatic rights and, in general, everything I have been able to earn by writing and whatever I may earn by writing from now on. I have given everything that I can count on and hope for, and have no more to give.

Until my death I shall be able to live at Rungstedlund and be able to use some of the monies of the Fund for my own living expenses.

As far as the old building that we are sitting in is concerned, its future is not fixed. It is possible or reasonable that the part the ornithologists do not need may be used for a museum about the history of Rungstedlund, and for a public library. In this way it would, true to tradition, unite nature and literature.

The specialists in Denmark with whom I have spoken about my intentions have shown the friendliest interest and understanding. The best of them are my allies.

From the start, I was afraid the area I could offer was too small for my purpose, and I asked Dr. Salomonsen of the Ornithological Society to come out and look at it. Dr. Salomonsen declared Rungstedlund was large enough to maintain a population of all the common Danish songbirds. And when he walked through the park and woods together with me, and saw how peaceful it is here, he said he thought that, by preservation and care, one might also attract less common species. I know by experience how the peculiarly sensitive animals react towards any protected area. When I was a child, swans were shot from the shore here, and it was rare to see a swan in the Sound. About thirty years ago the swans became a protected species, and now one sees here every spring hundreds of swans right down to the shore. In Africa I saw how the game knew the borders of the Masai Reserve almost to the very yard—one seldom saw buffalo or antelope beyond its dividing line.

Dr. Syrach-Larsen, who is known throughout the world as an authority on trees and plants, has been very kind to the Rungstedlund Fund, and has promised to assist me by acquiring those plants and kinds of grass which birds like and which will attract them here.

This spring we have started to dig and plant and to put up birdhouses. The Rungstedlund Fund bears the expenses but the Ornithological Society and Dr. Syrach-Larsen are planning and directing the work. To my great satisfaction, Dr. Syrach-Larsen advised me, particularly, where we should plant wild roses. There will be a direct line of succession leading up into today's activities from two hundred years ago. "In cooling shadows, in darkness which the roses spread."

I hope the work can be done so nicely and so well for the birds that Rungstedlund Bird Sanctuary will be comparable to others, and that ornithologists from foreign lands will sometimes come here to study Danish bird-life.

Rungstedlund will be open to the public as much as possible, while keeping the welfare of the birds in mind.

But fifty years are not eternity. I would not compare myself with the blessed Christian V, who established Dyrehaven—the animal park—but I should like in all modesty to have Rungstedlund, like the animal park, enter the life and consciousness of the people, at least in the surrounding area, for more than a hundred years, and to have the place remain for a long time in the future a haven for migratory birds.

Therefore I turn to you, my listeners, and ask you to join me in this undertaking. I ask every listener who is interested in protecting by law and preserving with care particular values in Denmark, and also every listener who, throughout the years, has derived pleasure from our meetings on the radio, to assist me today.

I should like to have it come about in the following way: that each of you who is now listening to my voice would give one Krone to the Rungstedlund Fund. For myself, it would be particularly pleasant to know how many understanding and kindly-disposed listeners I have had, how many of you remember me with some satisfaction and wish to give me satisfaction in return. I ask each of you listening to me now to send one Krone to the Rungstedlund Fund, at an address which will be announced after I have spoken.

There is one point in the matter which I regret. In order to contribute one Krone to the Rungstedlund Fund it will be necessary to pay thirty Øre in postage, and two Øre for a money-order blank: in sum, one Krone and thirty-two Øre. I have thought about the possibilities of trying to avoid this deplorable condition, but I haven't been able to get around it. I quite understand that it *is* more difficult to pay one Krone and thirty-two Øre than simply one Krone. But I beg you, do not let it be *too* difficult! I ask you to go tomorrow or the day after tomorrow to your post office, to fill out a money-order with the number that will be announced, and to put down the difficult sum of one Krone and thirty-two Øre on the counter.

I ask you, my listeners in Denmark who have their radios turned on now, to bear this expense and to go to this trouble for three reasons.

The first is this: so that the migratory birds, some spring, will not come from Amanzimtoti and find asphalt and flagstone where before was woodland floor. Instead, each summer far into the future Rungstedlund will be filled with new birdsong, "where the songstress builds and chirping reveals her nest."

Another reason is this: so that, for a hundred years, the children and grandchildren of my present listeners may walk in the woods that Ewald walked in. So that in the "listeners' park" at Rungstedlund, children will, for a hundred years, be able to play tag in the grass, young couples may kiss, and old people rest in the shadows. May they all think it is beautiful here and be happy.

The third reason is this: because I personally will feel that every Krone that comes in is a handclasp from an individual listener—from those to whom I am now speaking.

The radio people have asked me to return four weeks from today and tell you a story. At that time, I can also account for what the listeners have contributed to the Rungstedlund Fund and I shall have an opportunity to thank those who have contributed.

And you who now, as I hope, have pencil and paper in hand, I ask to guess what the sum contributed by listeners will be for my bird sanctuary and to write down the figure. Then four weeks from today, you can see how near you have come to the actual result. I shall do the same at random, for I really have no idea what the sum will be.

Of course, I hope that I shall hear some Kroner and

thirty-two Øre sounding on the counter, but I should prefer to shut off the radio tonight with the echo of birdsong in our ears.

Here at Rungstedlund there is a boy who was very young when he came here with his mother, who is my housekeeper. He is now twelve years old and plays the recorder. I am going to ask him to come to the fireplace and to play for you the old folk-song melody about *The Bird's Song*. Someone else in the house will accompany him by singing.

Notes

17 *Princess Caroline* (1793–1881), daughter of King Frederik Ferdinand VI of Denmark, was married to her cousin Prince Frederik Ferdinand (1792–1863) in 1829. No beauty, she suffered disfiguring burns the following year.

18 *Goethe's remark* "Wer nicht von dreitausand Jahren / Sich weiß Rechenschaft zu geben / Bleib im Dunkeln unerfahren / Mag von Tag zu Tage leben" *(West-Östlicher Divan, Buch des Unmuts)*.

19 *Estrup* J. B. S. Estrup (1825–1913), authoritarian prime minister of Denmark, 1875–94.

19 *A Doll's House* Ibsen's play *(Et Dukkehjem)* had its premiere at the Royal Theater in Copenhagen on 21 December 1879 and evoked an explosive public reaction. It was played twenty times more that same season. By February 1907 it had been given a hundred times at the Royal Theater alone.

19 *Emil Poulsen* (1842–1911), actor and director at the Royal Theater. None of his 250 roles was more popular than that of Ambrosius Stub in *Ambrosius* by C. K. F. Molbech (1821–88). Published in 1877, the play became one of the great successes of the Royal Theater during the last quarter of the nineteenth century.

20 *Admiral Bardenfleth* Rear Admiral Frederik Bardenfleth (1846–1935) was Head of the Royal Household for Queen Louise of Denmark, 1906–25. He was married to Ida Elise Catharine Meldal (1856–1946).

22 *Katholm* Estate dating in part from the sixteenth century in east central Jutland; was acquired by Karen Blixen's grandfather in 1839.

23 *Princess Dagmar* (1847–1928), daughter of King Christian IX of Denmark, married the later Czar Alexander III of Russia in St. Petersburg on 9 November 1866. As Empress of Russia she was known as Maria Feodorovna.

26 *Carolina Mathilda* (1751–75), daughter of Prince Frederick of Wales, was married at age fifteen to her demented cousin King Christian VII of Denmark. In 1770 she became the mistress of the German-born physician and Danish prime minister Count J. F. Struensee (born 1737), who was executed in 1772, the same year the queen was exiled.

26 *Carl Ploug* (1813–94). The passage is from Ploug's poem "Dronning Mathilde."

27 *Boganis* Karen Blixen's father, A. W. Dinesen (1845–95), published two volumes of *Jagtbreve*—"Letters from the Hunt"—in 1889 and 1892. His pseudonym was the name given him by American Indians with whom he had become acquainted during a long sojourn in the United States.

27 *Karl Gjellerup* (1857–1919) shared the Nobel Prize for literature with Henrik Pontoppidan (1857–1943) in 1917. Romulus is the name of a horse.

28 *"Who checks the king's evil counsel"* From the poem "Kong Frode og Gubben" ("King Frode and the Greybeard") contained in the collection *Digte,* 1804, by Adolph Wilhelm Schack Staffeldt (1769–1826). In the original, "thi den / Som styrer Kongens onde Raad / Er Kongens bedste Ven."

28 *Meïr Goldschmidt* (1819–87), classical Danish author, best known for his novel *En Jøde* (*A Jew,* 1845), and for his attack on Kierkegaard. *Homeless* (London, 1861), the English version of *Hjemløs* (1853–54), was at least in part translated by Goldschmidt.

29 *Viktor Rydberg* (1828–95). The words cited are spoken by King Frode in Rydberg's "Den nye Grottesången" (1891).

29 *"And on the sunny height"* by the Norwegian poet, dramatist, and agitator Bjørnstjerne Bjørnson (1832–1910). The second stanza of the poem "Barnet i vor sjæl" ("The Child in Our Soul") from the collection *Digte og Sange,* 1880.

35 *"black from Phoebus's pinch of love"* *Antony and Cleopatra* I, 27.

36 *Lady Colville* Olivia Spencer-Churchill, wife of Arthur Edward William Colville (1857–1942).

40 *Erik Glipping* (or Klipping, c. 1245–86), King of Denmark from 1259 until he was murdered—probably by his own retainers. The significance of the cognomen is uncertain.

40 *Erik Menved's Childhood* Erik Menveds Barndom (1828), a novel after the fashion of Sir Walter Scott by B.S. Ingemann (1789–1862).

50 *"You are more than your own power"* "Du er mere end Din egen Magt/og min Trøst er det, som Du betyder." From the poem "Trøst" ('Solace') in the collection *Djævlerier (Deviltries)*, 1904. Sophus Claussen, 1865–1931.

53 *"C'est le superflu..."* from Voltaire's satire "Le Mondain."

59 *"Other times, other birds"* "Andre Zeiten! andre Vögel! / Andre Vögel, andre Lieder! / Sie gefielen mir vielleicht, / Wenn ich andre Ohren hätte." The concluding verses of Heinrich Heine's *Atta Troll*, 1841.

62 *R.V.G.G.* "Reisender von Gottes Gnaden."

64 *Zahle's Seminary* Natalie Zahle (1827–1913) established a seminary for teachers in Copenhagen in 1851; it gradually became the largest in Denmark. She also established a well-known and highly respected girls' school.

66 *Estrid Hein* (1873–1935), opthalmologist, chairman of the Danish Women's Movement, Copenhagen Division, 1909–16; Karen Blixen's cousin.

70 *English clergyman Robertson* Frederick William Robertson (1816–53). The quotation is not found in his literary remains, although it is in Robertson's spirit.

70 *Leander and Henrik* Stock characters in the comedies of the Dano-Norwegian dramatist Ludvig Holberg (1684–1754): there are nineteen Leanders, seventeen Henriks, and nine Arvs in as many plays. Henrik and Arv are servants responsible for the action in the plays.

70 *Fanø* Island off the west coast of southern Jutland, known for its insular culture and folk costumes.

71 *Atalanta and Gefion* Atalanta was a legendary Greek huntress; Gefion, an Old Scandinavian goddess who is supposed to have ploughed out the island of Zealand from the Swedish peninsula.

72　*Aldous Huxley*　The quotation, from Crome Yellow (1921) is inexact. The text reads, "Parallel straight lines, Denis reflected, meet only at infinity. Did one ever establish contact with anyone? We are all parallel straight lines. Jenny was only a little more parallel than most" (p. 30).

72　*Johannes Ewald*　(1743–81) In his play *Pebersvenden (The Bachelor,* 1773) Ewald lets the servant Henrik say that when women are good they are angels, much more graceful than men—but when a woman is sly and false she is slyer and more false than a serpent. "We men do not climb so high but we do not fall so deep." Johannes Ewald, *Samlede Skrifter* (1915), 2:345–47.

73　*Storstrøm bridge*　Between the islands of Lolland and Zealand; it is about two miles long.

74　*Where'er you walk . . .*　Alexander Pope, "Pastorals," 1709, "Summer," ll. 73–74.

77　*Goethe said*　"Und des Mädchens frühe Künste / Werden nach und nach Natur." From the poem "Der Gott und die Bajadere."

78　*Captain Carlsen*　In January of 1952, Kurt Carlsen, captain of the freighter *Flying Enterprise,* held the attention of the world's press for several days by staying on board his listing ship in heavy weather. He received a hero's welcome both in New York and Copenhagen.

79　*Madame Heiberg*　Johanne Luise Heiberg, née Pätges (1812–90), the greatest actress in the history of the Danish theater, wife of the critic and dramatist Johann Ludvig Heiberg (1791–1860).

84　*the Norns*　Three sisters who were goddesses of fate in Old Scandinavian mythology.

85　*an observation made by Meïr Goldschmidt*　In the novel *Hjemløs (Homeless),* pt. I, chap. 5. See Goldschmidt's works edited by Julius Salomonsen (1907), 2:167–69.

86　*Kaj Hoffmann*　(1874–1949), traditionalist Danish poet.

87　*Paul la Cour*　(1902–56), known especially for his nature poetry and his aphorisms (*Fragmenter af en Dagbog,* 1948). Member of an originally French family that settled in Denmark in the eighteenth century.

88　*Tagea Brandt's traveling fellowship*　Established in 1905 by

Morten Vilhelm Brandt (1854–1921) in memory of his wife (née Rovsing). It is given to women "of liberal persuasion with a slightly conservative tendency."

89 *Politiken*   One of the two largest Copenhagen morning dailies; associated with the Liberal Party.

89 *Mr. Hasager*   Niels Hasager (1888–1969) had been employed at *Politiken* since 1918 and was known for his English sympathies.

89 *the German envoy, Renthe-Finck*   Cecil Renthe-Finck (1885–1964) had been the German minister to Denmark since 1936.

91 *the tenth of April*   Denmark was invaded by German troops early in the morning of 9 April 1940.

91 *Heretica*   The leading literary periodical of postwar Denmark, published 1948–53.

92 *General von Lettow-Vorbeck*   Paul Emil von Lettow Vorbeck (1870–1964).

92 *Let the saga of the past*   Not identified.

93 *"nothing left remarkable beneath the visiting moon"*   Antony and Cleopatra IV, 15, 67.

94 *Nis Kock's book*   The Danish title is *Sønderjyder vender hjem fra Østafrika* (Copenhagen, 1938). English translation by Eleanor Arkwright: *Blockade and Jungle* (London, 1940).

97 *Professor Horn*   Carl Horn (1874–1943) was the stepfather of Ilse Hess, née Pröhl. He was director of the Academy of Art in Bremen.

109 *Carlyle said*   Perhaps quoting from memory, Karen Blixen has partially obscured Carlyle's meaning. The passage in Carlyle is as follows: "The sword indeed: but where will you get your sword! Every new opinion, at its starting, is precisely in a *minority of one*.... One man alone of the whole world believes it; there is one man against all men. That *he* take a sword, and try to propagate with that, will do little for him. You must first get your sword!" (from "The Hero as Prophet," in *On Heroes, Hero-Worship, and the Heroic in History* [London, 1897], p. 61).

111 *Abd el Rhaman*   'Abd al Rahmān ibn 'Abd Allāh (dates unknown), governor of Andalusia, invaded Gaul in 732 and was defeated at Poitiers.

112 *Louise of Schaumburg-Lippe*   Louise of Denmark (1875–1906), daughter of King Frederik VIII, was the first wife of Prince Friedrich of Schaumburg-Lippe (1868–1945).

113 *Ich bin die Prinzessin Ilse* From *Die Harzreise* by Heinrich Heine.

117 *So fühlt man die Absicht* German proverb based on a line from Goethe's *Tasso*, II,1: "So fühlt man Absicht...."

118 *"when rightly run"* Given here is an English translation (copyright ©1978 by Piet Hein) furnished by the author, Karen Blixen's cousin Piet Hein (1905–), Danish poet, painter, and physicist, the son of the above-mentioned Estrid Hein. Karen Blixen had herself given a very free version of the original, "Hvor godt og stort / og efterspurgt / kun principielt / umuliggjort."

120 *Doctor Coué* Émile Coué (1857–1926), advocate of psychic self-improvement who coined the phrase "Every day in every way I am growing better and better," lectured widely in the United States and England.

121 *UFA* Universum Film Aktiengesellschaft

122 *Jud' Süß* Novel (1925) by the German Jewish writer Lion Feuchtwanger (1884–1958), who was living in France in 1940.

124 *And when all else fails* From the poem "Afrodites Dampe" ("Aphrodite's Vapours") in the collection *Den danske Sommer* (Copenhagen, 1921) by Sophus Claussen (1865–1931), p. 84.

127 *Jens Baggesen* (1764–1826) Danish poet who, in his travel book *Labyrinthen* (*The Labyrinth*, 1792), described a performance of *King Lear* given the first evening he was in Hamburg in June 1789. Friedrich Ludwig Schröder (1744–1816) played the title role and his wife Anna Christine, née Hart (†1829), Cordelia. Baggesen considered Schröder's acting incomparable.

127 *Peter Foersom* (1777–1817) Danish actor, published a four-volume set of translations from Shakespeare, 1807–16.

127 *Balser* Ewald Balser (1898–) had been attached to Berlin theaters since 1932 (and to Deutsches Theater since 1935).

127 *Bruno Hubner* (i.e., Hübner, 1899–) was on the staff of the Deutsches Theater in Berlin, 1934–44.

131 *Gründgens* Gustav Gründgens (1899–1963), the most

versatile actor and director in twentieth-century Germany. From 1934 he was in charge of the Schauspielhaus am Gendarmplatz in Berlin. He was renowned especially for the role of Mephistopheles in Goethe's *Faust* and for a production of *Die Zauberflöte*.

132 *Only as a blood-sucking leech . . .* From the poem "Napoleon Bonaparte" in *Krønike-Riim til Børne-Lærdom* (Chronicle Rhyme for Teaching Children) Copenhagen, 1829, p. 108, by the Danish clergyman, poet, educator, and politician Nikolai Frederik Severin Grundtvig (1783–1872).

135 *You, whom I love . . .* Found at the end of chapter 9 in Selma Lagerlöf's novel *Gösta Berlings Saga* (1891). The Swedish original reads, "Han, som du älskat så, som om han lärt dig att med vingar flyga i luftens rymnd."

137 *What chariots, what horses* From "An Astrologer's Song" by Rudyard Kipling.

140 *Aldous Huxley says* In the essay "Sir Christopher Wren" in *Essays New and Old* (New York, 1927), p. 185. Karen Blixen compressed Huxley's original text in Danish translation.

141 *Victory comes to the man* A source for this particular quotation has not been located; there are numerous variations of the concept in world literature.

145 *Nørrebro* Generally considered to be a less desirable quarter in Copenhagen. The Danish name of the letter *k* rhymes with the English word *hoe*.

145 *Albert Engström* (1869–1940), Swedish humorist and caricaturist.

153 *Niels Bukh* (1880–1950), Well-known Danish gymnast and the principal of the folk-high-school at Ollerup, southern Funen, that stressed gymnastics.

153 *Frederik VI* (1768–1839), King of Denmark from 1808—but he had already functioned as regent for twenty-four years.

157 *H. C.Branner: The Riding Master* *Rytteren* by Hans Christian Branner (1903–66) was originally published in the autumn of 1949.

157 *When Allah created the horse . . .* The passage is not a quotation from the Koran but merely lines suggested by Sutra 100 at the end of the Koran.

170 *The blood ran and the breast burned* From the ballad "Jom-

fruen i Fugleham" ("The Maiden Transformed into a Bird") found in the monumental collection of Danish ballads, *Danmarks gamle Folkeviser* (begun in 1875 by Svend Grundtvig [1824–83]), as No. 56C.

171 *Axel Olrik* (1864–1917), Danish folklorist and one of the editors of *Danmarks gamle Folkeviser*. His book *Nordens Trylleviser* was posthumously published in Copenhagen in 1934.

183 *Thorkild Bjørnvig's book* That is, *Martin A. Hansens Digtning* (Copenhagen, 1948), the earlier of two books about the Danish novelist and essayist Martin A. Hansen (1909–55) by Bjørnvig (1918–), one of Denmark's leading poets, a one-time protégé of Karen Blixen, and himself a critic and scholar.

183 *Dr. Kjærgaard* Hans Kjærgaard (1892–1957), author of a textbook for medical and nursing students; Danish title, *De almindelige Symptomer*, 1951.

188 *And nine is one* Goethe, *Faust* I ("Hexenküche"), ll. 2550–52.

191 *Jens Peter Jacobsen* (1847–85). The untitled, unfinished poem is found in Jacobsen's *Samlede Værker* IV (Copenhagen, 1928), pp. 102–3.

192 *Frank Jæger* (1926–77). His collection of short stories, *Hverdagshistorier*, appeared in 1951.

192 *Leif E. Christensen* (1924–). His story "Over alle Bredder" is included in the collection *Tyven i Tjørnstedet*, 1951.

192 *Svend Aage Clausen* (1917–) The story "Øksehug og Flora" appeared in *Heretica* V (1952), pp. 236–63.

193 *Jakob Knudsen* (1858–1917), one-time clergyman, lecturer, and novelist of a conservative if not reactionary stance.

193 *Here's the only way to fix . . .* A poem by Piet Hein (see above, note for p. 118). English translation furnished by Piet Hein and copyright ©1978 by him.

196 *Valdemar Vedel* (1865–1942), professor of the history of literature in the University of Copenhagen, was for many years the editor of the Danish periodical *Tilskueren* (*The Spectator*).

Notes to Pages 197–200

197 *Vesterport Station* One stop from the main Copenhagen railroad station on the underground/elevated line ("S-train").

198 *Gurre* Originally the name of a lake and castle in northeast Zealand. There are both folk ballads and more recent poetry that have some association with Gurre—the best known of which are by Jens Peter Jacobsen and Holger Drachmann (1846–1908). Drachmann was a prolific and popular Danish poet.

198 *Carl X Gustav* (1622–60), King of Sweden after 1654, when he succeeded his cousin Queen Christina upon her abdication. He occupied Jutland in 1657 and, because of the severity of the following winter, was able to cross the ice and attack Zealand in January 1658. The Peace of Roskilde resulted, but he attacked Denmark again later the same year.

198 *Charles XII* (1682–1718). Politically the most active of the Swedish kings, especially during the "Great Northern War" (1700–21). Charles was in Turkey between 1709 and 1714. He was subsequently killed in battle in Norway.

198 *Carolina Mathilda* Wife of King Christian VII, referred to in the essay "Daguerrotypes."

198 *Dyrehaven* Previously a royal hunting preserve north of Copenhagen, adjacent to Klampenborg. It has been a popular outing place for two centuries. The name literally means "The Animal Garden."

198 *Oehlenschläger's Midsummer Night's Play Sanct Hansaften-Spil* (1803) by Adam Oehlenschläger (1779–1850) is still given at the Royal Theater in Copenhagen. It depicts an outing to Dyrehaven and the events of a day there.

198 *Snekkersten . . . Skovshoved* Villages with small harbors along the Sound between Copenhagen and Elsinore.

199 *Professor Brøndsted* Johannes Brøndsted (1890–1965), sometime Danish national antiquarian.

200 *Christian II* (1481–1559), King of Denmark between 1513 and 1532.

200 *Christian IV* (1577–1648), ascended the throne in 1596 to

227

become the best known of Danish kings. During his reign many of the monumental older buildings of Copenhagen were constructed.

200 *Queen Sophie Amalie* (1628–85), born princess of Braunschweig-Lüneberg, wife of King Frederik III of Denmark (1597–1659), who ascended the throne in 1648.

202 *Steen Eiler Rasmussen* (1898–), prolific writer on architectural and related subjects.

202 *the state bankruptcy of 1813* The result of Denmark's alliance with Napoleon during the Napoleonic Wars.

203 *Kirstin(e) Munk* (1598–1658) was the second (and morganatic) wife of King Christian IV.

203 *the Rhinegrave* i.e., Otto Ludwig von Salm, with whom Kirstin Munk had a scandalous affair. The paternity of her daughter born in September, 1629, is unknown.

203 *Johann Fegræus* (dates unknown; knighted 1632), Swedish diplomat who assumed the name Strömfelt in 1632.

203 *Frans G. Bengtsson* (1894–1955), Swedish poet, essayist, and historian. Author of a life of King Charles XII, published 1935–36.

204 *Johannes Ewald* (1743–81), Denmark's greatest eighteenth-century lyric poet and, like Adam Oehlenschläger, author of one of the two Danish national anthems. He lived at Rungsted Inn betwen March 1773 and the autumn of 1775. Some of his verse was written here.

205 *Rungsted's Lyksaligheder* One of Ewald's best-known poems and read by every Danish schoolchild.

205 *Wilhelm Dinesen* (1845–95), Karen Blixen's father, mentioned above as the author of *Jagtbreve*—"Letters from the Hunt"—written under the pseudonym Boganis.

205 *Danevirke and Dybbøl* The former is the name given to the Danish defenses in southern Jutland from the Middle Ages until 1864. The latter is a strategically important site of a major battle between Prussia and Denmark in April 1864.

206 *Horsens* Provincial city on the eastern coast of Jutland.

208 *Pietermaritsburg* Capital of Natal in South Africa, about twenty miles northeast of Durban.

209 *Amanzimtoti* Town on the African coast about ten miles southwest of Durban.

212 *Count Stolberg* Christian Günther Stolberg (1714–65), father of two Danish German poets, spent his summers at Hørsholm, near Rungstedlund, after 1756.

214 *Dr. Salomonsen* Finn Salomonsen (1909–), authority on Danish bird life.

215 *Dr. Syrach-Larsen* C. Syrach-Larsen (1898–1979), internationally known Danish forester.

215 *Christian V* (1649–99), King of Denmark-Norway from 1670.